The Gathering of Gods:

Anubis

Derek E Pearson

First published 2017
Published by GB Publishing.org

Cover Design © 2017 Paul Collett

CBP
GB Publishing.org
www.gbpublishing.co.uk

To Sue, who is becoming intrigued, and to three women who have given me wonderful support. Thank you Catherine Domanski, Tracy Posner, and Erica Kilburn. Honest enthusiasm is a welcome spur to creativity.

Acknowledgement

George and the champions of GB Publishing corps make writing on my own in an hotel room when I could be enjoying free food and alcohol elsewhere seem like a good idea. Cheers guys.

CONTENTS

		Pages
Chapters		1 – 209
Author's note		210
Other Works by Derek E Pearson		211

'The media loves this guy. I tell you, they love him. On one page alone, they use more superlatives about him than a game show host uses about the crap prizes the contestants can win. The man's a living saint.'

'Where'd you learn words like "superlatives"? You been reading in the toilet again 'stead of jacking off like your sweet mommy showed you?'

'Girl, you're truly disgusting. You really kiss your husband with that mouth?'

'Sure do Lady, and you'd be next if you let me! Mwah! Come on baby; pucker up for the love machine.'

'In your dreams. Hey, seriously Sam, I'm telling you, they really love this guy. If you pulled your head out of that sweet black ass of yours for just five minutes you would have heard all about the Most Reverend Henry Puckling. They love him and his "heroic good works amongst the downtrodden and the needy". Take five minutes looking at the news and you'll find his lily-white fingerprints all over the residents in the poorest communities of this here parish. This man earns his column inches.'

'Yeah? news? Not my bowl of chocolada, lady friend. I want to listen to bullshit I can talk to you. Something I need to know about? Someone always tells me. Yeah, and even if there's something I *don't* need to know about there's always some douchebag lining up just aching to share it with me. Anyway, if he's such an all-fired saint what's he doing here in this godforsaken toilet?'

'Good point; well made. And where's the other half of his gut?'

'Probably with his pants and his underwear. I bet he never planned to go down looking like that.'

'Who does? Yeah, that's a nasty way to take your final bow.'

'Seen a training video once, dead guy looked just like him. Backpacker got himself killed by a bear which started to chow down, but she was scared off by hunters before she finished the first course. Ripped the guy's belly clean out to get to the good stuff. Looked just like him. That's an animal bite.'

'Shit, really? What were you training for? Forest rangers? And where would the Most Reverend Hugo Puckling find a bear around here? The bear wouldn't stand a chance. Hungry locals would have it killed and it carved up for a barbeque five minutes after it pulled its nose out of the garbage. There'd

1

be nothing left but its eyeballs and the smell of char-grilled bear steaks. And to be honest I wouldn't bet on the eyeballs. Soul food.'

'Feldman's gonna love this.'

The taller of the two women, homicide detective Prentiss, groaned, 'Feldman's gonna shit a baby. Hey, you see any CCTV cameras around here?'

'Nope.'

'He's sure to ask. We'll get uniform on it when they finally get here. We've got to stay put and protect the Most Reverend from rats, cats, dogs, and any other vermin that turn up with a camera or a smartphone. Don't want to see him looking like this on *Instagram*. Wish we could at least make him decent. Cover him up with something, get some clerical garb to give him back some sense of his so-called Holy office.'

'Yeah, right. Hey, you know, talking of column inches, would you say that thing was a big cock, a wowser, or just average?'

'Oh, please.'

'I'm just asking. I thought you would know.'

'Gross.'

When she finally reached her Rockaway Beach Boulevard apartment it was late and Prentiss was starving. She was in no mood to cook from fresh, there was nothing in the fridge but white wine and sliced cheese, and the idea of a microwaved TV dinner repelled her. As usual she decided to eat out. She took a few minutes to freshen up and change her blouse and jacket. She left her badge clipped to the side of her thin leather belt and her double action SIG Sauer P239 gun in the holster tucked into the small of her back. She was issued with this when off-duty. A detective with NYPD homicide must be careful. She has little time to socialise and few friends other than barkeeps, restaurant owners, and other cops. When she is also tall, slim, and beautiful with flawless, coffee-coloured skin, she can attract all kinds of the wrong attention. Especially when packs of two-legged street dogs have had enough time to get properly lubricated with intoxicants of their choice.

At that time in the evening the friendlier rowdies were most likely to hail her while pissing a bellyful of what made Milwaukee famous onto an unconscious drunk in a side alley. Dope-heads were mostly quieter but more insistent, even though they might be hopped to the rafters and impotent from long-term misuse. *As if that helped,* she thought. *The drugs empty their balls, but that doesn't stop them trying it on.*

She often reminded herself that she had moved to Averne for the atmosphere and the sea view. It was a cool, edgy place with a lively boho

2

vibe. And then she bitterly admitted to herself that she needed to be there during daytime on a good day to even see the sea. And it was the other side of the freeway. And what was the point of a 'cool, edgy scene' when she was mostly either too busy or too tired to take part. Paying the rent meant working overtime and taking double shifts whenever she could, making her life far too hard to waste valuable time on fun. Good genes kept her looking fine after ten hours on the job, but she wondered how long that would last at the brutal pace she was setting.

'Prentiss, a pleasure to see you here on a week night. Will madam be dining alone?'

'Good to see you too, Enzo. You got a table somewhere out of the way for a tired and hungry girl who just wants to eat without socialising?'

'Your favourite table will be ready in just a few minutes. Please, join me at the bar and I will get you a menu and today's specials board.'

They had played out the same comedy on countless occasions, usually at the same late hour on a weekday. Enzo was an avuncular, middle-aged, New York Italian whose family had originated from the hills around Milan. The few members of his family who had survived the war, including his widowed paternal grandmother and her three children, had left their ravaged homeland for the new country in 1946. He had once told Prentiss that he was the first son of his family who had not grown a moustache. When she asked why, he indicated his fine patrician nose.

'You see this replica of Mont Blanc? I ask you, what could flourish in the shadow of such a fine peak? I wish I took after my momma. A beautiful woman – and such a magnificent moustache.'

She had laughed aloud at this joke many times before, and they had been relaxed around each other ever since. He never flirted, which was a major point in his favour, but always acted towards her with gentle respect and good humour. He was easy company to be around, and he also knew when to fade into the background. She suspected she might have begun to value him as a true friend, and hoped that in his eyes she was more than just another hungry belly who needed feeding and helped fill his cash register.

Just as important, his kitchen was the best in the area. When she ate dinner at Enzo's she relaxed, almost regarding his place as her second home. It was comfortable there, although she was certain she would never clutter her own walls with acidly luminous prints of Mediterranean fishing villages, big green glass floats, fishing nets, and bright red, life-sized ceramic lobsters. Here in the restaurant it looked okay, it worked. In her minimalist apartment, it would look gross.

3

She gratefully sipped at a glass of house red so large she believed she could have housed a family of tropical fish in there and left room for a mangrove root and a sunken galleon, albeit a small one. As the level of the wine went down she began to feel the day's tensions easing from her shoulders. Her feet still hurt but at least she was sitting down.

She had made her choice from the menu before Enzo led her to her corner. It was her favourite seat, a place with a low ceiling lamp where she could sit in the shadows. She would be able to see her food and read her book without attracting attention from any hungry predators. Perfect. The knot in her belly unwound and she found herself becoming increasingly hungry. The aromas from Enzo's kitchen were always enticing, but that evening they had become maddeningly so.

To distract herself she picked up the novel that had become her dinner companion for the last few nights. It was a horror murder mystery set in the twelfth century and starred an English Franciscan monk called Brother Thomas. He was trying to unravel the secrets behind the killing of a young servant girl in the lord of the manor's ornamental 'kitchen herb and physic' garden. There seemed to be a connection between the girl's death and the symbolic plantings in the walled garden. Was the act of murder part of a message that might lead to details of a much greater crime? Perhaps even a conspiracy against the great King himself, Henry the second?

Her food arrived and she applied herself to her flash fried calves' liver in a sweet wine sauce, served with sage, prosciutto bacon, rosemary sautéed potatoes, and fine beans. She munched the wonderfully salty meat and started on her second glass of wine. She savoured the wonderful combination of flavours for a few mouthfuls before she returned to the page she had bookmarked and picked up the thread. The glass almost fell from her hand. *This was impossible!* She read it again. Brother Thomas had turned his keen eye toward Hagin, his novice, and said, 'Much as with Puckling, there's a great deal more to this killing than first meets the eye. Prentiss needs to watch the shadows. Her nemesis stalks her there.'

She read the passage twice more and the words doggedly remained on the page. She looked up at a sound and found Enzo hovering at the edge of the pool of light. He looked concerned.

'Miss Prentiss, is everything okay? You made a noise, is there something wrong with the food?'

'No, Enzo, it's fine, better than that. No, look here, please, read this passage for me.'

She indicated the offending paragraph and his dark eyes scanned the page.

'Ah, I have read some of these Brother Thomas books, very clever. Whodunit, yes? Always, all the clues are there if you know where to look.' He lowered his voice. 'Must be easy for you, yes? As a detective. Very easy. Me, I read right to the end scratching my head. I never know who did it until they tell me. Never.'

'Me too, but don't you see anything strange there?'

He read again. '*Was the girl drowned or poisoned? It isn't clear. That must surely be important*, yes?'

She took the book back and reread the passage. Now the words were innocent, all mention of her and Puckling had been erased. She gazed at the page with a baffled expression, then looked up at Enzo and smiled weakly.

'I probably need a vacation,' she said.

'We all do,' Enzo replied, sagely. 'We all do.'

Feldman filed a report stating that 'The cause of the Most Reverend Puckling's death is, to date, unknown, but the body demonstrates extreme trauma that looks like canid bite marks. Foul play is suspected'. Then he left his assistants to deal with the remaining workload while he went to find Officers Prentiss and Samantha Bolat.

He bearded them by the snack machine where they were arguing about the relative virtues of chocolate. As he approached he heard Prentiss say, very firmly, 'Strictly speaking a Hershey bar shouldn't be called chocolate. It would be more accurate to describe it as sweet, coloured lard. Lindt is chocolate, so is Montezuma and that really expensive stuff coming out of Ecuador these days, but Hershey just ain't.'

Feldman spoke up, 'These days talk like that will get you labelled as "Un-American" officer Prentiss. You are of course correct, but it won't win you any friends under the current administration. Expect a memo on the subject, plus the fact that Taco Bell three times a day is a healthy diet, and putting cheese on barbeque ribs is the slimmer's option. And don't forget to supersize the fries with that!'

Prentiss grinned, 'Most people try for a "good morning ladies" before diving headfirst into Sarcasm Lake. How you, doing, Feldman?'

'My balls are spinning like Catherine wheels, and that does nothing for my usual calm state of absolute Nirvana, for which I am justifiably famous. Nor does the fact that it's only Tuesday morning and I have what looks like the half-eaten remains of a wolf's lunch down in my lab. Couldn't you ladies at least have turned the other cheek, walked away? Maybe gone to find a local Tex-Mex diner or a delicatessen where they offer good salt beef on rye with sweet pickle and mustard? Did you really have to bring me shit like this so early in the week? You were the first officers on the scene, yes? So, it's you I have to blame for this mess?'

Sam answered, 'Somebody has to do the work 'round here. We can't all practice lookin' pretty for news broadcasts. You spend a lot of time in front of a mirror, Feldman? Man, you look just about edible when the cameras are on you. I mean it. I record the best bits for my more, how shall I put it, *private* moments.'

Prentiss raised a single perfect eyebrow and tilted her head towards the pathologist, 'You say wolf? Sam, here thought bear. She saw a training video once. Just the one, mind, she's waiting for the books with pictures to come out before she sees the rest. So, what makes you say wolf?'

'Bite marks, and those are vicious bite marks. I don't want to get too technical but a bear bites one way, a shark another and a wolf a third. We got some saliva for DNA analysis that will confirm or deny what I think. That is wolf or a powerful big dog. It wasn't done at the scene, of course, not enough blood, but it does look as if the bite was the primary cause of death. Any CCTV in the area?'

'Bingo, give the lady a cigar. Prentiss said you'd ask. We sent uniform on a CCTV hunt as soon as they turned up. They found one false box just there for show and a couple covering the entrance to the alleyway where we found him.'

Feldman stood patiently for about five seconds of silence, and then barked, 'Well?'

Prentiss answered, 'We've seen one disc from last night. Recording's blurry but it shows a van, dark coloured, a Mercedes-Benz Vito. Two maybe three years old. Backed into the alleyway at about the right time. No sign of witnesses and no-one came forward. Couldn't see the van's plates.'

Feldman shook his head. 'You want witnesses in Morrisania that time of night? Nobody sees anything along East One Sixty First street at midday, let alone midnight. All the single moms are in bed exhausted after chasing their kids around the block all day. That's why I chose the Forty-Second Precinct, people here in the Bronx are too poor and too hungry to cause trouble. Nice and quiet all day long.'

With a furious expression on her face Sam bent over and shoved her well-endowed buttocks in Feldman's direction. She had fine feminine curves and she knew it. She knew how to offer her body as a gift, or use it as a weapon. She pointed a finger at her protruding rear-end.

'See this? You see this? Prentiss here tells me I walk around with my head rammed up it. She's sweet like that. Well there's room up there for your fool head too, you want to go around spouting crap like that. You can't blame folk for being single parents and most of them are doing their best with what little they got. Don't you go saying shit like that where I can hear you. You understand what I'm saying, *Mr* Feldman?'

Blushing, Feldman opened his mouth like a beached fish, but no sound came out. He turned away and scurried out of range.

Prentiss grinned, 'Nobel Peace Prize awarded to Sam Bolat for her work with the under-privileged forensic pathologists of the NYPD. For a moment, there I thought he was going to grab your butt when you stuck it out at him like that. Damn, even I was tempted.'

'You'd be welcome, he'd need prosthetics. I'd bite his arms off at the neck, I would, so help me.' She grinned. 'Now that we've had our fun shall we take ourselves over to Wall Street?'

'Say what? Wall Street? Why?'

'Ain't that where we keep the wolves in New York City?'

'Hardy, har, har. A real, smartass and cute as a button too. No, I've a better idea and we're less likely to be robbed if we do what I say.'

'Which is?'

'We grab some pics of the bites from Feldman and we go ask an expert what he thinks.'

'What? Oh mom, we going to the zoo?'

'No, honey, no wolves in the zoo. We're going where the wild wolf roams. I'll drive.'

'Where we going?'

'You'll see.'

'Aw, mom, I wanna know? Are we there yet? Are we?'

'Hush, now.'

Just over an hour later the two officers climbed out of their car in the parking lot of the Wolf Sanctuary in Salem. Prentiss showed a man in the timber clad ticket booth her badge. He made a call on an internal line. Five minutes later a slender, lightly bearded man in his late twenties shook hands with them both and asked them to follow him. After the crowded streets of central New York, the peaceful, wide open, forested spaces of the Sanctuary came as something of a shock. Prentiss and Sam followed the man, who had introduced himself as 'Dr. Tabaqui Howlett, please, call me Tabaqui', along a tall chain-link fence. Trailing them on the other side of the fence were two, full-sized, wolves.

Howlett pointed at them, 'These are our ambassador wolves, Canis lupus, but don't be fooled by the lovely faces and the well-groomed pelt. This is not a petting zoo. We have one simple rule in the Sanctuary, don't touch the fence, ever. Those are wild animals and they're unpredictable. Gorgeous, but unpredictable. Much like some people.'

He smiled at his guests in a way that made Prentiss bridle. He seemed to be taking a lot of notice of her. Sam grinned from one to the other with hooded eyes. Prentiss fought down a sudden urge to slap her.

He led them into a lab that smelt of dog. Curled up in a large cage and fast asleep was a puppy. Howlett explained that the Sanctuary was part of an important conservation program for Mexican greys, which at one time numbered fewer than ten breeding animals. That number had been increased to more than four hundred but the cubs were still very carefully checked before being released back into the woodlands.

Seated in his office and sipping at an extremely good cup of coffee, Prentiss began to re-evaluate the scientist. He was an enthusiast for his subject and seemed to know what he was talking about.

He said, 'People have been villainising wolves for centuries, but they are an essential part of our eco-system. Preserving wolves is as important as preserving buffalo or dolphins, they all matter. But I'm rambling, sorry, soap box subject, you say you have a question for me? So, how can a humble wolf biologist help the NYPD?'

Sam answered, 'Frankly, Tabaqui, we think one of your wolves might have taken a bite out of a Catholic Bishop. Checkmated him, so to speak'

'Say what? Whoa, there, back up a spell, that can't happen. My wolves haven't been out of the Sanctuary trees, I can promise you that. You saw it, they're behind a high fence and its very secure. Keeps idiots out and the wolves in, and that keeps them safe. Wouldn't take much for people to start hunting wolves again, and rumours about them biting Catholic Bishops might just be the spark to set the tinder ablaze. So, tell me, what the hell are you talking about?'

Prentiss took three, eleven by seven inch photographs out of an envelope and handed them to Tabaqui. He studied them for several moments with a guarded expression on his face, then he left the room and returned almost instantly with a large, square magnifying glass on a lanyard around his neck. He studied them in more detail. A ruler had been included in the images. He used screw compasses to get a precise idea of bite width and then pulled another ruler out of his drawer to get a better idea of the size of the attacking creature's jaw in real terms. He left the room again, this time returning with a skull and a large reference book.

'Okay, ladies. It wasn't one of my wolves, nor was it what I thought it might be, a coywolf or eastern coyote.'

Sam was squinting at the skull Howlett had placed prominently on his table. She raised her eyes to the scientist.

'How can you be so sure? And what's a coywolf? One that gets embarrassed in mixed company?'

He chuckled. 'No, but that's a nice idea. A coywolf is a hybrid of three Canids, a wolf, a dog, and a coyote. They're becoming quite common in New York state and even NYC. The urban coywolf is a confident beast and sightings have been reported in densely populated areas.' He lifted the skull. 'This was not one of those. This is the skull of a mature grey wolf called Gregor, quite a big fellah when he died. He proves that your killer there was not a wolf. I'll show you why. Canids like Gregor live mainly but not exclusively on flesh. They have long muzzles, well developed jaws and a characteristic dental formula of three by three incisors, one by one canines, four by four pre-molars, and three by two molars. In total, they have forty-two teeth. The fourth upper premolar and first lower molar exhibit carnassial modification for the shearing of flesh, while crushing molars can handle vegetable foods. Your killer demonstrates a typical Canid pattern, much like a wolf, except for two vital differences. The jaw is longer and narrower dimensionally than a wolf's, that's the first thing. It looks more like a jackal to me. The second is the size.' He held up his ruler and placed it across the skull's jaw's widest point. 'You see here? The width of this is four inches and that's a fairly big average, it would normally be three to five inches. Your killer is more like ten or twelve inches and that makes it more than twice, even three times the size of a grey wolf like Gregor and up to four times the size of the average jackal. I'd love to see saliva samples from the bites if there are any. What you have here is a monster, the Canid equivalent of the shark from jaws.'

He tapped the photographs and then rubbed his eyes.

'It looks very clever, very clever, but it must be a stunt. What I'm seeing here is impossible. If it was standing up like a man, ignoring the length of its tail, your killer would need to be something like twenty feet tall. Where would you keep it, how would you feed it, and how did somebody breed the thing? Impossible. Your Bishop died for a practical joke, and frankly I don't think it's very funny.'

***

'Yeah, he was cute.'

'Who?'

'Tabaqui. You should have asked for his number. He wanted to ask for yours. I have an intuition about such man-lady things. He was interested.'

'What makes you *say* bad mouth shit like that?'

'The dribble on his chin every time he looked at you might have been a clue.'

'Bullshit. We're dealing with *Godzilla* and you think we're passengers on the *Love Boat*? Get with the parade, Sam. Anyway, I've got his number.'

'You do? Sweet.'

'Yeah, he wants to know the results of the saliva analysis. He gave me his number just in case anything new turns up. Business, honey, just business. Took mine too, so he could call me if he thought of anything.'

'Can I be maid of honour?'

'Only if you wear pink.'

'Man, I hate pink.'

'I know.'

The two friends laughed easily. Prentiss eased her way through the New York streets with practiced skill. She drove defensively, aware that people might do anything in the vehicular crush that passed for traffic in the city.

11

Over a thousand victims died on the roads in New York State every year, and seventy per cent of those were killed in the city. It put the Most Reverend Puckling's demise into stark perspective. Off to one side Prentiss saw a vehicle veering sideways towards her. The driver, a woman, was texting while she was at the wheel of her motor car. Prentiss switched on her lights and siren for a few seconds. The woman's smartphone flew out of her hands and she looked around frantically. Her SUV swerved while she scrabbled to regain control. She was evidently swearing and gestured angrily.

Sam grinned, 'Mom, you scared the naughty lady.'

'Silly bitch was about to cause a multi-vehicle incident. Smartphone manufacturers should get together with car manufacturers and work out a way to automatically turn the phones off when people get behind the wheel of an automobile. More people are killed by distracted driving than by drink or drugs, and, I'm informed, it's mostly down to using smartphones at the wheel.'

'1 Infinite Loop, Cupertino, CA 95014.'

'Say, what?'

'1 Infinite Loop, Cupertino, CA 95014.'

'What *is* that?'

'The Apple Campus. Let's go bust 'em for criminal irresponsibility.'

'Wish we could. What the fu...'

Their car juddered when the texting woman rammed into it from behind.

Prentiss yelled, 'Is that bitch crazy?'

'Shit, here she comes again!'

Sam switched on the lights and siren just as the SUV pounded into them again. Prentiss fought the wheel while her car tried to slew to the left into fast moving traffic. She hit the accelerator and pulled away. In her mirror, she could see the red-faced driver mouthing obscenities, her shoulders hunched forward over the wheel. Prentiss caught up with the car in front just as the lunatic came charging towards their rear bumper once again. There was nowhere to go.

Sam shouted, 'Fuck this!' She lowered the window and leaned out, pointing her pistol straight back towards the woman's head. She watched as cold realisation dawned on the woman's face and then mouthed, 'Pull over, now.'

One hour on the safety shoulder for the tow truck to arrive and two hours of paperwork later, they were still trying to work out how many laws Mrs Raluca Paceagiu had broken. Prentiss started with her texting while behind the wheel of a moving vehicle and worked her way along a list that included juicy little nuggets such as reckless endangerment, attempted homicide, driving without insurance, and aggravated assault on two police officers while in pursuit of their duties. Paceagiu would spend at least a night in the cells of the forty-second precinct. As soon as the cuffs had been clicked onto her wrists the furious lunatic had been transformed into a heap of weeping Jell-O. The tears were so copious they soaked the woman's pale blue blouse and revealed the cheap, flesh-coloured bra underneath.

The office comedian, one sergeant Morten, a painfully skinny man known universally as 'Fats', strolled to her desk and dropped a DVD on it.

'Present for ya.'

Prentiss sighed and picked up the box. Its cover featured a garish mix of blood spatter, some guy in leathers and extreme cars. Its title was *Death Race 2000*.

'What's the punchline, Fats?'

'Present for ya. You should watch it. Might give you some ideas about what to do the next time some loonytoons bats you in the ass on the freeway. Enjoy it.'

'Thanks, dude. I will.'

She wasn't in the mood to eat out that night. Her brain was still in a turmoil after the Mrs Paceagiu road rage incident, that and the fact that Howlett had rung her about the jackal photographs she'd left with him. His chat was both familiar and technical. After ten minutes, she had promised three things: she would get Feldman to call him, done; she would let him know if it happened again, okay, she would; and she would join him for dinner that coming Friday. He would pick her up at seven-thirty.

'Just to talk about the case, you know? Somewhere quiet I know about. Great fish. Do you like fish?'

'Yes, I like fish.'

'So, right, I'll pick you up at seven-thirty. What's the address?'

And she had told him. So now she had a date with a 'cute' scientist. No way would it work. It never worked. She was wed to the job, might as well be a nun. The familiar little voice in her head rattled away listing the reasons why all her relationships failed after a few months, weeks, or days. In some cases, hours. They called her a control freak, complained when she wouldn't 'put out' on a first date, not even the second, in fact, to date, never. She liked sleeping alone in her own bed, and she never knew when she might be free. Homicide was hungry, it devoured free time. Sam had summed it up once.

'Honey, you're busy, you're intense, and you're intelligent. You're beautiful, sure, and that draws them to you like flies to shit. Then you frighten them away. Smart *and* gorgeous, lethal combination. Scares the crap out of most men. They don't know what to make of you.'

'Sam, I wish you were a man. I'd marry you tomorrow.'

'I know, it's tempting, but life ain't that simple. Anyway, Jock and the boys don't know where anything is in the kitchen. They'd starve or get fat on KFC.'

Prentiss had opted for her favourite, fall-back, early evening at home scenario. She had bought an organic corn fed chicken, some lemons, and a bag of fresh mixed salad. A bottle of decent Chenin blanc was chilling in her fridge. She washed the chicken's skin in lemon juice, massaged it with olive oil and finished it with a generous twist of sea salt across the breasts. After it had been broiling in the oven for forty minutes the aroma was driving her crazy. She tossed the salad in a dressing of garlic, lemon juice and olive oil then threw in a few diced walnuts. She opened the wine and poured herself a generous glass. The chicken was almost cooked to perfection. It looked heavenly and smelled better. She opened her oven door slightly and turned off the heat. A ten-minute rest would tenderise the meat to perfection.

She had already loaded Morton's DVD into the player and turned on her TV. This was luxury, Prentiss style. Chunks of hot roast chicken, skin on, arranged on a big plate, and a bowl of salad with nuts. Something trashy on the TV, a bottle of cold wine, and lots of kitchen towel for greasy fingers. Enjoy the movie, pig out on good food, and drink. Bliss.

She had just assembled her tray when her phone began to ring. *Shit, no way, not now.* She would ignore it and check for voicemail once she had eaten. Cold chicken was good but hot chicken was glorious and she had endured a long day. She had earned it. She stuffed a piece of salty breast skin into her mouth and crunched it. She groaned with pleasure. *Too good.*

The phone stopped ringing, then began again. She put it where she wouldn't be able to hear it, fired up the DVD, and settled down for some seriously overdue 'me' time. Phone forgotten, she indulged all her senses.

The movie was better than she thought it was going to be. The image was clean and crisp, and she kept recognising people in the cast. Wasn't that Sly Stallone? Yes. And the guy in the mask with the weird skin, he was David Carradine from that *Kung Fu* thing they always repeat on the nostalgia channels.

She had finished her meal, washed grease from her fingers and chin and settled down with her wine to enjoy the rest of her movie. She rested a cushion on her lap as a prop for her glass of wine. She was a slow drinker, savouring the wine rather than seeking oblivion at the bottom of the bottle. She never wanted to feel that much out of control, bad things happen to girls under the influence. She had seen it at college parties, and had sometimes been called out to help with the aftermath when she was a younger, rookie police officer. Her sex, empathy and training had made her the obvious choice for comforting rape victims.

Then the scene on the TV screen changed. Instead of muscle cars on the rampage in clear sunshine she was watching a grainy nighttime scene. She looked out of her living room window. It was already dark in the mid-October streets of New York. The TV's POV was high and poorly lit but it looked like it was filming any urban alleyway from any town. She wondered if *Death Race 2000* had somehow been contaminated with footage from somebody's CCTV. A large square shadow slowly hoved into view from the lower right. A truck or a van was reversing into the alleyway. There was movement she couldn't quite make out. The doors at the back of the van opened and a hooded figure climbed in. Something bulky was pushed out.

15

The hooded figure jumped out of the van and closed the doors. It then stepped back into the dim light and raised its face to the lens. It pointed directly at her. Then it strode out of shot. The van pulled away. Barely discernible on the ground was the half-naked figure of a corpulent woman. Prentiss jolted out her seat and ran for her phone. She keyed in her voicemail and heard Sam.

'Playtime's over, honey. We got another one.' She rattled off an address in the Bronx and hung up. It had also been Sam's phone number the second time. And the third. Prentiss rang her back. She was answered instantly.

'Hi, honey. You on your way?'

'Just leaving. Who have we got.'

'You're going to love this, a newshound like you. We've got the charity dame from the Triangle Below Canal Street, TriBeCa. The famous Mrs Melanie Hart.'

'Yeah? I've seen her on the news.'

'Not like this you haven't. The Jackal Joker strikes again.'

'Shit. Okay, on my way.'

On her TV, the muscle car mayhem was back in lurid colour. She turned it off. Then she poured her wine back into the bottle and replaced it in the fridge before hustling down to her parking garage and heading east. She had to concentrate on the road, but she was distracted. In her mind's eye, she kept seeing the hooded figure gazing up at her as if it could see her through the CCTV lens. She saw the pointed finger directed straight at her. She saw the black mask on the figure's face, the long, pointed muzzle and vertical, spearhead shaped, pointed ears. She knew that face. She had only seen it for a few seconds but she knew it from somewhere. She wracked her brains while she drove.

It took fifteen minutes to reach the pandemonium of the crime scene. Sam was standing to one side sipping a takeaway coffee.

'You got here just as they're finishing the scene of crime. You want to see the vic'?'

'Sure, why not?'

Sam led her to a gurney that contained a zipped-up body bag. She opened it.

Mrs Melanie Hart was a well-nourished woman, most of it around her chins, belly, and thighs. She was naked from just below her substantial and cantilevered bra and something had taken a savage bite from her waist. The wound was deep and triangular. Prentiss nodded and Sam zipped the bag closed.

16

Prentiss walked over to where two technicians in environment suits were on their hands and knees combing the alleyway for evidence. She stood clear of the scene but looked up at the high wall next to where they were working. There it was. The yellow box of a CCTV camera.

Prentiss slept badly. Normally she fell into a dreamless state almost instantly, but that night she tossed fitfully in her bed. The image of the ruined grey sack of flesh that had once been a socialite fund raiser merged with the eerie masked face of the person in the hoodie. The way they had pointed at the camera seemed threatening, as if she was being singled out for special attention. She had asked Sam if she had been getting any weird visitations since the Puckling murder and got a typical reply.

'Lambkin, I've got a college professor for a husband and twin five-year old boys who have invented their own language. I can't think of a day when I *don't* get weird visitations. What are you talking about anyway?'

Prentiss brushed the subject away and they made a date for coffee and a catch up the next morning. She thought about calling Howlett about the latest development when she got home, but it was too late in the day, or too early in the following morning, to go ringing virtual strangers. Even cute ones.

At just after four in the morning she gave up on sleep, took a shower, made some coffee, and fired up her tablet. She couldn't get the masked face out of her mind. That dog-like apparition was nagging at her like a loose tooth. She had to find out what it was. She pushed the hair out of her eyes and keyed her search engine. What parameters to enter? She typed in 'dog masks' and spent a few minutes trawling through bizarre fetish websites. She decided there were some sick puppies out there – and chuckled at her own joke. Next she tried 'wolf faces'. She found an image library and studied the photographs with interest. She liked dogs and these wolf portraits were beautiful images of handsome creatures. There was no escaping the sense of intelligence and dignity in the animals' eyes, intelligence added to something primitive and yet somehow, noble. Then she hit on an image of a wolf baring its teeth as if about to attack, and she remembered Howlett talking about the human defensive mechanism that had seen wolves almost driven to extinction thanks to mans' fear. Wolves, tigers, lions, bears, coyotes, polar bears, and sharks barely survived in ever diminishing numbers because humans are afraid of them. More people die because of a panicking moose leaping through their car's windscreen than are killed and eaten by all the apex predators combined. Why aren't we more afraid of *them*? But moose thrived because they looked as if they belonged on *Sesame Street*. Moose on the highway. Dopy but deadly.

This was getting her nowhere. She typed in 'Jackal'. Instantly the hairs on the back of her neck stood on end. She was looking at an elegant creature with a pointed narrow muzzle and spearhead-shaped ears. The caption read 'Egyptian jackal'. She fed that into her search engine to narrow the parameters. What came onto her screen next brought a gasp to her lips. It was the mask. It was an exact replica of the hoodie's mask. She read the caption, 'Anubis, Egyptian God of the Dead'. She keyed in the name and a plethora of material filled her screen.

Turned out the jackal god was a superstar, with a ripped six-pack. She learned that the name Anubis, one of the most iconic gods of ancient Egypt, was, in fact, the later Greek version. Ancient Egyptians would have known him as Anpu or Inpu. Anubis was an extremely ancient deity whose name appears in the oldest mastabas of the Old Kingdom. In the Pyramid texts, he was listed as Guardian and Protector of the Dead. He was originally a god of the Underworld, but later he became associated more specifically with the embalming process and funeral rites. His name is from the same root as the word for a royal child, 'Inpu' and is also closely related to the word 'Inp' which means 'to decay'. *Royal child of death? Not helping me,* Prentiss thought as she read on. *Hart and Puckling were bitten, not embalmed.* There was a lot more about the god's relationship with the embalming process, including the fact that ancient embalmers would wear Anubis masks while they worked. It seemed the god had been a serial name collector. She discovered he was also known as 'Imy-ut' 'He who is in the place of embalming' and 'Nub-ta-Djser', 'Lord of the Sacred Land'. She liked that title. She carried her tablet into her little kitchen and carried on reading while she made more coffee.

Anubis was initially related to the Ogdoad of Hermopolis, the Ogdoad being a group of eight almost forgotten primordial deities worshipped in the ancient lands. So, he must have pre-dated the pyramids as the God of the Underworld. *Far out. Who makes this shit up?* She drank some coffee.

In the Pyramid Texts of Unas, she read, Anubis had been associated with the Eye of Horus, and acted as guide to the dead who helped them find Osiris, the king of the Underworld. Rather than being relegated to a miserable, dark place, the dead would be guided from the Underworld to paradise, which was also known as Duat or the Field of Celestial Offerings. It was described as a bright garden with fresh canals, good food and your friends all around you. *Oh, yes,* she remembered, *wives and handmaidens would be murdered and interred with a dead pharaoh, just so he would have*

19

someone he knew to play with in the next life. Nice. Want to bet it was a man who came up with that one?

But not for everyone. In other myths Anubis acted as judge and jury for the dead. He led the deceased to the halls of Ma´at, the Goddess of Truth, where they would be judged. Anubis watched over the whole process and ensured that the weighing of the heart, which represented the person's soul, was conducted correctly. This meant Anubis would literally weigh the deceased person's soul in the balance. The soul was weighed against a feather. If it was heavier the soul was rejected as unfit. The lightweight innocents were led to a heavenly existence in Duat, while Anubis abandoned the guilty to Ammit, an odd creature that, at first, looked to Prentiss like a cross between an alligator, a pig, and a dog. She was certain she had seen something like it in one of the episodes of *Star Wars*. A little more research showed her that in fact Ammit, also known as the Devourer of Millions and the Eater of Souls, was made up of the head of a crocodile, the body of a lion, and the hindquarters of a hippopotamus. It was female. So, then, the guilty souls would be devoured. *Devoured?* She was reminded of Puckling and Hart, both savaged by the jaws of a giant jackal. Or something.

Amongst Anubis' other names was 'Tpy-Djuf' which meant 'Man on his mountain'. Ancient Egyptians believed he kept watch on the places of the dead from a hill that overlooked the Theban necropolis. Somehow, he also guarded the entrance to the Underworld, the land of the dead, which was believed to be over in the west where the sun set at night. This earned him the title 'Khentyamentiu', or 'First among the Westerners', which meant he was 'First amongst the dead'.

Fascinated, her eye travelled down to the next paragraph. At what she read there her heart sank and the sour taste of too much coffee bubbled into her throat.

Prentiss, take what you have learned here and work with it. But be wary, be vigilant. He knows you. Ensure he does not judge you and find you wanting. He will weigh your heart in the balance. Be pure. Wash your soul in the light or you too will be devoured.

'Anubis? You want to call the giant jackal killer, *Anubis*? Why?'

Prentiss realised that explaining this was going to prove tricky. Could she tell Sam about the CCTV footage suddenly appearing in the movie she had been watching the previous evening? No. Rewinding the DVD had shown it had disappeared. The message had vanished from her book and the warning was gone from her online research. Sam would think she had slipped a cog.

'I was thinking about it last night, and about what Tabaqui told us about the giant jackal. I went online to research a few things and came up with some awesome stuff about the old Egyptian god Anubis. Made fireworks go off in my head. Listen to this...' Prentiss outlined some of the information she had uncovered, leaving out the embalming connections. That could wait until the next victim turned up mummified. Sam's eyes narrowed. She thought hard for a few moments.

'So, what? Where are you taking this? Anubis doesn't run around biting people. You said he leaves them to that Ammit thing after weighing them. Tabaqui never said anything about crocodile bites. He said jackal. Mind you, I like the sound of Anubis being the 'The First amongst Westerners'. That makes life very easy. We just take a squad to the White House and arrest the President. At least that would earn us a lot of likes on Facebook. Ah, okay, call it Anubis, why not? Anubis sounds a lot neater than 'giant jackal thing'. So, then, Sherlock, where does all this take us? Where do we go from here?'

Prentiss admired Sam. She was a good, hard-headed police officer, a woman who automatically looked for the strongest connections in a case. She personally hadn't thought of the President as the 'First Westerner' when she saw it on her tablet, she had preferred the idea of someone who considered themselves as 'First amongst the Dead'. But her line of reasoning had stalled before she could work out what that might mean.

She pursed her lips. 'I think we should explore the judgement angle. The devoured were souls who had been weighed in the balance and found wanting. Puckling and Hart were noted philanthropists. Surely, *they* were good guys and should have been taken to a heavenly afterlife in Duat, not murdered. They must have done something to earn it. The good Bishop and the saintly socialite. Was there something a little off-colour there? Did somebody hear too many skeletons rattling in their closets and killed them as a result? What if our killer's someone who takes philanthropy very seriously and punishes those who appear righteous on the surface but deep down are really shits?'

Sam grimaced. 'Why kill them? Why not just post the truth in the gossip columns or online? Leaving someone half-naked by a dumpster with half their guts missing is a bit extreme, don't you think?'

'Yeah, not exactly sane, is it? Okay, two things. One, we do as you suggest and we go talk with a gossip columnist, that's a good call. Two, we grab Feldman and have a chat about saliva samples. We still don't know what we're dealing with. Is it an animal or a lethal trickster?'

They found Feldman quizzically examining the filling in his breakfast bagel. When he spotted the grinning Sam marching towards him he groaned, put his bagel down on its bag and took up his coffee instead. He nodded at Prentiss and pulled a face at Sam. 'Good to see you. I'm meant to be on a diet and, thankfully, I've just lost my appetite. So, what can I do for you? Are you here for a reason? Or are you just on a mission to bust my balls before breakfast?'

Sam answered, 'Dr Feldman, your balls are not our concern, your customers are. Two things, have you any idea when Mrs Hart was killed? And what can you tell us about the Anubis killer?'

'Egyptian god of the Underworld? Jackal-headed guy, patron saint of embalmers? What? Oh, I get it. By the way, your guy Howlett is a godsend in a case like this. Knows his stuff. Thanks for putting him in touch. So, which one of you two came up with the new appellation?'

Sam poked a thumb towards Prentiss. Feldman nodded.

'Thought so, culturally sophisticated. Sounds better than the big jackal killer at any rate.'

Sam muttered, 'I called it the *Giant* jackal killer.' Feldman ignored her.

He continued, 'Dr Howlett has confirmed my findings. The bites appear to have been inflicted by a *canis aureus lupaster*, or Egyptian jackal, which, as no doubt you are aware, is a subspecies of the golden African jackal. Problem is the bites are exaggerated, they're much too big to have been meted out by a real animal, despite the traces of canid saliva we found in the wounds. Dr Howlett told me he had already shared his doubts with you. It makes a pretty puzzle, don't you think? Please, you must let me know how it turns out for you. Gosh, is that the time? I have coffee to drink and a morning to enjoy – without you in it. I must let you be on your way. Thanks for dropping by.'

Prentiss blurted, 'Wait. Are you saying there was animal saliva in the wounds?'

22

Feldman paused, 'I thought I made it quite clear. Yes, doggy dribble in the bites. We can only say "canid" saliva, we can't be more specific than that, but they are an inordinate size. Impossible for them to be real jackal bites, the thing would need to be the size of a T-rex. Good luck with it, ladies. Don't be strangers.'

He took up his coffee and his bagel and walked away across the room.

Prentiss shouted after him, 'But, that's impossible.'

He waved his bagel in the air and kept on walking.

More quietly Prentiss repeated, 'But, that's impossible.'

Sam sighed, 'At least he'll stand out in an identity parade. Come on, let's get out of here. Let's go listen to some juicy gossip.' She shouted after the pathologist. 'Hey, Feldman, where would you go to get the best gossip in town?'

He shouted back, 'I'd go where I always go, the end cubicle in the ladies' rest room. Oh, and to answer your first question, probably about eight o'clock. Not long before she was dumped. Gotta go now, byeee.'

Prentiss pulled a face, 'Do you think he's joking about the rest room?'

'Man, I hope so. He'll have heard what we say about him.'

'What *you* say about him.'

'Shit.'

A little research and a phone call brought them to the offices of *Dames & Dandies*, a fashion and lifestyle magazine based in Greenwich Village. Available for a fee online and almost independent of advertising, *D&D* was one of the most scathing and arch observers of the New York fashion and lifestyle scene. Its readers said its articles could only be published online, they were written with such extreme levels of vitriol they would have burned their way through the printed page. Its subscribers loved it and paid good money for their regular portion of bile and insight. Its contributors made sure to provide them with a healthy diet of well penned acid.

It was after lunchtime by the time they were led out of an elevator by a blandly pretty girl in a very short skirt, who left them in what looked and felt like a tropical greenhouse. A tall, bald, striking looking man in silk pyjamas strode out of the foliage and welcomed them. He held out a paw and delivered a surprisingly dry and firm handshake. He gave each of them an appraising once over and grinned.

'If NYPD has started recruiting fatales like you two I'm definitely covering the wrong end of the boulevard. Hello there, I'm Erskine, Gee Erskine. Gee for Gawain. If you want to know who put the knives in the backs of all the biggest shitballs in NYC look no further, it was me.' He held

23

out his wrists, 'Cuff me, darlings, and take me away. But first promise me something. All those stories about police officers sexually abusing their victims *are* true. They are, aren't they? Please say yes.'

Sam laughed like a hyena gagging on its supper. Prentiss decided she very much approved of Gee Erskine.

He let his wrists go limp and held his arms out at his sides.

'Well, if I can't talk you into a little recreational S&M I'd better offer you something to drink. What's your poison? Tea, coffee, tequila, mojitos?'

He swayed back into the foliage and vanished, then his head reappeared around a palm frond.

'Follow me girls, I don't bite you know, despite the rumours.'

Prentiss chuckled, 'Funny you should say that. That's pretty much why we're here.'

[7]

'Puckling and Hart, hush now, wash your mouths out. The bad boy Bishop and the bitch from TriBeCa. You want the full *D&D* down and dirty on two people who are probably offering unwelcome advice to Saint Peter even as we speak – or more likely assuming the position for a demon gang bang. Pants down and grab your ankles people, time to brace yourselves. What could they possibly have done to pin them onto NYPD's crap-o-meter and bring you lovely creatures to my door?'

Prentiss explained. 'We work homicide and they've both been murdered. You're probably aware of that. Other than that, we can't go into details...'

Erskine held up a hand to silence her, then said, 'They were both found butt naked from the waist down with half their guts torn out. Yes? Turned up in the kind of backstreet venues that they used to throw money at to heal the wounds, but had never actually visited before. Both were happy to raise a little money at society galas, but they never let their hands get shitty doing any real work. No, that's not true I'm doing Hart a disservice saying that. She *would* visit her recipients, in her own way and for her own reasons, but Puckling? No, he was too lily white, he wouldn't be seen dead...' He smiled at them. 'Oops, what am I saying? Silly me, of course, there he was.' He smiled pertly, 'Don't look so surprised, after all I'm a journalist. I get paid for knowing shit, it's what I do, and I'm good at it. So, then, they've been murdered, and not in a nice way. So, what? Why come to *D&D* Towers to see me? What cats would you like to see jumping out of the bag? Surely it's better to let the dead R-I-P, don't you think?'

His keen eyes opened wide when he said this. He smoothed a hand over his skull and then rested his chin on his fists. He pursed his lips.

'Please,' he said. 'Please, say no. I do so love to dish the dirt about the deceased.' He blinked disarmingly and offered a cherubic smile.

Prentiss sipped gratefully at her large, dirty mojito before she answered. The man was getting under her skin and she didn't know how she felt about it.

'We, that is...' She glanced at Sam who nodded. 'Yes, *we* have a theory about the killings. We believe they are ritualistic and based on ancient religious practices. We think the victims have somehow been judged by the killer, weighed in the balance if you like. We think they have been judged and found wanting. We can't be sure of the exact criteria, but, in my opinion,

25

it's probably because they previously painted such a clean picture of themselves as do-gooding sweethearts that it's pissed someone off bigtime.'

She took another sip, then continued. 'The killer's M.O. might be to take a close look at well-known philanthropists' secret lives and punish them if they have too much dirty laundry in the closet. If that's the case, we'll need to warn other potential victims. You might be able to help us there too, if you can.'

Erskine closed his eyes and took a deep breath through flared nostrils.

'*If* I can? *If*? What do you mean, *if*? Erskine's reach is long and Erskine is wise. I have ears at every rathole and eyes at every keyhole and I am the man who judges whether the laundry stinks enough to talk about. You want to know about Puckling and Hart? Darlings, ladies, where shall I start? Oops, sorry, sometimes I rhyme. It's a bad habit I know, but it amuses me. First let's do this and order some tea.'

He picked up a phone in the middle of the table and punched zero on its keyboard. 'Claudia, sweetie, Erskine. Really? You say the loveliest things. Yes, never mind. Boardroom three, I'm in it, is it free? The afternoon. I don't know, wait...'

He glanced at his guests, 'Have you eaten?' They shook their heads. 'Yes, Claudia, me again, order the usual from Strange and Ware, please, for three. Yes, I said S&W. My budget. Wait again...' His eyes found them again, 'Do either of you have problems with anything you might find on a plate: veggie, vegan, Kosher, anything like that?'

Prentiss shook her head, Sam said, 'I'm bad with Brussel sprouts and eggplant stew.'

Erskine nodded, 'Claudia, cancel the Brussel sprout and eggplant combo. No, really? Yes, I know they don't. I'm joshing you. Yes, dear, it was a *joke*. Sorry, I'll laugh first next time, shall I? Thank-you. Kisses and things, bye.'

He put the phone down and raised his eyebrows. 'Claudia's, a pet. Smart as a spaniel, pretty like October dawn, sense of humour of a paving slab. We really should put something about needing a sense of irony on the job application. Now then, where were we?'

Prentiss said, 'Dishing the dirt on Puckling and Hart.'

'Oh, yes.' Erskine licked his lips. 'Let's start with the Bishop. The Most Reverend Henry Puckling of recent memory. A careful man. When he's at home he covers his tracks like a native American hunter, but when he takes his little jaunts to the Philippines and Thailand he lets his hair down. I don't mean his behaviour gets posted on social media or we get sufficient proof to publish anything, no, no, no. If he had you wouldn't be here. You'd be

26

reading it in *D&D* and he'd be resigning from the church due to unforeseen personal circumstances. So, we're talking gossip from people who know the facts but can't be quoted. We're talking people, men, who share Puckling's taste for the younger girl. Pubescent or earlier. Not tots or babies, even to them that would be sick, but eight to twelve-year-olds. The sweeter the kid the neater the fit. Only smaller men need apply. I bet Puckling has a small gentleman in his trousers, tiny little appendage.' Erskine held up his little finger. 'A bitty, baby man weapon, or so I'm told.'

Sam butted in, 'Wait, no, that's not true. We saw it when we found the body. His wasn't the biggest candle in the sacristy, but he was no midget either. He could have made his way as a stunt cock on the porn circuit if things hadn't worked out behind the dog collar.'

'Really? Do tell. Most of the kiddy fiddler crowd are underprivileged in the gentleman department. There have been a few quite famous names linked to the practice. Juan Perón springs to mind. No wonder Evita wandered off the marital straight and narrow, Juan's gentleman part was too small to touch the sides. It has been rumoured that Dr Josef Mengele was welcomed to Argentina with open arms because Auschwitz's famous "angel of death" had no problem with performing abortions on underage girls. History records quite a few despoiled maidens that Perón's busy little pecker had impregnated. But I digress. Sorry, happens all the time. Head full of gossip like a gumbo, you never know which juicy little facts will float to the surface next. Leaving his penis aside for the moment, Puckling was a notorious face amongst the paedophile fraternity. That might skew the balance against him, do you think?'

At that moment, there came a cursory knock at the door and two young women pushed a trolley into the room. They unloaded some platters covered in foil followed by plates, napkins, and cutlery. Wine and glasses were also doled out. They made barely audible fluttering noises and left.

'Dig in, my dears' said Erskine. 'We can talk while we eat. Red or white wine?'

The food was hot, varied, and delicious. Prentiss was tempted to gorge herself but reined in her appetite so as not to appear greedy. Sam had no such compunction, she filled her plate and went back for more. Twice. Erskine also demonstrated his respect for food. He talked between bites but still managed to clear two platefuls.

'Mrs Melanie Hart. She was not one of the kiddy fiddle persuasion. She and Puckling knew each other on the charity circuit, but they didn't share the same interests. Again, nothing I've heard would stand up in court, but

Melanie was rumoured to be a hunter and gourmandiser. A very special kind of hunter and gourmandiser, a woman with particular tastes.'

He bit into a tempura shrimp and chewed reflectively.

'Hart is famous for her work with refugees from war zones, especially unaccompanied, child refugees. I'm sure you've done your homework on the saintly bitch. Unlike Puckling she did visit the recipients of her largesse. She's rolled up to the Middle East, dropped in on places in Africa. You know, anywhere people huddle together in fear. Been photographed feeding hungry children, talking with adults, finding out which of the children are orphans. She takes *special* care of orphans. Always has her favourites. They get to share her food, get treated with organic medicine. By the time she's finished with them, they're clean, dewormed, healthy, and happy. They have hope again.'

He fingered another shrimp into his mouth and chewed thoughtfully.

'She always takes her bow with her. She favours a Martin Archery takedown recurve bow with a fifty-pound draw. That's about one thousand dollars worth of stopping power, enough to bring down a moose from thirty yards. It will also bring down a running child from forty yards. She likes to give them a bit of headway before she kills them.'

Prentiss frowned, 'She's been murdering children?'

Erskine nodded. 'Yes. Then she and her band of cronies field dress, barbeque, and eat the evidence. They bury the bones. Predators, ah, yes, you've got to love them. Does anyone want that last shrimp?'

Erskine promised to put on his best thinking cap to come up with a list of potentials, 'wicked' philanthropists who might become the next jackal victims in NYC. He escorted them down to the bright atrium on the building's ground floor and air-kissed each on both cheeks.

'We must do this again. Such fun in the middle of a working week. Can I put special advisor to NYPD's finest on my CV? Shall I? Perhaps not, it might scare away the people I need to deal with during my day job.'

Prentiss shook her head. 'Mr Erskine, you remind me of Mycroft Holmes, Sherlock's smarter brother. He used to just sit in his club and feel the tug on his web from all over Europe. He knew about everything too.'

'Wasn't he the very fat man? That's a bit below the belt. I'm surprised at you. Really, my dear. And here, for a moment, I thought we were friends.' He grinned ruefully and kneaded his slender midriff. 'I suppose I could lose a few pounds without starving. But here I am, there you are, and here I go. Don't be strangers now, and I'll be in touch.'

He shimmied away and called an elevator with his pass card. He shook his fingers at them until the doors closed on him. Both women suddenly jerked as if they had been released from a fishing line.

Sam blinked a few times. 'Who am I? Who are you? Where are we and where did we leave the car? I feel as if I've been hypnotised. My mind's gone blank.'

Prentiss nodded, 'I know what you mean. Is that what they call charisma?'

Sam screwed up her nose. 'Is he gay, do you think?'

'Not a clue. Does it matter? You fancy your chances? If you do, can I get first dibs on your husband.'

'Hey, no, *no*! Look, I don't know why I said that. Forget it.'

Prentiss did know. Her friend was trying to put a label on a man who eluded nearly every definition in her vocabulary, and she wanted something she could pin on him. Gay was a label she could work with.

Sam moved towards the stairs that led down to the parking garage where they'd left their car. Prentiss spotted the bland, pretty girl who had directed them to Erskine scurrying towards them.

'He brought you down,' she said, breathlessly. 'Gee brought you down. He never brings people down. Never. He always gets me to do it. And he ordered a hot lunch from Strange and Ware. That's expensive. He must really like you. Who are you, anyway?'

Sam shrugged, 'Us? We're just simple homicide police officers going about our business. Mr Erskine has been helping us with our enquiries.'

'Oooh. Homicide? Really? Wow, really? Is Gee a suspect?'

'Sorry, miss. We can't discuss an ongoing case. Now, please, how do we get back to our car?'

Almost quivering with curiosity, the girl used her pass card to let them through the door to the garage and stood in the doorway watching them the whole time they walked to the visitor bays. Prentiss could feel the girl's intense gaze boring into her back. They remained mute while they climbed into their car. Prentiss was easing them into the flow of traffic before Sam broke the silence again.

'Hey, just a second. What do you mean, you get "first dibs on my husband"? You got eyes for my old man?'

'Sure. Who wouldn't. He's housebroken and trained already. And he appreciates a good cook. What's not to like? You take up with Erskine and your old man will be snapped up before you can apply for custody of the kids. Thought I'd throw my hat in the ring first is all.'

'Honey, don't you get it? Erskine was being nice to *me* because *I* was with *you*. I know who he was setting out to impress and it wasn't the sweet Mrs Samantha Bolat. No, sir. A lady understands these things. I got a nose for the things men like, and they like you. They like you a lot.'

Prentiss sighed, 'You think every man we meet has the hots for me. I'm saying you should take a long hard look at yourself sometime. You say you know what men like? I got news for you. You're a cute, sexy little bundle of fun, you know that? Feminine and luscious all the way from your *Nubian Hair* style to your *Kith Brooklyn* heels. You walk the walk well enough. Anyway, enough of all that. Do you believe him?'

'Erskine? Yeah, I guess I do. You?'

'Guess so. He was too specific to be making that shit up. So, what are we dealing with now? Are we calling Anubis a stone-cold killer? Or a supernatural vigilante?'

'From what "Gee" darling was saying it sounds like the world is a much better place without Puckling and Hart.'

'Maybe, but working without due process still breaks the law. We don't have capital punishment here in the Apple, but even if we did you can't go around snuffing people without due process, no matter what they've done.'

'What about Batman?'

'*Batman*? What?'

'Would you arrest Batman if he turned up here on the streets of New York? You know, if he took a break from Gotham and came to NYC? Would you arrest Batman? Would you?'

'Damn right I would. I'd slap his caped crusader ass straight into the pen.'

'What about Spiderman?'

'Catch the little webslinger on fly paper. Lock him up and throw away the key. I don't like spiders.'

'Okay, what about Superman? Would you arrest Superman?'

They were both silent for a few seconds, then Prentiss said, 'How the hell do you arrest Superman? With kryptonite handcuffs? Anyway, he's an alien. What's my authority?'

'Good point. Okay, Anubis. He's a twenty-foot jackal who devours bad people. If we leave him alone he'll clean up the city and we'll be out of a job. We've got to stop him or my children will starve.'

'We can hope he eats so many he gets too fat to catch the next one. Or maybe he'll get type two diabetes and suffer from underlying health issues.' Prentiss' face got serious. 'Forget it, Sam, it's not funny. We don't know what we're dealing with. Is this jackal creep just targeting bad philanthropists or bad people in general? Has he killed anyone else? The MO should make him easy to track down. Shit, girl, you can't hide a twenty-foot jackal in this city. What am I saying? No wonder weird shit keeps happening to me, I'm going crazy.'

'What weird shit?'

With an intense sense of relief Prentiss poured out the details about strange personal messages turning up in the pages of her book and on her search engine. She explained about the CCTV footage suddenly interrupting her movie.

'I saw him, I saw the hoodie with his Anubis mask dump Melanie Hart in that alleyway. And somehow, he saw me. He pointed straight at the camera before he left. He was warning me.'

'You checked the CCTV footage same as me. It was blurred okay, but that guy never pointed at the camera. We never saw his face.'

'I know. And Enzo didn't see the words in the Father Thomas novel. I tell you – I'm going nuts.'

Sam frowned. 'You talked to anyone else about this?'

'No, only you, so far.'

'Good. Don't. They'll lock you up in a rubber room and swap your knife and fork for a plastic spoon. Girl, you ever tried eating steak with a plastic spoon?'

31

'Am I losing my mind? What do you think, Sam? Really?'

'Me? I've always known you're crazy. Nothing surprises me anymore. Nada. But I'm used to you. You're like a mother to me. If that shit happens again you tell me. You have any more warnings, you tell me. I've grown used to your funny little ways and I don't want to lose you. Anyway, it would take too long to break in a new partner. We're in this together, honey, and maybe I'm as crazy as you are, but I believe you. Something strange is going on out there, something really freaking strange. But we're a team of three now, you, me, and Gee Erskine. What chance has a twenty-foot jackal got against firepower like that?'

'And Tabaqui.'

'Sure, yes, the cute Doctor Howlett. You ring him with the latest developments yet?'

'Not had a chance. I'll call him from the precinct. Then we can research to see if there have been any other murders like Puckling and Hart.'

'My money's on yes.'

'Yes, so's mine. But how many?'

[9]

'Prentiss, good to hear from you. Are you still okay for tomorrow evening?'

'Yes, I'm looking forward to it. By the way, I've been thinking about it. You don't need to come to my place. Tell me where we're going and I'll meet you there. You don't need to go to any trouble.'

'No way. Call me old fashioned but I believe there are ways to do things right. I'll be there at seven-thirty as we agreed. Now, what can I do for you?'

Prentiss was nonplussed for a moment, and then remembered that it was she who had called the biologist.

'Yes, of course. There's been another jackal killing.'

'What, since Mrs Hart yesterday?'

'You know about that?'

'Yes, Dr Feldman rang me this morning. Has there been a third?'

'No, no there hasn't. It's just I promised to stay in touch and we've been busy so this is the first chance I've had to call you. Glad to hear Feldman's keeping you in the loop.'

'Ha, yes he is. He said you're calling the killer Anubis. Great choice.'

Hoo, thought Prentiss, Feldman has a loose mouth. That's much more than Tabaqui needed to know.

'We are, but, Tabaqui, please, don't tell anyone, okay. It would be all over the media in hours.'

He chuckled, 'My lips are sealed. I promise. Even the wolves don't know. By the way, that was a strange thing yesterday evening.'

'What?'

'The wolves. I was working late. It was already dark when I left, I don't know, say seven-thirty or eight. I always say goodnight to the pack if they're about, or at least this side of the treeline. And you know something weird? They were all there, a dozen of them. They were sitting in a group, all of them completely silent, and they were all facing towards the centre of the city. I tell you I've never seen anything like that before. Gave me the creeps.'

Perhaps it was the way Howlett had said it, but Prentiss felt a pool of ice settle in the pit of her stomach. In her mind's eye, she saw the silent pack of wolves sitting in the darkness and staring towards New York City at precisely the moment Mrs Hart was being devoured by her unknown assailant.

She blurted out, 'What about two nights previously, were they doing it then? The wolves I mean.'

'Monday? I don't know. I left on time that day. I can check the monitors and give you a call back if you like.'

'Please, yes. That would be great.'

'Okay, laters, Prentiss.'

'Talk soon, and thanks. Really, thanks a million.'

His call came half an hour later. He asked for her email address and told her she would work it out when she saw some footage that was on its way over. And then he was gone. A panel appeared on her computer screen saying she had mail from Dr. Tabaqui Howlett. The text in the message box read 'Check this out'. She opened the attachment and was presented with a beautifully rendered video stream just over eight minutes long. The image looked to have been taken using an expensive infra-red camera at night, and she quickly recognised the tree line from the Wolf Sanctuary. There was no fence between her and the action, and she realised her point-of-view was higher than normal. She thought back and remembered a handy looking camera on top of a pole by the fence. There was a clock in the bottom left of the screen just under the date, which was the previous Monday. The time was nineteen fifty-eight. When the clock hit nineteen fifty-nine, black shapes flowed from the trees. Their eyes fluoresced like ghost lamps in the infrared. The wolves loped out into the open then sat as a group and gazed expectantly to the left of her screen, which would be their right. Prentiss knew they were looking precisely towards the centre of New York City. They sat unmoving and silent for all of five minutes, as if watching a show. The cone of active sound showed they were being recorded but they made not a whisper. They might have been a still photograph instead of living beasts. She felt the hair prickle on the back of her neck and gooseflesh chilled her forearms. At twenty zero five the pack got to their feet and melted back into the trees. The sequence flickered and ended with a transparent 'play' button in its centre.

'Sam,' she cried, 'Sam, you have got to see this. Get over here, look.'

Her friend bustled over to her side and Prentiss replayed the entire sequence while they both watched. At the end, Sam remembered to breathe with a gulping intake of air.

'That was freaking weird. That from Tabaqui?'

'Yes, he just sent it to me.'

'Go again.'

Eight minutes later Prentiss said, 'Tabaqui told me they did the exact same thing at about the time Hart died. This was recorded at the approximate

34

time when Feldman thinks Puckling was savaged. It looks like they're watching something, doesn't it? What would make a pack of wolves behave like that?'

Sam shuddered. 'Should we be talking to a different kind of specialist, now? We've got the wolf man and the society gossip plus two hard working and gorgeous homicide officers. Where do we go to find out more about shit like that? Looks like we're dealing with the supernatural.'

'Fats' Morton did a slow shuffle to the desk.

'Lemme see.'

Sam groaned, 'This is a murder enquiry, Fats, not a comic book. Not your sort of thing.'

'Come on, lemme see. Pretty please.'

Prentiss thought of Morton as an okay guy who, for some reason, always smelled vaguely of pear drops and vinegar. After a while standing next to him everyone wanted to move away and get some fresher air. She felt a little sorry for him.

'Okay, Fats.'

She played the sequence again and Fats watched, fascinated. After a few minutes, the smell of vinegar got stronger and Prentiss and Sam craned their heads away from him while trying not to appear too obvious. When the video finished, Fats straightened up and stroked his chin thoughtfully.

'You got anything else?'

Prentiss shook her head. 'Just this.'

Sam said, 'This and a twenty-foot jackal called Anubis.'

Prentiss glared at her. Fats looked interested.

'That a fact? What we talkin' about here? Twenny-foot jackal? What, Twenny-foot? For real? That would be so cool. Tell ol' Fats about it.'

Prentiss gave him the bare facts and he stood nodding, making 'uh-hu' sounds until she was finished. He whistled the wee-ooh, wee-ooh theme from the Twilight Zone.

'That is some grade A weird shit you ladies are dealing with and that's a gold bar facteroonie. You need to be talking with Aliya Petrus. You know her?'

Sam shrugged, 'The name rings a bell, but...'

'Spooky psychic chick, big girl. She helped with the Forster child abduction. Lucy Forster, remember? Aliya told the investigating officer, oh, who was he? Yes, Lloyd Hooper, that was him. Anyway, she told Lloyd where the poor kid was stashed in her teacher's house. Lloyd got straight around there and found Lucy under the bastard's bed, alive but terrified. The teacher only got five years, but that's a long time in solitary. Aliya's the real deal, trust me. She lives out in the projects. I got her number and address if'n you want it.'

Sam asked, 'Why have you got that? Need your horoscope reading?'

Fats chuckled, 'Nah, we went on a few dates back in the day, but it didn't work out. Nice girl and all, but between us,' he lowered his voice. 'Between us, she smells a bit funny. You know what I mean? But don't say anything. Okay?'

Prentiss shook her head, 'No, Fats, never.'

He scuttled back to his desk where he jotted some details onto a bright yellow Post-it note. He came back and presented it to Prentiss.

'Mention my name, it can't do any harm. Lemme know what happens, will ya?'

As ever Prentiss was astonished at the careful neatness of Morton's small, crisp penmanship. Every word and every number was clear as print. Morton was called from the office while Prentiss and Sam read the address and telephone number. Petrus lived in a quiet but run-down part of town.

Sam said, 'It can't hurt, and she helped with the Forster girl.'

Prentiss pulled a face but reached for the telephone and punched in the numbers.

The voice of a little girl answered, 'Hello, who is this?'

Prentiss said, 'Hello, this is detective Prentiss of the NYPD. Is your mommy there?'

'There's nobody here but me. Who are you looking for?'

'I need to speak with Aliya Petrus. Have I got the right number?'

'Yes, you have, detective Prentiss. I am Aliya Petrus. I've been expecting you to call. How can I help you?'

Prentiss raised her eyebrows to Sam who was listening in on the extension.

'I'm sorry, Ms Petrus, but, how do you know me? And, sorry, why were you expecting me to call?'

'Why, detective Prentiss, surely you want to talk with me about the judgement beast? You do, don't you? It is a very dangerous creature, and it knows you, detective Prentiss, it knows you. We need to talk.'

Suddenly the little girl voice vanished and was replaced by speech both deep and masculine that barrelled down the line so hard that both women jerked their heads away from the earpiece.

'I need to see you NOW, detective Prentiss, NOW. I am waiting.'

And the line went dead.

36

Sam put down the extension looking thunderstruck.

'And Fats split up with that dame because she *smelt* funny?'

'You as curious as me?'

'You bet, honey. Let's go. This I've got to see.'

[10]

Sam was of the opinion that most of New York City is beautiful but some places can put a damper on even the most glorious day. 'Others,' she continued, 'are just plain nasty, and help make a depressing day much worse. You sure won't find a toilet like this on no tourist maps.'

A fine drizzle greased the windscreen of the car and condensation fogged its interior, but it couldn't mask the gloomy melancholy of Aliya Petrus' home. Her apartment house looked as if it had been abandoned during a war.

The women parked in a visitor bay and sat quietly looking around until their breath steamed the windows. The project buildings either bulked around them like blocks of geometric misery made solid, or were separated by empty spaces paved with rotting tarmac and surrounded by a network of torn and pointless chicken wire fencing. Prentiss wondered which optimist had mounted basketball hoops at either end of one such gap in the landscape.

A swirling breeze lifted discarded scraps of paper and fast food wrappers in an exhausted mimicry of energy, then flung them back down as if even that feeble act had taken far too much effort. Even the graffiti was half-hearted, barely impacting on its environment. Hope had been dragged from that place by its heels, and then smothered under a thick blanket of despair.

Sam said, 'We can't just sit here. People are going to wonder what we're doing.'

Prentiss agreed, 'Every nerve in my body is screaming at me to get the hell out of here, and I'm a cop with a badge and a gun. What's it like for the poor bastards who live here?'

'Maybe we should do this another day, when the sun's shining?'

'That "I need to see you NOW" sounded pretty emphatic.'

'Yeah, but in geological terms, next spring might be plenty NOW enough.'

'You think?'

'No. You know something? I hate your sophisticated debating style; do you know that?'

'Come on, Plato. Let's move.'

They climbed out of the car and Prentiss made a deliberate show of checking her badge and holstering her pistol before she carefully locked the doors. She wanted to make sure any hidden but interested onlookers would know who and what they were dealing with. They hustled towards the entrance of a grey concrete apartment building which sported a sign bearing

38

the legend: *Prairie West*. Twelve stories of blank windows gazed down at them without a scrap of interest. The building slumped on its foundations like a tired old pit bull, too exhausted to bare its teeth. Prentiss had seen long-term prisoners in the penitentiary who had the same hopelessly blank expression in their eyes as the shrouded windows of those apartments. Men who had once been deadly predators but now had had the juice sucked out of them by terminal boredom. They would sit and watch anything that was moving without interest: the TV, a fly on the window, a prison guard, the pretty detective come to interview them about a cold case. Watching without thinking was something they could do without any effort. It was something to pass the time while they waited to die. Prentiss felt Prairie West was like that, it had been completely drained of joy right from the planning stage. She badly wanted to shoot the architect. Shoot him in the ass where he evidently did his thinking.

Sam was more succinct. 'If New York ever needed a coffee enema, I think we know where to stick the tube.'

'Amen to that.'

The entrance vestibule was gloomy and smelt of mould, stale food, and pine scented disinfectant. Prentiss wondered how she would describe the colour of the walls if somebody put her on the spot. She asked Sam. Her friend looked around and licked her lips in thought.

'Yeah, that's it. Fish belly mixed with drowned, white boy teenager. Been in the water at least a week. Dulux must have a new range out.'

'Tasteful.'

To their astonishment, the elevator quickly arrived when they pressed the call button. However, they were not so surprised at the condition of its interior and decided to take the stairs. Sam held her nose.

'I don't know if people who do that are trying to beautify their environment or scent mark their territory. I wish I hadn't said anything about an enema.'

Prentiss waved away lazy, bloated flies. 'Maybe they think smeared shit looks better on a wall than drowned teenager. You think number thirty-seven will be on the third floor?'

'We can but hope.'

It was on the fourth floor of the building. When they found the stairs they also found the ground floor had been marked with a six-foot letter 'G'. The air was thick with the stench from a pile of black garbage sacks that had been dropped down the stairwell to split on contact with the floor and empty their contents. The first floor was up three short flights of stairs. The same artist who had decorated the interior of the elevator had continued their theme up to the second floor of the stairwell. Sam offered her opinion that perhaps the guy had run out of raw materials. She said, 'I sometimes have mornings like that, what about you?'

'Ewww, gross.'

The light on the third floor seemed dimmer than on the ground. Prentiss checked her watch. Still over two hours to sundown. The stairs they had climbed were housed in a glazed tower built against one shoulder of the building. Apart from the elevator shaft, which ran up the centre, these stairs were the only way in or out of the building. She wondered what kind of person would choose to block their escape from this pallid hell with rotting garbage? Probably the same person who would smear faecal matter an inch deep on the elevator walls. That must have been a true labour of love. She thought tenderly about her own apartment complex and wished she was there.

Sam said, 'Is it me or is it getting darker?'

'Either that or I'm going blind.'

'You see any Japanese film directors or creepy wet kids around here?'

'Sam, I don't see *anyone* around here. Let's get this done and get the hell out of this toilet.'

'You scared?'

'Yes.'

'Good, I didn't want to be the wimpy sidekick.'

Sam leaned against the door and it noisily scraped open on one hinge. A deeply gouged arc cut into the floor demonstrated that this was not a recent problem.

She winced at the sound, 'This place is a real unique fixer-upper opportunity.'

Thirty was on the left. Ten identical doors were spaced either side of the murky, uninviting corridor. A cobweb blackened window at the end leaked a paltry flow of light across the last few feet of sweaty, oily looking linoleum. It was briefly illuminated by a brilliant flash of lightning followed by a booming roll of thunder. The growing tympani of a pounding deluge almost drowned Sam's shriek of fear. Then they were pitched into darkness.

Sam groaned, 'This is going too far. Let's call this off and get *Scooby Doo* in here instead.'

Prentiss looked around for a light switch and spotted a square box at shoulder height on the wall to her right. She pressed it and ceiling lights stuttered into life. They began to walk forward but had only gone a few yards before the lights failed again. They reluctantly decided to keep going and Prentiss used her fingers to count the odd numbered doors on her right.

'Thirty-one,' she muttered, 'thirty-three, thirty-five, thirty...' She stifled a scream when she felt a hand grip her wrist. A little girl's voice whispered gently in her ear.

'I thought it was you. I've been waiting. I think there's been a power-cut. I've got candles inside. Come in. Bring your friend. She's frightened.'

Prentiss allowed herself to be led forward, her heart pounding in her throat. She had the impression of a large mass moving before her, but the hand on her wrist felt small.

'Are you Aliya?'

'Yes, Prentiss. It is good to meet you, and you too, Samantha Bolat. Please, have you got any matches or a cigarette lighter?'

'No, sorry, I haven't.'

Sam said, 'Sorry, me neither.'

'Oh, what a shame. Neither have I. Silly of me. I have candles and no way to light them.' At that the masculine voice Prentiss had heard on the phone roared, 'Silly, stupid, BITCH!'

Another flash of lightning flared a burst of dusty grey light into the room and Prentiss fleetingly saw a bulking shape swathed in some diaphanous fabric. It didn't seem to have a head but instead a cone of material sat on its shoulders, like a beekeeper's protective mesh.

The little girl was whining, 'I'm sorry, I'll get some next time I go out. I promise. My mind's been on other things, you know that. It has been so hard to concentrate with the Beast abroad at night, and the man watching from his mountain.'

The voice paused in the darkness, then whispered. 'Prentiss, he knows you. He sees you. I must warn you that he isn't what you think. Watch the shadows. Look to the past and you will find him. Look to the future and he will find you. Wait long enough, and he will come to you.' She paused again, then continued, 'Give William my love. Tell him he didn't break my heart. It was my fault, I allowed him to smell himself and he didn't like it. Tell him hello from Aliya.'

The voice changed, becoming a sibilant hiss that sounded like escaping gas. 'Now you must leave, you must leave, you must leave, you must leave...'

Prentiss felt a firm hand at her elbow, Sam's voice came loud and insistent in her ear.

'Outstaying our welcome, honey. Time to go.'

41

'I hear you.'

They collided with the apartment's doorframe in their hurry to find the exit, and then fled down the corridor to the tower containing the stairwell. Behind them the hissing sound grew louder and louder, '...you must leave, you must leave, YOU MUST LEAVE.'

And then it was suddenly terminated as if someone had put a hand over the woman's mouth. Prentiss paused in the darkness and almost turned to find out if Aliya Petrus was all right. She took a single step back towards apartment thirty-seven. The man's voice roared, 'AND DON'T COME BACK!'

She heard Sam yelp, 'Fuck that! Let's get the Hell out of this madhouse.'

The broken door leading back to the stairwell had somehow closed once more and it took the strength of both women to lever it fully open. The opened doorway cast a dull orange light back into the corridor. Something large and pale hulked there and began to move towards them. The sight of it lent wings to their heels.

Back by the car they stood in the torrential rain for a moment while they caught their breath and Prentiss searched desperately for her key fob. For one panicky moment, she thought she had dropped it somewhere in the darkened building and whimpered at the idea of going back in to retrieve it. Then she found it tucked under a packet of tissues in her jacket pocket. She unlocked the doors and they climbed into the relative shelter of the vehicle. She locked the doors once they were both safely inside. She realised Sam was shaking and she wondered if it was due to cold, wetness, fear, or a combination of all three. With surprise, she realised her friend was shaking with silent laughter. It sparked her off too, and for a long minute the pair of them rocked in their seats while the toxic river of panic flowed out of them and away into the night. They were breathing hard and finally beginning to calm down when they perceived a shadowy figure approaching their car in the rain. He was lean and silhouetted by the sodium glare of streetlights. He was wearing low-slung baggy jeans, a metallic bomber jacket and a torn tee shirt. His young face was dirty with a beard and his wet hair slicked down his olive coloured face. When he reached the car, he pounded on the windscreen and then pointed at his crotch, waggling his hips towards them. Prentiss and Sam saw his erect penis in the same moment and their reaction was simultaneous. They drew their guns in unison and aimed them straight at the youth's tumescent flesh.

When he realised what they were doing the youth threw his hands in the air and then ran into the night, his stiff penis thrust out of his jeans like a hitchhiker's thumb. Sam shook her head.

'What made that boy think that bitty little thing was worth showing to two grown women?'

Prentiss grinned. 'Most normal thing that's happened since we got here. I don't know about you but I've had it. I'm going home. I want to have a shower and wash this crazy day out of my hair, and then I want to grab a red pen, open my diary, and write "Dear diary, what the fuck just happened" in capital letters three inches high right across the page. Can I give you a lift?'

'Mighty grateful, honey. I need to get out of the *The X-Files* and back to the madhouse my kids call home. Mind you, I can see what Fats liked about that woman. I bet that's the only time he's had three in the bed.'

Prentiss started the engine and glanced across at Prairie West. The building was still in darkness even though the streetlamps were lit.

'Sam, if there was a power cut shouldn't the streetlamps be out too? Want to go back and find out if anything...'

'Honey, nothing would compel me to spend another second in that dump. Put your detective head back in its holster and take me home. This girl's day is done.'

But for Prentiss it wasn't, as she discovered a few hours later when her cell phone rang while she was making a cursory meal of cold chicken, olives, and cheese washed down with a glass of Californian Sauvignon.

'Evening, Prentiss, it's Tabaqui. Sorry to bother you at home, but I thought you might like to know. They're doing it again.'

'The wolves?'

'Yes. Have you noticed the time?'

She looked at her clock, it was two minutes after eight. Somewhere, someone was being weighed in the balance. Her heart pounded in her chest.

'Prentiss? Prentiss, you still there?'

'Oh, Tabaqui, what does it mean?'

'I don't know, honestly I don't know. At least the rain has stopped.'

'Small mercies. Sam and I saw a medium this afternoon, she warned me about a creature she called the Beast, and something about a man on his mountain.'

'Say what? A medium? Why? Hey, they've stopped now, the wolves. It's over.'

Prentiss was sure it was. For someone. She wondered which celebrity would be on Feldman's slab the next morning.

'Prentiss, do you want me to come over? Keep you company? Just, you know, talk. I can be there in half an hour or so.'

'Thanks, but it's getting late... wait. How do you know it takes half an hour to get here?'

'What? Oh, I drove by your place the other day to make sure I know where it is. I'm seeing you tomorrow at seven thirty and there are two things I hate, being late and getting lost. It's a Howlett thing, I guess. My dad was the same, drove mum mad. We were both born wanting Sat Navs in our heads. Glad I've got one in the car, it's a lifesaver. Without it I'd go mad. Tell me about this medium woman, sounds freaky.'

'It was.'

They spoke easily for another ten minutes before she told him they'd best save something to talk about for the following evening and hung up. It had been a while since she'd felt anything like such familiarity with a man her own age. And, as Sam said, he was cute, despite her undercurrent of fear that he might be some sort of stalker. She remembered the boy called Phil Clancy when she was seventeen. He was a college jock, a few years older than her, and he had asked her out on a date. She had turned him down.

After that he took to hanging around her parents' house. At one time, Prentiss had been sunbathing in the backyard, a tidy lawned area with flowers and shrubs and a tall fence that kept it discreet from prying eyes. It was during summer vacation. Her father was at work and, although her mother was also on holiday, Prentiss was alone in the house while her mother was out running some errands.

Summer heat had made her drowsy and Prentiss feel asleep, face down on her lounger. She was relaxed, knowing she was safe, and secure in her own backyard. With a shock, she awoke to find hands stroking her shoulders. Clancy was by her side, touching her, whispering, 'It's all right, it's all right, it's only me.'

She had screamed and started shouting for him to get away from her. He started struggling with her and his breathing became laboured. Clancy began raising his voice while trying to wrest her bikini top away from her breasts. He kneaded her flesh with bruising fingers. She pounded at him but her fists were having no effect on her powerful attacker. She felt him tugging at her waistband, trying to touch her down there. He sucked saliva through his teeth and grinned. She was powerless to stop what was going to happen. He chuckled with a thick, wet sound.

And then he was gone, pulled away from her, his hands flailing wildly at the metal baseball bat gripped tight against his throat.

Her mother was suddenly there, hugging her, fury blazing in her eyes, but it was her next-door neighbour, Mr Wiśniewski, who had dragged Clancy away. Clancy was a strong youth but Wiśniewski was a marine, home on furlough, and he was furious.

His wife hurried to Wiśniewski's side. 'Don't kill him Pavel, don't kill him.'

'He's filth, look what he did to the poor kid. He's filth, the little shit.'

He tightened his grip on the bat and pulled it hard against Clancy's throat. The youth's face was turning purple.

Wiśniewski's wife held up her cell phone. 'Pavel, please, I've called the police, listen, they're here, they're here right now. Please, don't kill him.'

The doppler howl of sirens drew to a halt nearby and within seconds two uniformed officers had run up the drive and around the house to the scene. The lead officer eyed Wiśniewski. He spoke firmly.

'Thank-you, sir. We'll take him from here. You can let him go.'

45

'This filthy shit tried to rape the little girl.'

'Thank-you, sir, we'll deal with him now.'

Clancy was cuffed and taken away. During the trial, his father claimed Prentiss was a tease who had flaunted herself and tormented his son. He said the girl had led Clancy on, taunted him and then changed her mind at the last minute. He said she had deliberately been sunbathing half-naked in plain view.

Wiśniewski was the key prosecution witness. He had been up a ladder clearing his guttering, an annual chore, when he saw the Clancy youth sneaking around the house. He saw Clancy's attack on a 'defenceless sleeping girl half his size' and ran to her defence, pausing only to pick up his baseball bat.

Wiśniewski's wife had seen his charge from the kitchen window, grabbed her phone and ran after him, arriving just as Prentiss' mother pulled into the drive and flung herself out of her car to race to her daughter's side.

Prentiss' mother had had a premonition while standing at the chilled fish counter of the big store in the retail park a mile outside town. She had dropped everything, left her shopping in the trolley, and raced home. In fact, the officers who had attended the scene hadn't at first been responding to Mrs Wiśniewski's call but had been racing after the speeding vehicle driven by Mrs Prentiss. Her speeding charge was later quietly dropped.

Clancy eventually changed his plea to guilty and received a plea-bargained, suspended three-year sentence for assault and sexual assault with intent to rape. He was also given an injunction that he must never be found within three hundred yards of either Prentiss or her home.

He was dropped by his football team and suspended from college. Sometimes Prentiss thought she could see him in the distance. It looked as if his big, hard-trained frame was turning to fat. She heard he got a job with his father's company as a sales rep. To date Clancy had been Prentiss' only personal experience of stalking and physical assault, but he had coloured her view of the male sex ever since. At the age of twenty-five she was still a virgin. It was a status she would, perhaps, relinquish to just one man, and she hoped she would know him when she met him. She had also gained a blackbelt second Dan in TaeKwon-do. She vowed that if anyone tried it on with her again he wouldn't walk away without crutches.

Prentiss found her mind drifting back to that day eight years before and felt a shiver run up her spine. Clancy had tried to tell his friends that he and Prentiss had had consensual sex on a regular basis and she had loved it, took it everywhere, couldn't get enough. He said she only panicked that day because she thought her mother was due back and she didn't want to get caught. Everything the neighbour said in court was a lie, and she had put out for him to get him to perjure himself. Prentiss, said Clancy, was nothing but a little slut and one day she would get hers. Some of his friends believed him, others thought he was a sick creep and told her what he had been saying. His words had hurt and embarrassed her for a while, but she had never told her parents for fear of what her father might do.

She idly wondered what she would do if she met Clancy again. She picked up her pistol and idly aimed it across the room at her TV, which had been showing a popular quiz show with the sound off. On the screen stood a hooded figure in a jackal mask pointing back at her. She gasped in fright.

Her cell phone began to ring.

12

The body had been found near a dumpster in the corner of a vacant car lot by a man whose dog, he explained, had 'troublesome guts' and as a result was keeping him out at all hours, 'no matter how lousy the weather'. The victim had been identified as Errol M, a retired rapper famous for his charitable work with both gifted musical children and the disabled young. More recently he had starred in a daytime show called *Ask Errol* during which he would grant some lucky children their dearest wish, and had since become as celebrated for his bling as he was for his booming baritone voice and catchphrase 'The kids gotta have it and Errol's gonna give it'.

The killer's MO was the same as it had been for Puckling and Hart. Half his bowel had been sheered away but he was otherwise untouched. No defensive marks on his hands or arms, just plenty of heavy gold chains and rings. His neck was carrying the entire stock of an expensive jewellery store window. From the waist down he was naked, including his feet. Sam eyed his exposed and diminutive genitals. She took a sly look at Prentiss.

'Look at that bitty little thing. Want to bet Erskine would say he was a kiddy fiddler?'

'No bet. Is that always the first thing you look at?'

'Got to keep your eyes on the prize. Can't stir no coffee without no spoon, you hear what I'm saying?'

'Ewww, gross. Bet you there's going to be canid DNA in the bites, but Feldman's still convinced it's some sort of weapon or device.'

'Ask him, he's over there.'

Feldman was sniffing dubiously at a grande paper cup of steaming take-out coffee. He eyed Prentiss mournfully as she approached.

'What do they do with coffee in Seattle? The French make good coffee look easy and the Italians treat it as an art form. What do they do with it in Seattle that sucks all the life out of it? How can I help you? I suppose the good officer Bolat sent you over to break my balls?'

'Anything new?'

Feldman indicated his team who were working in their all enclosing environment suits under bright, tripod mounted LED lamps.

'Too early to tell, the urban spacemen are conducting a fingertip search even as we speak. I presume there's no CCTV?'

Prentiss pointed to a camera on a pole, one of three in the car lot.

'Uniform is trying to find out where they feed to. My bet is, if we see anything from those, we'll see Errol over there getting dumped by a guy in a hoodie driving a black, or dark, Mercedes Vito van. I'd estimate the body was dumped between eight thirty and nine forty-five. Time of death eight o'clock near as damn it.'

'You want to sign the death certificate while you're doing the rest of my job?'

'This killing is a carbon copy of the other two. That makes three this week and its only Thursday. And so far, we have nothing to go on but the van. It's too frustrating.'

Feldman sniffed. 'The killer has to have an agenda. How's he selecting his victims? Maybe he hates celebrities? Maybe he's on welfare and wished someone would hand him some easy money? Maybe he's a psycho freak who built a big artificial dog and likes to let it bite people? You're the detective, I'm the pathologist, you tell me.'

'Jackal. It's a jackal not a dog. Dr. Howlett said jackal.'

'Yes, yes he did. And he confirmed the saliva as definitely canid, but you already know all that. Prentiss, the only jackals you'll find around here play ice hockey, and they don't go around biting lumps out of famous people for the fun of it. There has to be some freak out there getting his rocks off by doing this. Check out the fanzines and chat rooms, see what comes up. This creep needs to be stopped or every charity gala will be filled with nothing but empty seats and the poor kiddies will have to go without Christmas this year.'

'Yeah? Well maybe Anubis hates hypocrites. Question is, who is he? Where is he? In fact, is he even a he? We don't know squat.' She changed tack. 'Hey, where's the nearest mountain to here?'

'Mountain? Nearest? I'm not sure, Catamounts, Adirondacks, Overlook. Why?'

'How long would it take to get from any of those to here?'

'I've been to Overlook, it takes over two hours. Say maybe three from the others. How do mountains come into it?'

She felt deflated. She had hoped Aliya's mention of the man on his mountain might be a clue, but it could also be a red herring. Wherever the killings took place had to be within a radius of no more than half an hour from the Bronx by van. She remembered Tabaqui telling her it took him half an hour to get from the Sanctuary to her place, that would make it roughly the same for him to get to the Bronx. Was that a clue? She berated herself.

49

Was she treating Tabaqui Howlett as a suspect now? That was insane. She was finally going crazy.

Feldman looked away from the LED lamps blazing around the crime scene.

'Prentiss, you don't need to look for mountains around New York City. You want to get high off the ground you're standing in the middle of one of the biggest man-made mountain ranges in the world. How many buildings in the Big Apple are over a thousand feet tall? If they were natural that would make them mountains. It's nuts to think that way but this whole thing is nuts. Why the sudden interest in mountains anyway?'

Prentiss grabbed him and planted a kiss on his mouth.

'Feldman, you're a genius and I love you.'

He raised his eyebrows and touched his mouth.

'You're very welcome, and whatever I did I hope to do it again someday.'

'You will, don't worry.'

Prentiss loped back to where Sam was chatting with a woman in uniform. The woman pointed to a service station adjoining the car lot.

'That's the place, detective Bolat, the cameras feed to the back office in there. The owner sometimes parks customers' automobiles here and his insurance insists he provides at least the absolute minimum of security so he invested in the cameras. He's got the recordings set up for you now.'

Sam nodded, 'You seen them?'

'Yes, they're not brilliant. Not much light around here, but you can see the van arrive. Worth a look.'

The detectives hustled to the service station. Prentiss told Sam she had an idea that might bear fruit but that it could wait until after they'd seen the footage. They found the owner stacking packets of cigarettes into the shelves behind his counter and had to thread their way through densely packed aisles packed with groceries and candy to reach him. He was a slender balding Asian with a thick black moustache. He looked as if he was permanently exhausted. As they approached he waved out of his window towards the forensic team's LED lamps.

'This is all I need. All I need. It's such a damned bother. People will come to look at the place Errol M's body was found but they won't spend a cent in here. Why couldn't they have dumped the poor man outside Walmart? They don't need the trade like I do. Such a bother.'

Sam said, 'I'm sorry, sir. Sorry, could I take your name?'

'I told the uniformed officer. It's Patel, Clinton Patel. You can call me Clint if you can keep the stupid grin off your face.'

'I'm sorry for your trouble, Clint...' She was fighting a smile. 'Really sorry. We're told you have footage of the scene, may we see it, please?'

'Yes, of course. Will your friend stay here while I turn it on please? I can't leave my store unattended for so much as a heartbeat. They'll steal me blind in seconds. Junkies you know, the whole block is filthy with them. They're out there, out in the shadows. Always looking for an opportunity.' He raised his voice and looked back behind them into the rear of his store. 'Yes, sir? Can I help you? Please, don't worry about my friends here, I'm just helping these very fine police officers with their enquiries.'

The greasy looking young black man who had silently slipped into the store pulled his long coat tightly around his scrawny body and bobbed his head urgently. He mumbled something incoherent and tumbled back out into the night.

Patel sighed. 'And so, it starts. Every night the same. Welcome to my world ladies. When you leave, I shall lock that door behind you and serve people through that armoured window, so much for customer relations.'

He reached under his counter and showed them his pistol.

'And my little friend here will always be within reach. It is all properly licenced, don't worry about that. I am a member of the American Retailers' Gun Executive of National Traders. I think they made that work a bit too hard for a funky acronym, don't you? ARGENT. I truly believe such rubbish is invented by Cretins Ripping American to Pieces, don't you? Now, let me show you the CCTV footage. After you officer.'

He followed Sam into the back room while a bemused Prentiss was seeing the acronym CRAP glow in her mind's eye and chuckled to herself. Patel was back moments later and grinned at her.

'I see you got it, not everyone does. Thank-you for minding the store for me, please, join your friend.'

It was dark in the back room and crowded with stock. Two chairs had been wedged together in front of a bank of three TV screens. On each the empty car lot glowed dimly. An empty white carrier bag caught in an errant gust of wind made its way across the screens from right to left, performing almost a wide 'U' shape due to the positions of the cameras, and then vanished from view.

Seconds later a black van came in from the left and stopped midway across the centre screen, which left its front half on one screen pointing at an acute angle to its rear on another. A dark figure in a hoodie climbed down from its cabin and made its way to the back doors, which were in plain view. He opened one of the doors and climbed inside. Seconds later a figure

51

tumbled to the ground and lay sprawled and unmoving. The person in the hoodie jumped to the ground and closed the door. Then they looked directly up at the camera and lifted their gloved right hand in the classic two fingers extended gun shape.

Sam gasped, 'Bingo. There it is, the jackal mask. Prentiss, we've got Anubis on film. This is perfect.'

They watched until the van pulled away, and then Sam went to tell Patel they would need copies of the recordings. Prentiss wondered if that briefly disclosing sequence would still be there when they checked later. She doubted it.

13

'So, now *I'm* seeing this weird shit too?'

'Yes, Sam. It must be catching. Sorry about that.'

'How can it just disappear like that?'

'Your guess is as good as mine.'

'They think we're losing it, you know that, don't you? They already think you're *Looney Toons* and now they're mentally measuring me for a straightjacket.'

The gun finger sequence had vanished from the footage, as had the jackal mask reveal. On replay, back at the precinct in front of an eager audience of fellow officers who had been told what Sam and Prentiss had seen, everything played as it had at Patel's store. Right up until M's corpse flopped out of the back of the van. The hoodie followed it, closed the door, and just as Sam breathed 'Now' kept its face down and angled towards the vehicle until they had climbed back into the darkness of the cab. Prentiss thought there might have been a faintly muzzle-like silhouette briefly outlined in the dim dashboard light when the hoodie started the engine, but didn't want to mention it in front of the disappointed crowd who were confronting them with baffled questions.

Sam held her arms out, asking for patience. 'Okay, sorry. We were mistaken. What can I say? How about you cut us some slack here, guys? You telling me you bozos never, ever made a mistake? We said sorry, okay? Sorry. Look, its late, let's go home and reconvene in the morning. Okay? Goodnight. Yeah? Goodnight. Ciao. Go home, we love ya, now get outta here'

When they were finally alone together Sam breathed a deep sigh.

'Well, that could have been a little less embarrassing.'

'As Clint said, "Welcome to my world". You're right, Sam. It's late and we're tired, but look at this...'

Prentiss rewound the footage until she found the few seconds of the hoodie's profile in the dashboard lights. She froze it. The grainy image seemed to crawl across the screen but there it was. A muzzle.

Sam, squinted. 'Am I seeing things or is there a dog driving that van? Do we tell anyone or wait to see if it's still there in the morning?'

'It's been a long day. Tomorrow's plenty soon enough.'

Sam ran a hand through her hair and shook her head then worked her shoulders as if to loosen them. 'I could sleep for a year. This case started weird and then got worse. We need to see if Manchester was on Erskine's naughty boy list. That reminds me, you said you had an idea for a possible lead, what was it?'

'It can wait for the morning. And anyway, it's probably mad as Feldman's twenty-foot clockwork jackal. My head needs to be spending time in a padded cell. I need a shower and glass of wine and my bed. Let's hit the road Mrs Bolat.'

'Forget the wine and come to my place. Eat pizza, wonder why I ever married the big galoot who shares my bed, and then take a sniff at my boys' heads. They smell just wonderful, especially when they're washed and asleep. Like a drug to a mother and solid therapy. Just as good as your bottle of wine I promise you.'

'Sounds great, I'll take a rain check on all of it, I promise. I'll even order the pizza. But tonight, I need to go home and enjoy that glass of wine. Walk you to the garage?'

Her silent apartment welcomed her with open arms, or so it felt when Prentiss walked through the door, slipped off her shoes, and stretched until her shoulders popped. She padded into her kitchen and poured herself the promised glass of wine. There was another half glass left in the bottle so she took that with her into her lounge and put it on a coaster within easy reach. She climbed into her black leather *Stressless* recliner, tucked her feet under her bottom, and relaxed, taking her first welcome sip of the wine. She took a deep breath and rubbed her neck. Lassitude threatened to steal her away from wakefulness, so she put her wine down and luxuriated under a quick shower. She went back to her wine in her white cotton nightshirt and a white robe. She could hear the siren call of her bed from across the hall and sipped from her glass before adding the remains of her bottle. She regarded the wall-mounted black screen of her TV and the remote on the table. The red stand-by light glowed balefully at her. She decided against a trawl through the late-night oddness that made up the content of most channels at approaching midnight. Her days were odd enough without any help, thank-you. She thought of Sam sniffing at her sleeping son's heads and bantering with her other half. She would probably be putting toys away while telling her man, Marty, about her day. Prentiss wondered if she would mention the disappearing jackal mask footage. Police officers were asked to refrain from discussing active cases with loved ones, especially murder cases, but it happened all the time, she knew it. She didn't envy Sam, but she did wonder what it would be like to share her private life with a special person. She loved the look that came into Sam's eyes when she spoke about her family. They

54

were the hub around which the rest of her world revolved. She would be lost without them.

Prentiss' eyes began to close and her head sank to her chest. She fought against exhaustion just long enough to take her empty glass and bottle back into her kitchen, brush her teeth, shuck off her robe, and climb into bed. Sleep claimed her in minutes.

She was still wearing her white cotton nightshirt, but on her feet were sandals woven from yellow grasses or reeds. A hot wind lifted the hem of her garment and blew flint scented dust into her face and around her bare legs. Rising above her was a brown ridge of mountains framed by a flat blue sky. She was on a pale stretch of road leading up towards the tallest conical peak in the ridge. Brown-skinned men and women toiled up the road with heavy baskets filled with produce, or loped down with similar baskets but empty. She was reminded of a busy double line of ants she had seen in her parents' yard as a child. Both men and women were naked except for a little skirt, a rope belt, and sandals like hers. Despite the breeze the air was arid. She looked around. In the distance to either side of the great shoulder of stone flowed silver ribbons of water. She was standing in a land between two rivers. Why was that important? Prentiss felt compelled to follow the labourers and began to climb. She sweated in the heat and her thin cotton nightdress stuck to her nakedness in a revealing way. She felt embarrassed at first but nobody was looking at her. It was as if she had become invisible. For the first time since she was a teenager people were ignoring her. Even so she was glad that she always slept in her panties. The scanty garment preserved some of her modesty. She continued her climb, leaning into the ascent.

Her path took her between two black sculptures that somehow looked both ancient and recently carved. She thought they had been fashioned from basalt, a notoriously hard material to work with. Both stood about fifteen feet tall above stepped plinths. The sculptures depicted snarling winged demons, bandy legged creatures with well-proportioned human torsos and heads like jaguars or lions. Each was wearing a skirt like that of the labourers around her, but instead of sandals they had clawed feet. Each was holding a weapon that looked like a bolt of lightning, or a series of waves made solid, she couldn't quite make out which. She wondered why she was taking the sculptures so very seriously, but they seemed important and threatening. The labourers crouched lower when they passed between them, as if afraid of being struck. She quickened her step until she had stepped out of their shadow. She looked ahead and paused, dumbfounded by awe. Her path ended in a great pillared doorway carved from the living stone of the mountain. It was massive. The lintel looked heavy enough to crush everyone scurrying under it. Six more basalt demons, three on each side of the path, towered over the stream of people passing to and from the black portal. Despite the blinding sunshine not a single ray of light illuminated into the portal's darkness. Her belly tightened with fear, but she couldn't resist the charisma of the doorway. She knew she must enter. She stepped to one side of the stream of people and hurried forward. The nearer she got to the doorway the bigger it seemed, until it dwarfed her and she felt the sheer weight of it press down on her. A cold breath of air was expelled from the interior and she felt the hair on her arms spring to attention.

She entered the shadows. One of them moved at her side. A great black hand gripped her shoulder firmly. The ebon eyes of Anubis gazed deeply into hers.

'Are you ready to be weighed in the balance?'

He reached forward and plucked at her chest. She felt a wrenching pain. When he withdrew his hand, it contained her beating heart.

She woke up in her bedroom. Her sheets were drenched in cold sweat and her hair matted to her skull. The shadows in the room seemed to mill around her as if they wanted to touch her. A great figure seemed to tower over her. She switched on her sidelight and the shadows fled back to the corners of the room. She placed her hand firmly against her ribs and with relief felt her heart still pounding in its allotted place.

[14]

The next day she woke up feeling exhausted and rang in sick then retired back to her bed. But she couldn't sleep. Her cell phone rang, it was Sam.

'Hi, honey, they tell me you're poorly. Need a bowl of soup?'

'No, Sam, thanks. Really, I'm fine. Had a rough night, you know? I'm seeing Tabaqui tonight and I didn't want to greet him looking like the frightmare witch. And anyway, you and me, we've got the weekend off, so I thought I deserved a little extra me time. Make it a long weekend. Get some rest.'

'Okay, but you said you had an idea that might be worth following up. I like your ideas, they usually make sense. What was it? Might give me something to do today.'

Prentiss told her friend about the buildings as mountains theory that Feldman had posited.

'Remember, Aliya talked about the "Man on his mountain". Anubis was called that back in the day. What if *our* Anubis lives in one of the thousand foot plus high rises within a half hour radius of the Bronx by van. That might work, and still fit in with the Anubis legend.'

'That means real money, you won't get into one of those condos without a credit rating would make a banker's eyes water.'

'Told you it was just an idea. I know it's lean.'

'Positively anorexic, but worth a thought. Okay, I'll do some research, oh, by the way, the muzzle was still there this morning.'

'Muzzle? Oh, the muzzle. Really? That's great, we're vindicated.'

'Not really, Fats was the only guy who could see it. The rest are still measuring me for the straightjacket.'

'Keep your head down. Let's see what we can turn up. Fancy lunch?'

'Sure, where?'

'How about the Metropolitan Museum? We can go to the roof garden bar.'

'Why not, the sun's shining for once. And I'm sure you'll tell me why when I get there. One o'clock?'

'See you then.'

Prentiss had one of those minds that sometimes surprised its owner by throwing up ideas that she hadn't completely thought through – but somehow still made perfect sense. She had visited an exhibition of Egyptian artefacts at the Metropolitan Museum of Art during the previous fall and had spent a

57

fascinating afternoon browsing the displays. If she wanted to beard Anubis in his den, she thought, that would be the place to start.

An hour later she was climbing the steps to one of the finest buildings on Fifth Avenue and one of the greatest art museums in the world. She was proud of her breathtaking city, proud of its confidence and energy. You need powerful shoulders to carry a place like The Met with anything approaching the right level of swagger, and New York was built like a linebacker.

Her long stride quickly carried her through the vast halls. In her dream, she had been invisible to the labourers. Such was not the case in The Met. She was drawing attention as if she was one of the artworks. Hungry eyes followed her progress with interest. She was inured to it. Her mission was to track down a jackal god, the Guardian of the Underworld. Horny little devils were five cents the bushel. She tried to remember what she had learned during her last visit. The Met had thousands of Egyptian artefacts from the Middle Kingdom, a time when the Nile delta flourished as one of the five great defining ancient civilisations of mankind, which also included Mesopotamia, Persia, Anatolia, and China. Rome and Greece were toddlers by comparison.

She entered gallery 131 of the Sackler Wing, the hall of Egyptian antiquities, and almost instantly her eyes were drawn to an arch and a stone building some twenty feet tall. She approached it until her progress was halted by a little moat. The plaque informed her that she was looking at the Temple of Dendur from the West Bank of the Nile. It had been completed in ten BC, when Egypt was ruled from Rome by Augustus Caesar. The great nation had become a puppet state. The little temple had seen a lot since it first opened its doors. Prentiss wondered if the most famous Cleopatra had ever cast her shadow on its walls, if Julius Caesar had ever turned his appraising glance towards its pillars. It was a miniature version of the vast portal in her dream. She heard again the voice asking if she was ready to be weighed in the balance, and shivered at the memory of her heart being plucked from her chest.

'Why, detective Prentiss, you look as if you've seen a ghost. Are you, all right?'

She jumped and muffled a slight scream. Gee Erskine had walked to her side, and she had been so absorbed in her thoughts that she hadn't noticed his approach. His wide, hawk-like eyes studied her face with concerned interest. She compared his scrutiny with that of the men she had passed during her walk through the museum and found none of their heat in him, just genuine concern.

'Mr Erskine. Good to see you. What a surprise to find you here.'

'Gee, please. And I was about to say the same thing. I come here all the time, this is one of my favourite haunts, but I don't think I've ever seen you here before. And, believe me, I would have noticed such a charming woman even if I hadn't been formally introduced, which, by the way, I consider we have.' He smiled to disarm his statement. 'So, then, what brings you to my second home? Is it the little temple or are you interested in Egypt in general?'

She couldn't stop herself, she blurted out 'I want to see Anubis, the jackal god.'

He nodded his understanding. 'Then let me introduce you to him.'

And he took her hand.

He led her to a display case that contained a figure over sixteen inches tall.

'Here he is, Anubis lite I think of him. Painted plaster on wood. They say he's meant to be greeting and calming the spirit of a recently deceased pharaoh, but to me he looks like a game show host telling his audience to settle down. *That* is not the face of the god who guards the underworld and must judge fresh souls in the halls of truth. Will that jolly little fellow lead the dead to immortal life in paradise? Would he damn them to an eternity of torment in the belly of a hybrid monster? Of course not, he's a stand-up comedian delivering his punchline. Look at that outfit, more Harlequin than harbinger of hell, don't you think?'

Prentiss could understand what Erskine was saying. This was not the awesome creature of her dreams, that dark spectre was not like this friendly little Dude, who was wearing a fetching mini dress detailed with a red and blue diamond pattern. Nor did her dream jackal display the gentle smile of a teacher pacifying a roomful of over-excited first graders.

Erskine continued his monologue. 'This was made over two thousand three hundred years ago, but it is quite modern really. Look at this...'

They walked to another gallery where he showed her the carved figure of a recumbent jackal. 'There we are, that one's about three hundred years older. Dog waiting for its master to come home. These are not the manifestations of true deity. These are brand images meant to reassure customers that the embalmer and his team are on personal and friendly terms with the afterlife. They even wore Anubis masks while they worked. I bet they came off as soon as the public left the workshop. Now, look at this...'

He fetched his smartphone from an inside pocket and tapped on its screen for a few moments. Finally, 'There, what about him?'

59

She found herself face-to-face with a solemn basalt figurine. It had gravity and power. Erskine smiled at her expression.

'Yes, that's the Anubis you're looking for. And that look in your eyes, that's recognition, isn't it?'

She nodded, 'Is that here?'

'No, that one's in Paris, in the Louvre. Powerful looking chap, isn't he? So then, what's attracting one of the most beautiful homicide detectives in New York's forty-second precinct to one of the most mysterious characters in ancient religion?'

Prentiss looked at her watch, the time was just after eleven.

She said, 'Mr Erskine, I'm meeting my friend here, up in the roof bar, at one. Can we go somewhere to talk, please? I think you can be a great help to our investigation. If you have the time?'

'I'm a freelancer. My time is my own. It would be a great pleasure to spend a few hours in such delightful company. Shall we retire to the cafeteria? The view of Central Park on a day like this will help sweeten the taste of extremely average coffee. And please, as I said, call me Gee. What shall I call you?'

She shrugged, 'Prentiss. It's my name.'

15

'Of course, I'm interested in Egyptian culture, why not? I was born there and I spent a lot of my childhood there, I still visit whenever I can. There's a lot more to the Nile delta than tourists will ever see, and there are still many treasures to be found if you know where to look. Mystery and romance has always run through the veins of every Egyptian, but these days the ancient magic has been diluted by a sad mixture of politics and extremism. Very sad, Rameses would be spinning in his sarcophagus.'

Erskine had been proved right about the disappointing coffee, but the view of the park was also everything he had promised. Prentiss sipped at the lukewarm, mud coloured beverage cradled in her hands. She idly wondered what Feldman would say about it. Nothing flattering she was sure.

Erskine was in his stride. 'Anubis is the Greek version of his name, of course, but I think you know that. Ancient Egyptians would have recognised him by a host of other names: Anpu, Anupu or even Wip. But I guess that would be like trying to call Jesus Christ by the name Yeshua bar Yoseph. Who would know who you meant? So, Anubis it is. Jackal headed god, protector, and guide for the souls of the dead. Judge and jury of a soul's purity. He isn't Egyptian you know, and he isn't really a jackal.'

This last brought Prentiss' attention fully into the room.

'He isn't? Then what is he?'

Erskine shrugged, 'A fascinating enigma, a rebus, perhaps an angel? You are asking me to encapsulate years of study into an hour's conversation. Some would say that Anubis is an alien and that his jackal mask is actually a type of breathing apparatus, like Darth Vader, you know?'

He placed his cupped hand over his mouth and made asthmatic breathing sounds, then grinned at her.

'Was God a spaceman? It's a theory, but it fails to acknowledge human imagination and intelligence. Gods were probably created by mankind to answer big questions: where do we come from when we're born, where do we go when we die? Where does the sun go at night, and what eats the moon during the phases of the month? Jackals were seen haunting burial sites but they weren't digging up the bodies, so were they there guarding the dead? It isn't that much of a stretch to go from that to a jackal god caring for souls in the Underworld. Is that where Anubis comes from? His name was found in the earliest mastabas in Egypt, and he had been linked to judgement from the very beginning. That "god and protector of embalmers" nonsense can be ignored as pure vanity on behalf of the embalmers. No, like the sphinx, he pre-dates the pyramids. I wonder if he might have once become Melek Taus, the peacock angel of the Yazadi Kurds.'

'I don't know that one.'

'Oh, but you do. Christians and Muslims call him Shaitan. Or Satan. If you've become interested in the mysteries you should consider studying Yazdânism, highly recommended. But I digress, you must stop me if I become boring. Now, where was I? Ah, yes... Religious belief predates writing, and sacred sites predate settlements. For instance, Göbekli Tepe in present-day Turkey is a massive monolithic temple that makes Stonehenge look like a gazebo, but it was built by hunter gatherers in around nine thousand BC – or BCE in new money. Or, I know, better yet, dip into the mythology of ancient Sumer. Sumerian religion starts with the Anunnaki, who were a pantheon of good and evil gods and goddesses who, in the writings of the Sumerians, came down to Earth to create humanity. According to some sources, these gods came from a place called Nibiru, or the "Planet of the Crossing". The Sumerians claimed that one year on planet Nibiru, a period known as a sar, was equivalent to three thousand six hundred Earth years. Anunnaki lifespans were immense. They lived for one hundred and twenty sars, which is about four hundred and thirty-two thousand years. That means an Anunnaki alive at the time of the Sumerians could easily still be alive today. According to the Sumer King List one hundred and twenty sars had passed from the time the Anunnaki arrived on Earth to the time of the Great Flood.'

Erskine's eye glittered, 'According to the *"Was God an astronaut"* theories propounded by people like Erich von Daniken, the Anunnaki, and other alien species, came to Earth and seeded humans in many variations, and always for their own purposes. Unfortunately, we poor humans have always had a way of pissing off our bosses and our behaviour during the reign of the Anunnaki was no better. Our vile and questionable behaviour inspired our prudish alien rulers to put an end to us with a great flood. Sumerian writings include the first recorded incidence of the Noah story, as far as we know.

'There were three principal Anunnaki kings who ruled Earth in the Antediluvian period. The highest was Anu – the god of the heavens – and the oldest god in the Sumerian pantheon. The other two were the sons of Anu, and they were Enlil, god of the sky and Enki, or Ea, god of water. In our hunt for the origins of Anubis it's this third figure, Enki we're most interested in. In his position as Lord of everything watery he becomes Shar Apsi, King of the Apsu or "the deep". Sumerians describe the Apsu as an immense abyss of water beneath the Earth, which is right next door to a place called Aralu, and yes, I know, there's a lot of new names to remember in all this but Aralu is important to the story. Enki was also lord of Aralu, which was the gathering place of the dead, the Underworld. Which means Enki becomes hyphenated to En-Ki, which changes his title to "lord of that which is below". Are you with me so far?'

Prentiss nodded weakly and made a mental note to get on her search engine when she got home and look up ancient Sumerian mythology.

'It was our hero En-Ki who rescued humanity from the great flood. Some say he saved the good man Ziusudra by instructing him to build an ark, a large vessel designed to house his family and animals, you know the story. Others say he did it by bringing them all safely into the heavens in a magic ship. And there's more, En-Ki's youngest son, Ningizzida, was listed as Lord of the Tree of Truth in Mesopotamia, and was later adopted into the role of the great god Thoth in Egypt. The ancient teachings of Thoth were passed down to his initiates who became the priests of the old Egyptian death cult. They are said to have hidden the secret wisdom of creation itself, passing it down through the ages. So, in En-Ki we have the Lord of the Underworld whose son is the Lord of the Tree of Truth. With Anubis, we have a god who leads the souls of the dead to the halls of truth where they are weighed in the balance. In En-Ki, we are approaching the aegis of the Egyptian god Anubis are we not?'

'Sure.' Prentiss shook her head, back to business, 'hey, Gee, that reminds me. Before I forget, was Errol M on your "naughty boy but we can't prove it" list?'

'Errol? Wow, was he! Flaxen haired boys were his preference, prettier and younger the better.'

'Sam thought so. He was very underdeveloped in the trouser department.'

'Good reason to keep him away from anyone under eighteen. Say, what's going on out there?'

Prentiss had been aware of joggers loping both ways past the window the whole time they had been talking; now she saw that everyone was running the same way. Most of them were in street clothes. The numbers increased while she watched.

She said, 'They aren't just running, Gee, they're *running away*. Something out there is spooking them.'

The big windows in the café were double glazed, but even so she could just make out the rattling sounds of a machine pistol.

'Shit! Gee, get away from the window.' She stood up, raising her voice, and holding up a hand containing her badge.

'I am a police officer. Please, everybody, remain calm. Nobody panic. There is a good reason to believe you might be in danger if you remain by these windows. I must ask everyone to move away from the windows and get under cover.'

A big man yelled at her, 'I'm trying to eat my freakin' lunch here.'

She drew her pistol, 'Then I suggest you take it with you. MOVE!'

She spotted a fire escape leading to the park in the corner of the café and ran to push it open. Alarms sounded all around her but she ignored them. People were running past her in panic, some had blood on their clothes. Her heart sank, people had been hurt. To her right the machine pistol rattled its deadly tympani. She ran towards it. She saw a tall man with a full beard stalking through the meadows of Central Park. He held a gun in his right hand and was spraying bullets randomly around himself. She was struck by how calm he seemed. *Just taking a little walk in the park.*

She positioned herself to keep the trunk of a tree between her and the gunman and ran to it. He was just a few yards away now. She took deep breaths to steady herself and held her pistol in the double-handed grip that had proved most effective at the range. Safety off, chambered round. She heard the chatter of the machine pistol followed by bullets striking her tree and then moving away. She stepped into the open.

'Armed police officer, drop your weapon NOW!'

She could swear he grinned at her while he swung the barrel of his Uzi in her direction. She fired twice and the man dropped like a falling log. She crouched low in a defensive posture and ran to his side, all the while scanning the landscape for accomplices. When she drew close the man lifted his gun in her direction once more and screamed. She shot him in the face and he jerked back, his head slapping flat on the grass.

She cautiously holstered her pistol and drew out her cell phone.

'Hi, Sam, we'll have to forget lunch. Yes, sorry, where are you? I'm in Central Park by the Met, I've got at least one fatality here, maybe more. No, nothing to do with jackals, I shot him. Yeah, I'm having one of those days. See you in about fifteen minutes. Can you handle despatch? Cool, thanks, honey.'

She stood up and looked back towards the museum windows. She was certain she could just make out Gee Erskine staring back at her.

16

'Nobody's claimed your John Doe gunman yet. The media got hold of it of course. They're trying to link him with any number of terror groups, but we don't recognise his face, what's left of it, which would make it highly unlikely, albeit not impossible. Current analysis, detective Prentiss? We can't rule it out, but we don't think he's on our radar. Dollar on the barrel says this is another case of "suicide by cop". This time the lunatic got you to pull the trigger. Sorry about that. Hope you enjoy the rest of your day.'

The nondescript man from Homeland Security, who had introduced himself as 'Peter, just plain Peter will do' stood up, shook her hand and that of Chief Lewis, and then left.

Lewis came around his desk. He was a man who wore his age well, and although he was close to retirement his close cut, full head of hair was still its natural honey colour and his broad-shouldered figure still trim. He sighed and took the seat 'Peter' had vacated.

'John Doe shot and killed three people today, injured two. He would have killed more if you hadn't stopped him. Somebody with a smartphone was stupid enough to hang around and film you in action. The whole thing has been repeated ad nauseam on CNN and just about every other news channel and platform.'

'Shit! Sorry sir.'

'No, I think "shit" sums up the situation very well. But you're not in it. You might be able to smell it from your pedestal but you're well out of the sewage. You're a hero. Luckily, nobody knows you were officially on a day's sick leave. We'll keep that quiet. The Commissioner has requested I put you in for the Police Combat Cross, and I will.'

'No, need. I was just doing my job, sir.'

'No, you went in and acted intelligently against an armed adversary, knowing the risks. Ticks all the right boxes, Prentiss. Mind you, others might say your job would have been to call it in and wait for back-up.'

'There was no time, sir, I saw people had been hurt, and he might have heard me. I reckoned enough people knew about him to have made the call.'

'Yes, you're right. Nine-one-one was in meltdown. You made your report?'

'Yes, sir. Typed it up as soon as I got in.'

'Good, we'll share it with the Central Park Precinct and anyone else who wants a piece of John Doe. So then, why were you on the scene?'

'Sir?'

'You call in sick then turn up playing super cop in Central Park. How is that? Were you out getting a breath of fresh air?'

'No, sir. I worked very late the night before and I hadn't slept well. I felt lousy and planned a day in bed, but I couldn't settle. The case I'm working on kept gnawing at me, you know what I mean, sir?'

'Yeah, I do, bought that tee-shirt years ago. So, what took you to Central Park?'

'Research. I've been working on the celebrity philanthropist killings and we're getting nowhere. I had an idea and went to The Met to do some research. I met an acquaintance there and we were having coffee in the café that overlooks the park. The rest you know, sir.'

'I know the case very well. We're under pressure to make some headway but doctor Feldman tells me we're finding zero tell-tales other than dog spit in the bites, which he believes to be artificial.'

'I've heard doctor Feldman's theories. I believe them to be a little far-fetched.'

'He says the alternative is to believe in a twenty-foot jackal stalking the city. A jackal with a taste for celebrity meat. That's also far-fetched, wouldn't you agree?'

'Yes. Yes, it is. But I have an idea that might provide a motive, or at least a direction for our investigations. Let me explain...'

She took fifteen minutes to outline her researches into Anubis, the weighing in the balance, the devouring of the unjustified. She explained the 'wicked victim' list Erskine was compiling and what the gossip columnist had said about Puckling, Hart and Errol M. Lewis pulled a disapproving face when she went into detail. She left out the strange appearances and disappearances of the hooded masked figure and the mysterious text in her book and on her tablet. She made no mention at all of Aliya Petrus.

Lewis growled at her conclusion. 'You're thinking some sort of vigilante cult, maybe more than one person involved?'

She hadn't been, but it was an idea. She gave a non-committal shrug.

'It is a line of enquiry, sir. We have people looking for the van but all we know for sure is that it's a dark coloured Mercedes-Benz Vito driven by a person in a hoodie. It must be the cleanest van in history because it leaves no trace, neither on the body or at the crime scene. We both know that if several people get involved in any crime it increases the chances that one of them will make a mistake and then we've got them. A lone vigilante may take longer to find. Perhaps, once we've got Erskine's list we can stake out the potential victims and the killer might walk into our arms, and some people might be more likely victims than others. We know that all the victims to date have exploited minors, that might prove to be the trigger factor.'

'Innocent until proven guilty, Prentiss, innocent until proven guilty. Follow your line of enquiry and let me know what you find when you get to the end. If it's a twenty-foot man-eating jackal, promise me you'll call for back-up and not go it alone?'

'I'll have Sam Bolat with me, sir.'

'Not much more than an appetiser and a snack between the two of you. Go on then, Prentiss. Sorry about the medal, it will mean publicity but the precinct thrives on that sort of thing. Well done. By the way, you ever killed anybody before? I haven't had time to check your file.'

'No, sir. Wounded a few, when I had to, but I never needed to stop someone like that before.'

'You okay? Need to talk to a counsellor?'

'Thanks, but no. I'm good. I had no choice, it was him or them. It says, "To serve and protect" on the badge.'

Sam hugged her when she got back to their office.

'Phones been ringing. Our press people want to talk to the hero of the hour. Saw you on TV, girl you were *cold*! Talk about *ice, ice, baby*. You deserve a medal.'

'The commissioner agrees with you. Chief's putting me in for the Combat Cross.'

'That's awesome! Is that why you came in here looking like someone kicked your favourite puppy?'

'I don't know what I feel, Sam. I shot a man directly in the face today. I was as close to him as I am to you. I saw what the bullet did to his head. Surely, I should be feeling something other than just tired? But that's all I'm feeling, you know? Tired and flat – and confused about the whole Anubis thing. My brain feels like a rat in a barrel. John Doe got what was coming to him. It felt great to catch a killer in action, get him out in the open and do something about him. Pop! Stop him before he did anything else, before he could hurt anyone else, you know? No brain sweat, no weird shit, no ancient Sumerian spaceman with an agenda.'

'Whoa, there! No ancient *what* did you just say?'

Prentiss shared what she remembered of the mini-lecture by Erskine, which was more than she thought she had. Sam's eyes grew huge.

67

'Girl, we're on a trip. We're going from a jackal the size of T-rex to Darth Vader in the same movie. We're cooking with gas but nobody gave us the recipe, we're just making this shit up as we go along.'

'Yeah, and I am so not in the mood for a date tonight.'

'You got a date? Shee-it, yeah! You got a *date*!'

'I'll call him and say I've got my period.'

'You can't do that. He'll think you only date when it's okay to put out, and he'll get lucky as soon as your monthly's stop. No way. And anyway, dinner with the cute wolf man is just what doctor Sam orders. Relax for once, let someone be nice to you. Shit, look at the time. I've got a date to spend the weekend with two little demons and a hot college professor. See you Monday, get some rest and enjoy this evening. Promise me?'

'I promise, now go home and hug the boys for me.'

Sam grabbed her bag and rushed for the door. Before she reached it, she stopped and walked slowly back. She hugged Prentiss, hard.

'You know I love you. If you need me, call, okay?'

'Okay. I love you too. Now go before the hero bursts into tears.'

'See you Monday.'

'See you Monday. Those three magic words that mean so much.'

[17]

Prentiss watched the second hand of her watch as it ticked towards the half hour. In twenty seconds, the punctual Dr. Howlett was going to be late, fifteen, ten, five...

Her entry-phone buzzed on the precise stroke of seven thirty. *No way.*

She answered with, 'Hi, Tabaqui. I'll be right down.'

'No, sorry, I brought flowers. Is it okay to bring them up?'

'Sure, that's sweet. Second floor.'

'Cool, yeah, I know.'

You know?

She opened her front door and waited for less than a minute. An artful array of hot house flowers exited the lift followed by Howlett who looked around before spotting her. *At least he didn't know where my door is,* she thought.

He hustled up to her and thrust the flowers towards her.

'Here, I hope they're okay.'

'They're lovely. Thank-you. Come in for a minute and I'll find a vase.'

He stepped into the hallway and stood just a few feet inside the door, hovering expectantly. She smiled, he hadn't just barged in but had waited to be invited. Tick in the box.

'The living room is just there. Take a seat. I won't be long.'

The only vase big enough was in her kitchen closet, tucked at the back behind her vacuum cleaner and a plastic bucket filled with cleaning products. She dug it out, rinsed it in the sink, filled it, poured the tube of plant food attached to the flowers into the water and arranged the bouquet to her satisfaction. She carried the full vase into her living room where she found Howlett gazing quizzically at a beautifully framed etching of a Victorian London street scene. She placed the flowers on a coaster in the exact centre of her coffee table, turning them until she felt they were right. Then she stood back and admired them.

Howlett grinned, 'I asked for flowers to go with any décor, a bit of a mixture. I didn't know what your place looked like so I told the girl to be eclectic. She asked if I expected her to stick her finger in a power socket.' He grinned and shrugged. 'This etching, is it really by who it says it is?'

'Whistler? Yes, and yes, it's real. I couldn't afford it but I had to have it. It's an etching and dry point portrait of St James' Street. See, there's his butterfly signature with its stinger. I call it a portrait because I think

69

everything he did was a portrait, even buildings and street scenes. He drew it from life straight onto the copper so it's reversed. I love it, it's my most prized possession. I ate spaghetti for a month after I bought it, it was all I could afford.'

Howlett blurted, 'And you look very good on it, if I may say so.'

He blushed slightly when he said this. Prentiss mentally compared him with the practiced socialite, flirt, and flatterer Erskine. She put another tick in a box.

He looked at his watch. 'We'd better go or we'll be late, and you know...'

'I know. You hate to be late. I'm ready, I'll grab my bag.'

Their table was in a quiet and discreet Italian restaurant called La Campagna. Prentiss had heard of it but never been there before. It smelt appetising as soon as they walked through the door. Lighting was low, and it was reassuringly busy. Howlett asked her what she would like then ordered drinks from the waitress. A carafe of water was placed on the table along with a basket of warm artisanal breads and a small bowl of balsamic vinegar in olive oil.

They talked their way through the menu, pleased to discover they had similar tastes, and their conversation ranged across food, wine, and theatre to work and, inevitably, the jackal killer. They made their choices, both plumping for two light dishes. A tall, striking woman came to their table with a bottle of Prosecco, an ice bucket, and two tall glasses. She uncorked the wine and poured it out. Prentiss held her hand out.

'Sorry, wait, please. We didn't order this, there's been some mistake.'

The woman smiled warmly, 'There's no mistake, Officer Prentiss. The wine is on the house. This is my restaurant, I am Anna Bianchi. This lunchtime I was in Central Park with my daughter, taking a little walk near The Met. This is a small token to say thank-you from all of us who were there. It is the very least I can do. As for dinner tonight, you are our guests. I insist. I know mister Howlett booked the table, but I'm sure he will understand and appreciate the gesture. Please, enjoy your meal.'

Anna Bianchi glided away just as their waitress brought their antipasto. Howlett watched her retreating back, and then turned a quizzical gaze on Prentiss. He frowned, and then his eyes widened as if a light bulb had suddenly switched on inside his head.

'I heard something about a shooting in Central Park on the radio on my way over. They said a lone NYPD officer shot the man dead, at considerable risk to themselves. Saved a lot of lives. That, was *you*?'

'It's my day job.'

'Wow. Prentiss, you are simply, awesome.' He raised his glass of sparkling wine. 'And you sit here talking about food as if nothing happened today. Here's to you, you're one in a million. I mean it, wow.'

She tapped her glass to his and sipped. It was excellent.

'Tabaqui, I'm not here to talk about work, please. Can we change the subject?'

'Of course, I'm sorry to be such a boor. It's just that I've never... Forget it, ignore me. The floor's all yours. Pick a subject, any subject. Where would you like our conversation to flow next? Not the NYPD, so where else? Culture, science, politics, religion? Pick a heading and let's see where our fancy takes us. I'm all ears, but, you know, that comes from my mother's side of the family.'

She grinned at his silly remark. *Self-deprecating. Tick.*

'Okay, religion I guess. What do you know about Anubis?'

'Anubis? Wow, that came out of left field. Hum, ancient Egyptian, jackal-headed god. Something to do with death cults. Hold on...' He raised his hand, palm out.

'You said we're not to talk about work and you instantly break your own rule. Anubis and giant jackal bites, is there a connection? Am I warm?'

'Piping hot. Give that man a cee-gar!'

'Thanks, but I don't smoke.'

'Don't drink much, don't smoke. What do you do for fun? And don't say anything scary.'

'Right at this moment? I'm going to have a great dinner courtesy of a crazy hero police detective. The way I see it I still owe you a dinner. Is there anywhere we can go they won't mob you in the street and I get to pay my way?'

There always Canada?'

'Too Canadian.'

'The Adirondacks?'

'Too Adirondackian.'

'Anywhere beyond the Turnpike?'

'Wow, do we really want to go that far for dinner? Don't worry, I'll think of somewhere. Anyway, if you really want to know about Anubis, I'm not your man. He was a god before my time, my guy came thousands of years later. Tell you what, I *can* look him up for you if you like. Research is what I do. I done me some book larnin' back in the day, and I larned me how to spell a touch too. I can sign my own name, and I know near on two hunnert

71

words. See, I can count to twenty if'n I take my boots off. But, miss, I never do that in an enclosed space because the court order.'

She went along with it. 'Court order?'

'Yass'm the one about my socks being a public nuisance – and an offence against the clean indoor air act of 2003.'

He nodded gravely and then joined in with her laughter.

'I mean it, you want me to dig the dirt on Anubis I got friends in the belief business who know about the occult the right side of an upside-down crucifix and a bunch of black candles. Somebody will know.'

She smiled, 'Thank-you, I appreciate it. I had my earwax boiled out by a friend today at The Met. He seemed to know a lot more about Anubis than I thought was usual. A whole lot more...'

Their antipasto plates were cleared away and their first courses arrived. Prentiss' calamari looked too delicious to hold back and she forked herself a mouthful. Hot and tender. Howlett regarded her with worried eyes.

'Friend? Man friend? Should I...'

She swallowed hastily, 'No, honestly, no. Okay, look, I said friend but he's an acquaintance really. He's helping me with the case. Gee Erskine? You know? The online gossip guy? He knows everything about everybody; he knows where the skeletons are buried. He's creating a list for me of apparently good guys who do bad things. They seem to be the target for Anubis, the jackal killer.'

'What, Puckling did bad things? But... He was a *bishop*?'

'Quiet. Keep your voice down. We don't want everyone to hear us. This is an ongoing investigation, I shouldn't be discussing it with you, but yes, all of them were child abusers of one kind or another. Now, forget I said anything.'

Howlett nodded and pressed fresh anchovies onto a slice of bread, bit it and chewed thoughtfully. Prentiss took her chance to address her squid while it was still hot, she squeezed more lemon onto it and a twist of black pepper. As she did so she wondered why she had been so quick to explain Erskine as an acquaintance rather than a friend. Had Howlett begun to matter that quickly? She watched him eat for a moment and he looked back into her eyes. There was something honest in his gaze.

He said, 'I hope you don't mind me saying but I'm really enjoying this evening. Thanks for agreeing to have dinner with me. I don't do this much, you know, this sort of thing.'

'No,' she said. 'Me too, and I don't do it much either. This sort of thing.'

[18]

Prentiss surprised herself by inviting Tabaqui up to her apartment for coffee. He surprised her just as much when he said he'd love to, but with a caveat.

'I can't stay long, early start with the wolves tomorrow. Work, you know? I try to get eight hours every night and I've got to meet some people at eight thirty to talk about the international breeding programme. They've come all the way down from Alaska, so, the least I can do is be there to meet them.'

Mentally she put another tick in the box. Physically she grinned.

'You know something? I've got a rare weekend off. Maybe I should come see your wolves as a tourist rather than as a police officer on a case?'

'Forget being a tourist you'll be there as my guest, that would be so cool. I could introduce you to the guys.'

'Really, you want me to meet your colleagues? Isn't it a bit soon?'

'My colleagues? No, sorry, no, I meant the pack. You know, the wolves.'

'Oh, well, that would be brilliant too, nice. Should I bring salt or do they bring their own?'

'Salt?'

'For when they try to eat me.'

Howlett had held back from drinking too much wine with his meal and Prentiss hadn't wanted to waste it, finishing most of the bottle. She felt a little giddy, but in a good way. She directed Howlett to the visitor parking bays and they chatted warmly about wolves while waiting for the elevator in the lobby. When they reached her floor Howlett insisted she exit first, and she thanked him with a throaty chuckle before stepping out onto the corridor. She pulled up short. A stocky, dark figure was fidgeting directly outside her door. Howlett stood at her shoulder.

'Who's that?'

'I don't know. Shall we find out?' She raised her voice. 'Hello, can I help you?'

The figure stopped fidgeting and raced angrily towards them.

'Are you the resident of 204?'

'Well, yes I am. Why?'

The man pointed back at her door.

'I live under you, in 104, and I have water flooding down my living room walls. I've been waiting for you for an hour at least. You must have left a tap running. It's just too bad. I've been waiting an hour...'

Prentiss ran to her door, unlocked it, and tore it open, Howlett and her neighbour close at her heels. They paddled into almost an inch of water in her living room. She splashed across the room and opened the door to her kitchen. No taps were running there and the floor was dry. It was the same in her bathroom. Her bedroom was also untouched. She glanced thankfully at the mahogany door bars her father had fitted across the floor between each internal door lining in case of just such an eventuality. He had needed to take over an inch from the bottom of each door for them to close properly. She hadn't needed to get used to them and there was no danger of her tripping over them. She had grown up in a house where they were at the base of every door. It was her father's 'thing'. She remembered him kneeling on his sponge pad, drill in hand, and she could hear his placid voice as if he was still there in the room.

'Five minutes of work today can save a mountain of trouble in the future. I hope it never happens but one day you might thank me for this.'

Thank-you, daddy.

Howlett asked where her stop valve was hidden. She admitted she didn't know but her neighbour told him it would be at the back of the closet in the kitchen.

'All these apartments are the same,' he explained. 'But give me five minutes to check out the situation. There's something odd about this. May I?'

Prentiss thanked him. She tried to assess the damage, but the saturation seemed to have stopped at ground level. Her rugs were soaked and probably ruined, but her other furniture had legs or bases of varnished solid wood and would likely be fine. Even though the flooding seemed to have been confined to her living room, the gloss had been scoured from her perfect evening with a coarse file. She would probably need to spend at least an hour mopping her floor.

Her neighbour, whom she had learned after a rapid exchange of names was called Laurie, returned looking baffled.

He was apologetic. 'My dear, Prentiss. This is impossible. I'm an engineer by profession and this is impossible. Some vindictive bastard must have stuffed a hosepipe through your mail slot and deliberately flooded your apartment. I'm so sorry I accused you of leaving a tap running, can I help you mop it up? Have you got a spare bucket?'

She protested that he was too kind and needn't bother, but he waved her protests away.

'I'm acting in my own best interests, my dear. The sooner we mop your place up the sooner my place can start drying out. But, this is impossible. How could it happen?'

He left after half an hour, promising to return in the morning with a dehumidifier.

'I have two, very useful in unexpected cases like this. Soon have things back to normal.' He paused at the door, examining it. 'Of course, you don't have a mail slot any more than I do. Stupid of me. Where *is* my head these days? What we have here is a mystery. I'll be back in the morning about nine if that's okay.'

Howlett followed shortly after. 'I'm sorry to leave you like this but I do have an early morning. Will you be okay?'

'I'll be fine, really. Thanks for your help, and for a lovely evening. Sorry you had to get involved with all this. Bet you wish you'd said no to the coffee.' Then she realised and burst out laughing, 'But you never even got a coffee, just wet shoes. Oh, Tabaqui, what a horrible end to a perfect evening.'

'Yes, well, at least we had the evening. Will I see you tomorrow? The Alaskans will keep me busy until eleven and then I'm all yours.'

'I hope so. I'll have to wait for Laurie and his dehumiddy thing, but I'll call you as soon as I'm on the way.'

'Dehumidifier. He seems a nice enough guy. I'll see you tomorrow.'

He kissed her warmly yet chastely. Neither opened their lips in invitation for more but there was a promise there. When they parted, he smiled.

'I'll see you tomorrow.'

She nodded and watched him walk to the elevators. He waved, and was gone.

She shut her door behind her and walked into her living room. She could smell the damp in the rugs, which had been slung over the bars of her airer to dry. She hoped Laurie was getting things sorted out. She realised she had lived there for more than two years without ever meeting him. *What a great introduction.*

It was too late for coffee and she'd had enough alcohol for one evening. She drank a tumbler of water, set her alarm for eight and got ready for bed. It had been a long day. Despite everything, sleep claimed her in minutes.

She dreamed it was pitch black, a blackness so oppressive it pressed like squeezing thumbs against her eyeballs. She closed her eyes and then opened them again. It made no difference. There was the sound of running water in the darkness. It could have been someone urinating, she thought, but they would have needed a bladder the size of a house. She was deep underground,

75

without knowing how she knew that. She could feel the pressure of miles of rock above her head. The darkness was total, but she wasn't afraid. The lack of light won't hurt you, she reasoned, whatever was hiding in the darkness will be as blind as you. She moved a few paces towards the sound of running water and almost instantly dashed her head against something unyielding. Bright sparks of light exploded across her vision. She reeled back and pressed her hand against her forehead. She felt blood there, a flap of skin had been slashed away. The pain made her want to cry out, but she didn't want to attract unwanted attention in the darkness, and so bit her lip.

She started towards the sound of running water once more, reaching out with questing hands to protect her fragile body. The sound got louder. After a while she began to see an orange, flickering glow some way ahead. It looked like firelight. At last she could make out some details of her surroundings. As she suspected she was in a tunnel. The ceiling seemed to be natural rock with protruding knobs of wet limestone descending into her path. The walls on either side had been carved with the same open jawed and winged demons she had seen on her climb up the mountain path. She had time to notice that the demons had four wings each, two pointing up and two pointing down. They formed an X shape. Each of the demons gripped a weapon that might have been stylised water or lightning. Around their wrists they wore amulets that could easily have been modern wristwatches. The demons looked immensely powerful, and expressions she had at first thought were angry now looked stern and masterful, filled with resolve. Prentiss wondered what those implacable creatures had been meant to represent.

The tunnel reached a turn to the right and she approached with caution. She was dressed only in the big tee and panties she had worn to bed, and the woven sandals she had found on her feet before. Something told her she had been invited to this place, but natural caution made her wary. Slowly, she poked her head around the corner. What met her gaze made her gasp in surprise.

19

The chamber was vast. The distant far wall was lost in shadows and mist. It was high enough for great birds to flap around overhead, and massive iron braziers provided the only sources of heat and light. She found herself standing at the edge of a beach made up of fine grey sand and white boulders. The languid roll of flat, black waves licked at the shore as if probing at it. She imagined it as a beast with a thousand oily tongues, all licking at the land, tasting it before taking a bite. The great chamber held an underground sea between its walls, its surface barely moving under a sluggish breeze. A waterfall fell from high up on one wall and cascaded down onto a heap of giant boulders that had been carved into recoiling shapes by the action of the water. The beach was a hive of activity. Lines of labourers like those she had seen on the mountain road passed to-and-fro across the beach to huge stone tables at the base of a broad, ornate staircase. Its balustrades were beautiful things made from finely curved stone. Fine spars passed through a series of complex geometric shapes. She recognised the shapes, they reminded her of the models of atoms and molecules she had seen in class at college. Because of the complexity of its design the staircase looked very modern, but everything else looked ancient. The labourers emptying their workloads onto the tables were the well-muscled men and women she had walked with on the mountain path, and were well-fed by the look of them. They wore short modesty skirts to cover their genitals, sandals like hers, and cloth scarves on their heads. They were otherwise naked and their skins had been sun-darkened until they appeared almost black in the firelight.

The staircase led up over thirty, perhaps as much as forty feet, to an arched portal. Beautifully carved, winged demons held burning torches that cast white light into its shadowed interior. Shadows boiled and massed in there as if on the brink of ejecting some horror out into the light. Her attention was drawn to the two columns of creatures on the staircase, one column carrying laden trays up to the portal, the other carrying empty platters back down to be refilled at the tables.

All this activity, she thought, to feed whatever lives up there. What manner of person would have such servants? The creatures on the stairs were muscled like hormone heavy gym addicts. They were dark grey and winged like the stone demons in the tunnel behind her. She couldn't quite see how the wings were attached to their backs, but the lower set almost touched the floor and the upper towered over their heads. These too were almost naked apart from stiff belted skirts that looked heavily starched to make them stand away in a 'V' shape from their powerful legs. Broad, brightly coloured straps of some thick material looped over their shoulders, under the wings at the back, and fixed to the belts at their waists, looking a little like suspenders. Each of them wore an amulet on their left wrist, just as the carved demons did. They looked even more incongruous in life than they did in the carvings, too much like the Rolex watch that keen-eyed viewers had spotted on a Roman soldier in an historical movie.

Their heads looked human from where she stood. Large, bald, blocky, and muscular, but human all the same. Their faces were the same shade of pewter as their bodies, and their eyes seemed to be heavily made-up. Their eyes looked black, but she also caught a hint of what looked like gold framed surrounds or metallic tattoos. Part of her wanted to get closer to see what was happening in greater detail, but the wiser element of her mind was more cautious and chose to stay well clear in the safety of the shadows. Then one of the birdlike beasts swooped down next to the tables at the base of the staircase and landed on its powerful legs. Prentiss' mind reeled. What had landed wasn't a bird, she realised, it was one of the winged men. She watched the grey skinned, black-eyed man mount the centre of the staircase. While he climbed his brothers passed either side of him making respectful bowing gestures which he returned. Before too long he had ascended to the torch-lit portal. He entered the clotted shadows. When he re-emerged, he was wearing a full-face helmet that resembled the idealised head of an eagle, or perhaps a vulture. He held a staff that looked like frozen lightning in his left hand. He pointed it towards the sea. His amulet glowed white, like phosphorescent flame, and his staff emitted a crackling bar of light that burned into the black waves like a laser beam. The light threw everything around him into sharp relief and Prentiss had to protect her eyes from its brilliance.

I must be dreaming, this must be a dream. What am I seeing here?

The staff's light winked out and Prentiss was momentarily blinded, until her eyes had adjusted and she could see what was happening once more. Where the beam of light had struck the water, the sea had begun to swirl and spin anticlockwise as if a giant invisible hand was stirring it. The motion created a whirlpool that funnelled deep towards the seabed. Labourers and winged men alike ceased their toils to watch events unfold. Prentiss held her breath and wrapped her arms around her torso. Cold sweat trickled down her spine and her mouth became achingly dry. She hugged herself but found little comfort in it. She needed to pee but didn't dare move. Her unblinking eyes became dry and sore making her squint and blink rapidly, but she couldn't drag her gaze away.

The sea became calm once more, but the peace was fleeting. After a few moments, it rose into a dome that foamed and glowed inside with an eerie gold light. The dome became a column and then a pillar fully ten feet across and over thirty feet high. It moved towards the beach. Prentiss could smell a caustic chemical stench that strengthened as the pillar drew closer, and she could hear a spitting, crackling noise like fat on a hot griddle. The labourers knelt and pressed their heads to the sand, the winged men bent stiffly at the waist. Prentiss stepped back, moving closer to the tunnel mouth and ready to flee.

The column sparked and emitted little arcs of electrical discharge when it reached dry land. It advanced towards the column of labourers before it stopped, as if considering its next move. Prentiss eased herself forward and closer to the column – while making sure she remained shielded behind a boulder – to get a better view of events. Something dark was moving in the column's watery interior. It seemed to be casting off orbs of golden light and ribbons of inky black material. Suddenly, everything in the column shrank down to a single, central point, and the tower of water cascaded to the ground.

What emerged was a man; at least he was from the neck down. He was skirted like the winged men and well-muscled, yet he was leaner, tall, and square shouldered. He held out his right hand and a long ebon staff seemed to grow from it. He turned his head to the right and she saw the long snout and gilt-edged, midnight black eyes of Anubis.

Prentiss thought back to Erskine's comments about the little statuette in the display cabinet at The Met. In the face of the awesome figure before her, the memory of that slight, tartan clad model in the showcase became a joke. This version was the truth of the ancient god, the awe-inspiring Lord of the Underworld and Shar Apsi, King of the body of water, the Apsu. She fully understood why the labourers knelt in obeisance and the winged men bowed. She moved again for a better look. That was a mistake.

Anubis spun and covered the distance between them in the blink of an eye. Before she could so much as twitch he was towering over her. She fell backwards in terror, landing hard on the impacted sand, and grazing her elbow against the boulder. The great head with its spear-like ears and gold limned eyes came close and its lips drew back from white, deadly looking fangs.

It spoke, its voice an oddly inflected hiss. 'I smell a killer. Do you hunt me, killer? Am I to be your prey?'

20

It was too much. Too operatic, too Grand Guignol. The entrance had simply been too showy to be convincing. This Anubis had stepped from 'awesome' to 'showman' the very moment he had spoken. The long jackal's muzzle had never been designed for speech and his opening act smacked of a clever conjuror at work not an ancient god.

Prentiss sat up. 'Is this you. Erskine?'

The creature hissed, 'Erskine? What are you suggesting, little killer?'

'What is this, hypnotic suggestion? Did you suggest all this shit to me so it would pop into my head when I fell asleep? Did you put this crap in my head while we were at The Met? You're blown Erskine. Hey, I bet that's why you know so much about people. They tell you while they think they're just having a friendly chat, but you hypnotise them and without knowing it they tell you their deepest, darkest secrets. This is some clever shit, Erskine, but it won't work on me.'

The creature reached out and took her throat in its hand. She grabbed at its wrist to pull its hand away but it was like trying to move solid rock.

'Are you ready to be weighed in the balance, little killer?'

'Hell, yeah! Are you?'

Its hand moved down until it was between her breasts, its fingers extended like a blade. It growled, 'You, first.'

Her fear spiked when its hand plunged into her chest and then tugged at what it found there. There came an exquisite agony of tearing, a torture of hot knives that ripped through her body. Her body arced upwards, trying to blunt the pain, but it only got worse. Then, through her tears, Prentiss saw the clawed black hand held open before her eyes. In its palm was a beating heart, pounding, and pounding but disconnected from any living body. She cast her eyes down to her chest, and then quickly looked away from the empty, blood filled cavity she saw there. *This must be a magic trick.*

She found she couldn't take her eyes from the organ still beating in the creature's left hand like a slick, gory pump. She could feel the pulse throbbing with it in her ears, behind her eyes, and in her constricted throat. But her living heart lay there in Anubis' hand like a messenger of imminent death.

I'm going to die in my sleep.

'You shot a man. Was he worthy of death?'

81

Anubis' staff was gone and in its place, in his right hand, was a large and simple set of scales. He held them up before her eyes. One of the winged men was at his side. It walked forward and took a white feather from its upper set of wings and placed it on the right-hand balance. The balance barely moved.

Anubis showed its teeth. 'The cohort makes its own rules. The feathers of their upper wings are lighter. It is their way of making a statement about the judgement. He says he believes you are guilty. The rest is up to me. It has always been up to me. Now, are you to be judged as guilty or justified?'

Slowly and with great precision he placed her pulsating heart onto the left-hand balance. He was weighing a mass of pounding, powerful meat against almost nothing. To Prentiss the result seemed to be a foregone conclusion. Her heart looked heavy as lead.

A heart is a powerful muscle. It has gravity and mass. What is a feather? It flies. She considered the attributes that might add more weight to her soul. She found regret, shame, desire, and anger, but no evil. She closed her eyes and prayed. *Forgive me, Lord, if I have sinned in protecting your people, but I did what I believed to be right. If I was wrong, punish me now, do not torment me. I may be a poor foolish sinner but please, at least let me die in your grace. Amen.*

She heard a shout of wonder and opened her eyes.

The showman jackal held up his balance. The feather was tilted towards the earth and her heart was lifted skywards. She was redeemed. *She was redeemed.* She got to her feet and held her arms out to the rejoicing labourers and they cheered and danced, men and women lifting their skirts to display their genitals.

Their dance turned them into a column of spinning, singing dervishes, all celebrating her acceptance into the elite band of the justified. The winged men moved amongst them and took some of the women into the shadows. They didn't struggle, but neither did they look happy.

Anubis grimaced. 'Would you care to join the breeding program?'

Prentiss glanced across at the column of labourers. *What breeding program?*

She answered, 'No, thanks. But please, tell me, when they fail the test, do you devour the guilty?'

'Of course. The judge makes the decision, he must make the kill. Would anything else be fair?'

'Then, what was the creature called Ammit?'

The jackal god snarled. 'Ammit is nothing but a made-up puppet created by priests to scare the congregation. It is stitched together from all the animals Egyptians knew as likely to eat humans. Look at Horus, Isis, and Osiris, look at me. Are we jigsaw puzzle creations made from pieces of the things men fear most? Ammit was an invention, and a clumsy one at that. A show god built by men in order to frighten the gullible.'

'You're changing. You look different. What am I seeing now?'

'Sleep well, Prentiss. Time enough for change tomorrow. Sleep well, little angel.'

'No, stop, I want to talk to you...'

And then he was standing still while she sped away. An irresistible force pulled her backwards into the tunnel she had left. She became nothing more than a vector targeting a place she didn't know how to reach, but she thought of it as home and that was enough. She hurtled through the deepest depths of darkness and back to her own bed. She sighed, turned her body to her preferred sweet spot, and descended into a gentle night of unbroken slumber. In her dreams, she heard laughter. Whoever, or whatever, was laughing they were doing so with her own voice.

...

'No shit. What else happened? It sounds amazing. You must have one hell of an imagination.'

Prentiss was gazing at a half pound burger and fries Howlett had bought her in the Sanctuary café, and was wondering how much ketchup she would need to politely get through the monolith of meat, bread, and potatoes. She took a tentative bite, and then an interested second.

'Are you involved in the catering here? This is good.'

'Of course, I have to eat here. Why put up with crap when good can be done for the same money? I've never managed to work out why every venue like ours can't produce decent food. It isn't the cost. Bean counting shouldn't make beans taste like shit.'

He was spooning a bowl of chilli and taco hulls into his mouth, liberally dosed with sour cream and harissa. Prentiss looked at his meal.

'May I?'

'Of course.'

She forked a portion of dark red meat and beans into her mouth. Then she grabbed at her cola.

'No,' said Howlett. 'Take some of the sour cream.'

She did. The sting subsided.

Howlett smiled, 'Dairy takes the punch out of peppers. Your mom wasn't Mexican, was she?'

'WASP enough for two nests.'

'Tension in the house?'

'Can we drop the subject?'

He looked up. 'Hear that noise?'

'Hmm?'

'Kerchunk. Subject dropped. Let's get back to dreams.'

'I don't want to be boring.'

'Are you kidding? This is like any minute you're going to spin like one of those dancers and change into a Lady Fantastic costume.'

'Who? Who's Lady Fantastic?'

'Wait here.'

Howlett left the table and vanished through one of the side doors of the café. Prentiss enjoyed another bite of her burger. *Steak and toasted sourdough, cool!*

She had opened the bun and was examining the salad of shredded apple, red cabbage, and mooli on top of her meat patty, when he returned. He flopped a graphic novel on her side of the table.

'There you are. Lady Fantastic. Werewolf superhero lady. The science is crap but the illustrator, a guy called Rex, really knows his stuff and he's a brilliant artist. Look here.'

He spent the next five minutes pointing out how the draughtsman, a man apparently called 'Rex T. O'Saurus' knew his way around the wolf – and the human female – anatomy. He spoke with a degree of evident familiarity.

'You know this guy?'

'Rex? Sure. We went to college together. Same classes. He dived off into the arts and I chose to stick with the science. Why?'

'Call me a lady of intuition, but I think I need to speak with this friend of yours. Will you introduce us?'

'Sure, I can make a call after lunch. What are you doing this afternoon?'

'I was thinking of going back to The Met.'

'Take a rain check. You're going to love Rex, and I promise he's really going to love you. By the way, how did you get that bruise on your forehead?'

'I'll tell you later. Let's eat first.'

21

It was Prentiss' first foray into a home that was also a modern graphic arts studio and she had little idea about what to expect. She had thought to find a chaotic place filled with drawing boards and easels, bundles of brushes, pens and pencils in eccentric jars, a litter of paper on the floor or overflowing from cavernous bins, and perhaps canvases leaning against the walls. What met her surprised gaze was clean and minimalist. She liked it immediately. Rex T. O'Saurus welcomed them into his loft apartment home and workplace by offering them a choice of alcohol, tea, coffee, or soft drinks.

'This is a first,' he grinned. 'I've been showing beautiful women to the Wolfman for years, at least on the printed page, but this is the first time he's brought a live one to my lair. You've been worth the wait, Prentiss. What did you do to your head?'

'Forget my head, where on Earth did you get your name?'

'Hm, well said. Nothing if not to the point. I appreciate that. Okay. Once upon a time a publisher thought the name Rex Chappell was too ordinary for the work I was doing, and she told me to think of something more outlandish, something more like Moebius or Giger, you know? Wolfman here and I got together over pizza. We sucked a few beers and threw a few ideas into the hat. And we came up with Mr T. O'Saurus, a name we considered the most stupid, irritating and annoying. We thought the fool woman would get a burr under her saddle when she heard it, that she'd hate it so much she'd shut the fuck up and let me keep on working as momma Chappell's little boy. Bingo, that's when the plan backfired like a bellyful of refried beans. Fool bitch loved it, she used it, and now that Rex T. O'Saurus has been firmly established on the graphic novel stage – I'm stuck with it. Pays the rent and lets me enjoy a few little luxuries, plus I love the work of course.' He raised a glass of chilled wine, 'To the man T. O'Saurus, may his scaly hide never fade from the public view.'

His guests joined the toast, and Prentiss took stock of her host. He was slender as a reed and just over six feet two inches tall, about the same height as Howlett but without the shoulders. His face was lean with high cheekbones and beautiful, long lashed, oval eyes. His dark chocolate complexion was highlighted by his loose cream shirt and light blue baggy pants, which were cinched tight at his waist. His skull was covered with black peach fuzz and he had a gold stud in his left ear. He was immaculate. She thought he looked like a fashion plate from an up-market magazine.

'Senegal,' he said, enigmatically.

She started. 'I'm sorry.'

'If you're wondering where my looks come from. Mom's from Senegal, I take after her. Dad's New York Jewish, which makes him handsome enough to catch a woman like mom, but I take after her. Lucky flip of the genetic coin. That mark on your forehead is fading fast, even as I watch. You put miracle cream on there or something? Whatever you did, it's working.'

When she had checked out her forehead that morning while waiting for Laurie to bring up his dehumidifier the gash was still plainly evident. There had also been a quantity of blood on her pillow. She had showered and applied some medicated gel to the wound. There was little pain, more of a dull ache that subsided after she took a few paracetamol. While washing she had winced at the graze on her right elbow, remembering her collision with the boulder when Anubis had confronted her. By the time Laurie knocked at her door, the facial wound was fading to a nasty bruise, and while her elbow still sported a yellowish purple area the skin itself had healed.

Laurie commented while he set up the humming, three-foot box in the middle of her living room.

'Have you been in the wars, Prentiss?'

'Tired and I got careless. Walked into a door. Stupid of me.'

The stocky little man had reached out as if he was going to touch her face, his face a mask of concern. He shook his head.

'When the Lord gifts us with beauty we should do our best to preserve it as long as we can, not go around ramming it into doors. Is it painful?'

'Embarrassing, really. I'll be more careful in future, I promise, Laurie.'

'Make sure you do.'

And now, hours later, she told the truth to Howlett and Chappell. Chappell listened while sketching, his eyes darting from his pad to her face.

'Don't mind me,' he explained. 'I do this all the time, helps me concentrate.'

She told her story from the moment she fell asleep the first time to the instant she had returned to her bed. She talked about the blood on her pillow from her head, and on her sheet from the graze. She showed them her elbow. The skin was unmarked. Howlett reached out and stroked her arm. His touch sent a jolt of electricity through her and he snatched his hand away in surprise.

'Wow, that was some static charge you built up there.'

Chappell's eyes widened, 'I saw the spark! Make sure you two don't touch while you're pumping gas, you could burn the place down.'

Prentiss had a sudden urge to weep, something she hated to do in front of people. She fought the impulse but tears glittered on her lashes. She dabbed at them with her knuckles and sighed. Outside the sky was a curtain of massing clouds. The light it cast was cool and forensically precise, shining on the three figures in the room in such a way that it created a sense of heightened reality. The loft's living room had a solid wall of large, north facing windows, which, Chappell explained, was one of the principal reasons he had selected it. The windows angled inwards with the roof's camber and framed an unusually vast area of empty sky.

There came a flash of light that made the three look up at the same time, and they were instantly bathed in the actinic glare of an immense bolt of lightning that traversed all four windows. They were still blinking away the red after-images when the window-frames rattled under a clap of thunder that made them duck in their seats for fear they would be showered with shattered glass. And then it started raining in earnest with a pounding drumming sound that declared itself to be settling in for the duration.

Chappell raised his voice to be heard, 'My mother would say that flowing rain washes away stagnant water, but she is a pragmatist. She also says that if the hut is on fire you should bake yams for the survivors. I say, I can't send friends out in filthy weather like this; the house's roof fights the rain and those sheltering under it can tell bad weather to go fuck itself. Would you like to join me for dinner? I want to hear more about your research, Prentiss, and the Wolfman is always good value when he sings for his supper. Have we got a deal?'

The torrent of water redoubled overhead and they accepted with thanks. Chappell stood up, 'Bring your drinks, I want to show you something. Please, come with me.'

He led them through to another room that also had big, north facing windows. These were double-glazed and the sound of the downpour had been deadened somewhat. The walls were covered in framed artworks; including a mixture of detailed graphic art and impressionistic drawings. A few fine watercolours stood out, as did some etchings. Prentiss recognised Howlett in two ink portraits that had been framed and mounted next to each other. There was a tenderness of touch in the portrayals that she thought denoted something more than just friendship.

An honest portrait says as much about the artist as it does the sitter, she thought.

'Sorry about the clutter,' said Chappell, 'this is where I like to perch when I work. I call it the nest.'

87

The lower half of one wall was taken up with deep wooden shelving which was covered with books, drawing pads, boxes of pencils, and portfolios. The wall by the door contained a massive flat screen monitor under which was a powerful computer with a keyboard, a wireless mouse and a Wacom tablet and pen. On a nearby table lay a scanner and a deep lightbox, plus graphic magazines and acrylic slips filled with pencilled layouts. Everything was precisely in its place. Prentiss thought the room was enchanting, a place where dreams could come true. Dragons could fly here and wolf women spring to life. No wonder Chappell hadn't questioned her sanity after her dreams about flying men and jackal-headed gods. He lived them every day of his life.

The artist said, 'Pull up some chairs,' then settled himself before his workstation. The great screen sprang to life to display an intricate yet organic looking spaceship, floating against the hard, black virtual vacuum of space. The image disappeared.

'Sorry,' said Chappell. 'Work in progress, you shouldn't have seen that, embarrassing. Sorry about that.'

The screen of a search engine Prentiss recognised came up and Chappell clicked into its question box.

'Right then, Prentiss' he said. 'Let's see what the Strangeness Forum has to say about your adventures. Are you happy for me to share with them?'

22

Prentiss tilted her head quizzically. 'Strangeness Forum? What's that?'

Chappell looked at her archly. 'It's a place where suspect characters like me can go to prove to themselves that they're not crazy, and that they're not working in a vacuum. Let me demonstrate.'

His fingers rattled on his keyboard and a simple panel appeared asking for his username and password. He keyed in T. O'Saurus in the top box and muttered, 'T hyphen Rex hyphen nineteen ninety-three' as a series of little dots appeared in the lower.

Howlett asked, 'Why nineteen ninety-three? That's not your birth year.'

Chappell sighed. 'Doh! Of course, it isn't. It's the year Spielberg's *Jurassic Park* came out. Probably the greatest film ever made. Now, watch.'

The home page opened to a sunlit glade in a forest and the sound of horse's hooves. A white shape flickered through the trees and then burst out into the open. It was a superbly realised unicorn.

Prentiss gasped, 'That's beautiful.'

Chappell smiled to himself. 'Thank-you.'

The legendary creature bent its head to the tender grass in the glade and nibbled delicately. It was a peaceful, heart touching scene. And then the unicorn looked up in alarm, it made as if to bolt. It was too late. A man-like wolf beast leapt onto its back and with savage strength it tore bloody grooves into its victim's throat. The unicorn reared and kicked. Gore smeared its neck and shoulders and blood sprayed around the glade. Its movements became weaker. The point of view closed in on one of the unicorn's eyes as it glazed and died. The werewolf hulked forward, reflected in the unicorn's dead pupil. The scene faded to black to a soundtrack of tearing flesh and wet, chewing noises.

Prentiss said, 'That's horrible.'

Chappell agreed, 'Yes, you're right, it is. I made the beginning sequence and someone else extended it to include the werewolf attack. *She* said it represented the inevitable demise of female innocence once a girl has been confronted by unbridled male lust. I think there's more than a touch of wishful thinking in there, don't you?'

Prentiss queried, 'She? A woman made that? Really?'

'Yes, really. You'd be surprised. And we endure all that just to get to here.' A new page opened. He gestured with an open palm. 'Welcome to the forum.'

A beautifully detailed dragon curled right around the screen, its tail in its mouth. Large flat spines rose from the dragon's back and circled a group of antique looking metallic letters that spelled out, 'To join a current conversation click HERE. To start a new topic, ignite the dragon's breath.'

Chappell hit control and clicked on the dragon's head at the same time. It was a practiced move and he did it without a moment's hesitation.

Prentiss murmured, 'You must do this a lot.'

'One of the tools of my trade. Keeps me sane. Well, you know, almost.'

The dragon belched a ball of yellow white flame and vanished, to be replaced by a hunched, black robed and hooded figure standing in a pale beam of light that was the only illumination in an otherwise darkened scene. The figure limped towards them holding out something in its long-fingered hands. As it drew closer Prentiss saw that it was holding a smoky looking crystalline globe. It came closer and closer until the globe filled the screen. Formless midnight mist coiled around its interior and then slowly resolved itself into a string of undecipherable words. They were too dark to make out against the sable background. As if a taper had been lit the text suddenly glowed bright silver. Prentiss read, 'They who would begin a new topic must enter the Strangeness vow, HERE.'

Chappell clicked on it and tapped out, 'I swear I am pure of heart, dark of mind, and an arcane traveller in Strangeness.'

'Enter new topic.'

'What is Anubis? When did he begin? When shall he end?'

Prentiss considered his questions to be a highly esoteric approach to information gathering. She wondered what answers Chappell was likely to get, and doubted they were going to prove useful. But at least the site had proved entertaining – once they got past its horrific introductory sequence.

Chappell leaned back in his seat. 'That pours the lamp oil into the tinder box. Now we wait to see if anyone strikes a big enough spark to make it burn. Right then, fellow diners, follow me into the kitchen and let's see what we can find for dinner. We leave the Strangeness members to chow down on our subject. I'm curious to see what colour juice they spit out.'

The rain was still pounding at the windows and the sky shone like polished pewter. It looked as if Chappell's loft had been encased in lead and sounded like workmen were busy hammering it home. The result would have been claustrophobic if the rooms hadn't offered so much space and so many artfully concealed light sources. Despite the muted roar of the storm Prentiss felt safe and relaxed. She liked Chappell's loft, his taste was very like her own. He had evidently bent his home to his will, and impressed his love of culture on it. She wondered how he would cope with finding a partly eaten, half naked celebrity by a dumpster. It might not fit well with his geometrically precise worldview. At that moment, she noticed a small yet exquisite, cream coloured bowl in a carefully lit niche. Despite its simplicity, she felt herself compelled to look more closely. It was breathtaking. Chappell came to her side.

'Can you hear the music in its form? True artistic genius creates music made solid. Can you believe someone made that by hand?'

She looked at him wide eyed. 'It's beautiful.'

'Yes, it is. I couldn't really afford it but I had to have it. Song dynasty, Chinese, over a thousand years old. It completes the room, don't you think?'

'It makes me want to cry.'

'Wolfman told me about your Whistler etching. What does that make you feel?'

She blushed a little. 'He told you about that? I guess he would have done. My etching makes me want to walk there in old London town, or read something by Dickens. Something like *Our Mutual Friend* or *Oliver Twist*. Something set in the stews and the smoke.'

'Taste as well as beauty. Wolfman *is* a lucky boy.'

Howlett interrupted, 'I am standing here, you know. And stop judging her like a prize heifer at a state fair. You're better than that.'

Chappell clasped his hand to his breast and reeled as if stabbed. 'A hit, a palpable hit. Prentiss, my dear, please forgive me if I have offended you. I do not think of you as a heifer or any other kind of domestic beast. And the Wolfman is become very defensive of you. I like that, I like that very much.'

He grinned like an artful urchin, a picture of mischief. She grinned back. Howlett scowled. Chappell threaded his arm through hers.

'I believe we must find red meat for the Wolfman before he bites us. This way.'

The kitchen was as neat and stylish as every other room. The first thing Prentiss noticed was a row of bright, wicked looking knives, their blades glued to a wall mounted magnet. They had been arranged in descending size order. Then she took in the rest of the room. If a farmhouse had been built with a well-trained eye and with respect to harmonised colour and texture, this would be its kitchen. Wine coloured tiles were set against honeyed woods and black marble work surfaces. A solid oak table and chairs looked perfect in the centre. On a good day, the table would have been lit by dormer windows mounted deep into the gabled ceiling. On that cloud covered, late afternoon the windows were dark and work surfaces glowed below recessed

91

LED downlighters all around the walls. Chappell switched on a faux storm lamp he had fetched from a closet and placed it in the centre of the table. Orange light glowed bright.

He spoke clearly. 'Albert, a little Brahms Cello Sonata would be nice, please.'

Mellow tones flowed from discreet speakers.

'Thank you.'

Chappell was very much the master in his kitchen, as he was in every other room of his house. He prepared and cooked them a meal of tender, breaded veal escalopes with patatas bravas, hot breads, and mixed salads as if he had been expecting them and laid in supplies. They ate, drank, and talked around a dazzling range of subjects. Even when the topic was out of her comfort zone the two men made sure she felt included in the conversation. She was invited to go into detail about her Anubis research. Howlett joined in with his jackal observations. Chappell listened mutely and nodded frequently, his eyes thoughtful. Afterwards their host cleared away the dishes into the washer, topped up their glasses despite Howlett's protest, and ushered them back towards his studio. As they left the kitchen he said, 'Lights out and music off thanks, Albert.' And the room descended into silent darkness.

The screen in his studio was dark until he twitched his mouse and a message board appeared.

He tilted his head at Prentiss. 'Well now, lookee here. I didn't expect that.'

23

The same message was being repeated over and over, scrolling down the screen.

'You shall first find Anubis under a dying star. Tell Prentiss to close her eyes.'

'That's interesting,' said Chappell, dryly. 'Looks like someone's hacked the Strangeness Forum. That would take real talent. The Strangeness site has been encrypted like Fort Knox, better than Homeland. Wonder if I should answer it? Wonder if I could answer it without infecting my whole system with a virus? And it looks like you're a celebrity, Prentiss. What do you want me to do? This should be your call I think. Shall I turn it off, answer it, or burst into tears and run screaming from the room?'

The message appeared, and scrolled down, appeared, and scrolled down. It had an almost hypnotic effect on the group. Prentiss sat in her chair and looked at the two men. 'Keep an eye on me, please. This is just another big step up the weirdness ladder and I'm already way out of my comfort zone.' She held her arms out. 'Would you hold my hands, please guys? I'm going to shut my eyes for a moment. You know, see what happens.'

Howlett leaned towards her and took her hand, concern written plainly on his face. 'Are you sure? You don't have to do this.'

'I'll have to close my eyes sometime, even if it's just to sleep. I'd be happier with you guys here while I did it. Call it a controlled experiment if you like. Okay? Rex, it's your apartment. You okay with this? It could get freaky.'

Chappell took her other hand. 'I normally illustrate this stuff, but this is the first time I've had to live through it. Ready when you are, but remember, I'm a virgin to this sort of thing. Be gentle with me.'

Prentiss closed her eyes and leaned back. Chappell noticed that almost at the same instant the scrolling message disappeared from his screen.

'How the fu...?'

Prentiss sat with her eyes closed and waited vainly for something to happen. After a few seconds, she began to feel a little foolish about making such a dramatic performance out the simple act of shutting her eyes. And then she began to feel profoundly calm. Her breathing deepened while she entered a meditative state. She could no longer feel the men's hands holding hers. There followed a gentle sensation of dizziness as if she had been spinning very fast and had suddenly stopped. She felt weightless as if floating on a warm, salty sea. She couldn't bear the suspense any longer. *What was happening?* She opened her eyes.

A bloated red sun filled an orange sky. She was floating above a carbon black and featureless landscape that stretched to the curve of a far horizon. Nothing moved except ripples of heat haze that distorted her vision, and crackles of yellow flame spreading like broken veins across the red face of the sun. She knew the heat from the distended red orb should have rendered her to a charred crisp in an instant, but she was protected in her cocoon of cool air. At first, she thought she was travelling across a dead land, a barren place burned by a dying star, and she wondered why she was there. Then something clean and white caught at the edges of her sight. She turned to face it. Something winked brightly and glided towards her. It looked like a snowflake, an impossible snowflake surviving in a furnace under a sky on fire. And then she recognised the pattern. It was identical to one of the geometrically carved nodes in the balustrades of the great staircase on the shores of the Apsu. As it came closer she realised the structure was vast and much more complex than it had at first appeared. And it was achingly beautiful, an exercise in exquisite harmony. Subtly coloured fractal patterns and crevasses began to emerge in the intricate patterns, and Prentiss' point of view fell towards one of these. It opened out and swallowed her. She entered the structure, floating gently into an airy, well-lit space of arches and delicate, lacelike spars. Something about the architecture made her think of photon-microscopic images she had seen of bleached bone tissue and she would have liked to pause and study it, but she kept moving and had no chance to look more closely. Something had her firmly in its grip. Her passage took her inevitably towards a wall containing a mass of slowly moving fibres. They looked perhaps like fine, wind-blown hair, or sea anemones on coral, or nothing she had ever seen or experienced before. The pale fronds reached out to her as if sensing her approach. She could do nothing except accept their probing touch. When they stroked her, she became numb and a pleasant coolness radiated through her. The fronds wound around her body, holding her firmly yet gently. Her vision became lost in a sea of pearlescent white. And then she heard the voice. It was a voice she knew from her dreams. It had somehow insinuated itself into her mind without entering her ears.

'The sun is dying and the Earth must die with her, Prentiss. We choose not to die. This city is in stasis, held in the eternal instant by a time vortex that stretches from the city's core back to the beginning of all existence. The city is frozen in this last moment of this last day under a dying star. Just a few moments after this immortal *now* the sun will explode and its core shrink back to become a remnant of its former self. Little more than a short lived white dwarf. It will not matter to Earth. She will have been destroyed in the explosion. Most of our people have left the solar system behind and moved on to fresh horizons, but some of us decided to stay. We feel we have a duty of care for those who went before. We believe we are shepherds who would protect our flock from the wolves in the forest, but it would be just as true to say we are the dead.'

'And, you. You speak for your people. Are you the first among the dead?'

'You want to know if this is the ultimate land to the west? If that is your question, then yes, perhaps. Open your eyes, Prentiss. Open your eyes and see the truth at last.'

She blinked once and saw black, gold-rimmed orbs gazing back at her from her reflection in polished grey stone. She screamed, blinked again, and found Tabaqui Howlett looking down at her, Rex Chappell at his shoulder. She shook with fright, her teeth chattering, and looked around wildly. The men still held both of her hands. She pulled them away and ran her fingers down the skin of her arms and across her cheeks.

She gasped, 'Mirror. Is there a mirror? I need a mirror.' Her voice quavered.

Chappell vanished from view and returned seconds later with a small mirror, framed in black lacquered wood. He thrust it at her. She held it glass down in both hands for a second, and then raised it to her face. Her own panicked eyes looked back.

She let the mirror fall onto her lap and looked from Howlett to Chappell.

'How long were my eyes shut? Please, tell me, did anything happen? How long were my eyes shut? I have to know.'

Howlett cast a quick look at his friend and then back to her.

'What do you remember? Do you remember anything? Anything at all?'

'Of course, I remember everything. I was in a scorched landscape under an obese, red sun...'

She told them of her experience in the white, fractal city. The touch of the numbing fronds, the voice. The polished ebony eyes gazing at her from her own reflection, and returning to the here and now.

'I must have fallen asleep and dreamt it all, but where is all this coming from? Am I going mad, or has my head been filled with auto-suggestions by someone?'

Chappell took her shoulder in his hand and squeezed it.

95

'I wouldn't have believed it if I hadn't seen it with my own eyes. Honest to God, I nearly pissed myself with fright. I'm telling the truth here aren't I, Tabaqui?'

She looked at Howlett. 'What truth? What happened? Come on, you must tell me. What?'

Howlett took a shaky breath. 'You levitated. Your hand gripped mine so hard I thought the bones would break. I felt them grinding together. And then you floated up into the air. You went as high as you could go without losing your grip on our hands. And then you started to drift from side to side. I don't know, it was like you were caught up in invisible waves or some sort of current in a stream. I've never seen anything like it. Your hair was floating around your head like it was alive. And then it was over, after about ten minutes, maybe more. I don't know. You floated back down to the chair and slumped forward. That was when you screamed, and woke up asking for a mirror.'

Chappell said, 'I'll just be a second,' and vanished from the room once more. Howlett took the opportunity to take Prentiss in his arms and try to comfort her quivering body. She accepted his gesture with gratitude and surrendered to his warmth. She felt safe in his embrace.

Chappell returned. 'They do this in the movies when someone's had a bit of a shock. Not a clue if it works but it made me feel better. You're not meant to do it in cases of hypothermia, or so I'm told, so God only knows how much damage those dogs do up in the Alps. Anyway, you two look warm enough so no harm done. Bottoms up.'

He distributed thick bottomed glasses with an inch of dark amber liquid in the bottom of each. Prentiss took a sniff and almost reeled away from the densely alcoholic fumes.

'What is this stuff? Rocket fuel?'

Chappell looked offended. 'No! It's very fine Cognac. It was a gift from my publisher. I've never opened it but I thought, you know, needs must. Take a sip.'

Howlett did as he was told and sighed. 'Smooth,' he said.

Prentiss gingerly took a sip, and then a second. The Cognac filled her mouth and body with a rich warmth unlike anything she had experienced before. She drained the glass and felt a blanket of drowsiness drop around her shoulders.

She stuttered, 'I need to... need to... go home I think. Been a long day.'

A flare of lightning and an almost instant roll of thunder highlighted the fact that the storm still held the city in its grip. Chappell took her arm.

'Prentiss, my girl. I don't want to think of you all alone in your apartment. I've got a spare bedroom here that has its own bathroom, and that leather thing over there is a sofa-bed that can easily manage Tabaqui's height. I can't let you risk the streets in this terrible weather and I'm told I do a fair breakfast. Why don't you stay? Keep me company?'

Prentiss looked drowsily at Howlett, who stifled a yawn behind his fist. She nodded at Chappell.

'Thank-you, Rex. You're a lovely man. But I must warn you that the weirdest shit happens at night, so be prepared.'

Chappell grinned. 'Now she tells me,' and he drained his glass.

24

Prentiss decided Chappell must be a frustrated hotelier. He had even supplied her with a little wash bag containing a fresh toothbrush plus a miniature tube of toothpaste, a small bottle of shampoo, shower gel, and a little block of soap.

'I stay in hotels during Comic Cons,' he explained. 'I always use my own stuff but I like to keep the freebies. I don't think of it as being cheap, I just feel like I've already paid for them, you know?'

She smiled and nodded. He pointed to a small black box on her bedside cabinet.

'All the rooms are connected by those sound boxes. The people before me had little kids and they were paranoid something bad might happen to them, so they had the whole place wired for sound. I've never bothered to have them removed, it would cause too much disruption. Anyway, there they are. If you need anything, just shout and we'll hear you. Okay?'

'Okay, and thanks. Good night, I really appreciate this, Rex.'

'Good night.'

She used the bathroom then undressed to her panties. The thoughtful Chappell had given her a choice of big tees to use as a nightshirt and she had gone for the *Spiderman* version. It seemed only fair, especially after admitting she would have arrested the web-slinging vigilante if she got the chance. She regarded herself in the mirror. It had been a long day, but she still looked fresh, if heavy eyed. She heard her mother's voice in her mind's ear.

'Don't matter what you do to yourself, girl, you'll always be so damn beautiful you stop my heart. You take the shine off a rose's pride. If I was you I could never stop looking in that mirror, but you don't even know, do you?'

And her mother would buss her on the cheek then fuss her way back into the garden, or the kitchen, or the utility room; wherever her next chore took her. Prentiss' mom was always busy. Sometimes too busy for her little girl. Prentiss settled herself in the bed and turned off the light.

'Good night, Wolfman, good night, Prentiss.' Chappell's voice issued in a slightly tinny fashion from the box on the cabinet.

'Shut up and go to sleep, dude.' Howlett's voice sounded drowsy.

Prentiss joined in, 'Good night, guys. See you in the morning.'

She felt a little foolish talking aloud to an empty room. She closed her eyes and sought the sweet spot in her unfamiliar bed. Something disturbed her, what was it? She sat up. Beside her the sound box emitted a soft humming sound. She picked it up and shook it. She called out, 'Hey, guys, can you hear that buzzing noise?' She got no answer. 'Hello, can you hear me? Hello?'

And then she felt something like a hard gust of wind, as if a window had opened to the storm outside and then closed again. She tasted ozone and her skin tingled. That was when the clotted shadows in the corner of the room moved. She had almost been on the point of sleep but suddenly she snapped awake, adrenaline jolting her body to a state of readiness.

'Who's there?'

In a futile reaction, her hand clawed for the light switch. She couldn't find it. Almost panicked she had to calm herself long enough to remember she was no longer at home. The shadows in the corner flowed. *Where was that damned light switch?* She finally found it and pressed. Nothing happened. She pressed again. Nothing. She whimpered.

'It won't work. Neither will your communication device.'

That voice. 'Anubis?'

'As good a name as any other. It will do for now.'

'How did you...? What do you want?'

'I would talk with you. I know you are tired, I am sorry about that. But I need to know something.'

'What?'

'What links us?'

'I don't understand.'

'I remember you visiting me many thousands of years ago, I also remember you visiting me billions of years from now. How is that possible? What links us?'

She answered its question with one of her own.

'They call you a god? Are you?'

'Many have thought so. Some still do. But, no. I am not a god.'

'Are you human?'

'I am as much human as you are three point seven billion-year-old simple-celled bacteria from the Nuvvuagittuq Supracrustal Belt. However, I have no doubt that I share a fraction of my DNA with humans, at least in some small part of what you might loosely call my anatomy. I like mankind. Some of it is aesthetically pleasing, and it believes in good, despite all the evidence to the contrary. But what is it that links us, Betsy Mae Prentiss?'

'Just Prentiss, okay.'

'As you wish. As you wish. But, what links us?'

'I don't understand the question. What do you mean by "link"? I don't know what you are or where you're from, or even how you're here. Why are you killing people? Where are you hiding? Why are you even in New York? Why are you here?'

'You believe you're telling the truth, Prentiss. How fascinating. You are unique, my hunter. Throughout the entire vortex of the current Earth time you are the only creature who has come to me to be judged and lived. The only one. You are also the only one who has witnessed the results of my judgements and hunted me in turn. There must be a clue there. And you found me. You called to me. You ask what I am? The answer is complex. I am one of the last of a small group of evolved minds living in the last city during the last days of Earth. I exist there but my consciousness also spans throughout all time, as do we all. You have seen the ruin of my world. It is a dead and dark place under a blood red sun. It is the land of the dead. It can be hard to remain positive under such conditions, but we try. We find joy in the goodness in the past. Good brings us joy and evil brings us pain and great suffering. One we worship as a sign the creator has touched his work once more. The other we reward with death, as you have seen.' The shadow in the shadows moved closer. She heard its breathing, felt it cold on her skin.

'You ask why I am here in New York? Why not? I am also in London, Moscow, Brasilia, and Beijing. Wherever evil festers you will find me. Wherever children are harmed and innocence suffers there you will find me. I take many forms but the dark combination of wolf and jackal pleases me most. Where do I hide? Where I am most needed. In shadows, in an empty glass, in a memory. In a place where hope has been sucked away and replaced by torment. In a heart that would see a child bleed and smile with pleasure at the sight. I will take such a heart and I will weigh it in the balance. If it fails I will devour the sinner's soul and send them to endure that last day of a barren planet where they will burn in torment for all remaining time – which I estimate to be about three hours from the moment they arrive. Knowing all that, little hunter, what do you think links us?'

Prentiss was silent for a long moment. Something teased at the very fringes of her mind. She shut her eyes in the darkness and focused her thoughts. The reflected image of ebon eyes surrounded by gold came back to her. How had she seen herself reflected with Anubis' face? How had it happened?

'Perhaps,' she said. 'I will one day be the one who judges you and chooses your punishment. Perhaps I am more like you than you could believe possible. Perhaps I am your nemesis.'

The orange light of a burning sky filled the room and the darkest shadows flowed together and curdled to form a tall figure silhouetted against the blood red brilliance of a bloated and dying star. It was dark and slender with the head of a jackal and the naked body of a man. Its shoulders were broad and its arms powerful. She could not help but notice the tumescence of its penis. Whatever else it might think itself to be, the creature was certainly male. Its shadowed face turned towards her. She got the feeling it was smiling fondly at her.

'I once lay with women in the lost temples of the Zagros mountains. They worshiped and feared the winged priests of a cult who believed vultures to be the undertakers of the creator, and jackals and wolves were the guardians of the dead. We shaped ourselves in the forms of beast creatures and divine, winged messengers. It was a simpler time then, a time of survival and warriors and farmers. It had its sophistications and its rulers and its followers, but it was a simpler time. The belly of modern mankind is not now as it was then. People worked for their food but they would share what they had without hesitation. Now, some kill themselves with excess while others starve. Such imbalance causes a disturbance that we can feel in the vortex. It is like pain for us, it breaks our hearts and we reach out to cure the pain at source. Such a disturbance attracts evil to it in the same way street dogs would be drawn to the body of a dead child in ancient Egypt. The effect is that evil thrives like worms in a wound and civilisations fall from grace then collapse. When your civilisation collapses, Prentiss, it will take the world with it. Would you judge me for trying to stop that? Would you?'

'Then what links us?'

'I wonder. As I said, I once lay with women in the temple. Some of them conceived. It was many thousands of years ago. Are you, perhaps a daughter of that distant temple reborn in America? Are you born of the line of blood of my hearth? Are you a child from the line of Anubis?

25

The next morning Prentiss was subdued over breakfast and remained quiet while Howlett drove her back to her apartment, only responding to direct questions. Her head was in turmoil. She wanted to believe her encounter the night before had been a dream, but in her heart she knew it had been real, no matter how impossible and fantastic it seemed. If a witness had told her they had received important information from an ancient Egyptian deity who had visited them in their bedroom in the middle of the night, she would have thanked them, wished them well, and not believed a word of it. She wondered if she needed therapy, or at least a long girly chat with Sam, mujer a mujer. It seemed an age since she had last seen her friend, but with surprise she realised it had only been one day and two nights.

'Rex told me he would keep an eye on the Strangeness posts for you and report anything he considers worthwhile.'

Howlett's comment dragged her back to the here and now.

'He's a good friend of yours isn't he.'

'He is, yes. We were at college together, roomies, you know.'

'Does he have many friends?'

'I guess not. He's a very private person, shy. You really brought him out of his shell last night. I've never seen him so relaxed with another person in the room. He can be very intense – he frightens people away sometimes.'

'Does he have a girlfriend?'

'I don't think that's his thing. Oh, sorry, he gave me this for you.'

The car was stationary in the Sunday morning traffic, which allowed Howlett to reach onto his back seat and fetch a large manila envelope.

He handed it to her. 'He made me promise not to give it to you until we were well away from his loft. He gets embarrassed about people saying thank-you for some reason. Anyway, go on, open it.'

With a curious rush of nerves Prentiss peeled up the flap and pulled out two sheets of heavy cartridge paper. On one was a portrait of her, sensitively drawn, the work of a keen eye and a brilliantly talented hand. She had once had her portrait drawn by a professional at the insistence of her parents. She loathed the clumsy result, which they kept framed under glass over the mantel shelf in their living room. And she hated it when they drew their guests' attention to it, as if Rembrandt had signed it rather than some talentless hack. Chappell had talent.

The next sheet was breathtaking. Anubis gazed out at her, ancient, wise, and implacable. She got a real sense of power and presence from the portrait. This creature could be coldly judgemental but never shallow or cruel.

The car began to move. Howlett said, his eyes on the road, 'Do you like it?'

'They're astonishing. I can't accept these. A gallery would charge a fortune for something like this.'

'They? I thought he'd given you a little sketch or something. He always gives me a comic sketch of a werewolf doing odd things like the washing up or sitting on the can. I've got dozens of them in my condo, and they're all signed so they're worth something. What's he given you?'

'There's a fine portrait of me and a drawing of Anubis. They're exquisite, much too good to give away like this. And they're signed.'

The traffic drew to a halt. 'Please, let me see.'

Howlett studied the portraits in silence then handed them back carefully when he needed to take the wheel once more.

He smiled oddly. 'I've known Rex for more than eight years. I think of him as my best friend. He's a professional artist, a graphic genius whose work is on the walls of some very select galleries. He's highly collectable but he rarely sells anything. He doesn't need to. He makes his money from royalties from the graphic novels he illustrates, and the design work he gets commissioned to do for science fiction movies. Go into any large bookshop and you'll find a shelf full of books about his work, all listed under that silly "O'Saurus" name of his. Go to another shelf and you'll see stacks of the graphic novels he's illustrated. In his own world, he's famous, but to me he's a friend. I've been there when he needed a hand to hold and a shoulder to cry on. He made those drawings of me, he said, so that I would always be there if he needed me. But he's never given me drawings like those. He's known you for one evening... Wow, you really got to him, Prentiss. You have true star quality.'

She didn't know what to say. She sat looking at her drawings. Even though she felt she should give them back she couldn't bear to part with them. Anubis looked at her across thousands of years of history. The portrait had a quality of stillness but it was also charged with life. The lines had been laid down with confidence, she could feel the speed with which Chappell worked, but there was not a single wasted stroke of the pen. Her respect for the artist increased while she examined his work. Howlett broke into her train of thought.

'Are you still planning on a trip to The Met today?'

'It's a good place to go and think.'

'Fancy some company?'

'Yes, please, that would be nice.'

'Okay, great, good. Is it all right if I drop you at your place and go visit a clothing store? I'm feeling a little funky and I need a change of clothes and things. That cool with you? I hadn't planned on an overnighter with Rex, and, well, you know.'

'Great thinking, there's a place just around the corner. It'll take you about five minutes on foot. Park your car in the visitor bays and I'll show you how to get there. I'll be changed and have some coffee ready by the time you get back.'

'Sounds like a plan. Sunday lunch at The Met. How very civilised.'

When Prentiss let herself in she was startled by a strange humming sound and it took her a moment to remember that she'd left Laurie's dehumidifier working the whole time she was out. She rushed into her living room and turned it off, wondering what leaving it working for over twenty-four hours was going to do to her electricity bill. On a more positive note it had proved very effective. The floor and furniture was as good as new, but she had been right about her rugs. They were stained beyond recovery. She bagged them up in bin liners and put them by the front door to take them down to the garbage when they left for The Met later that morning.

She changed her clothes rapidly, pulling on a pair of jeans and a favourite cotton blouse. The apartment was redolent with the rich scent of freshly brewed coffee by the time her buzzer told her she had a visitor.

'Hi, honey, I'm home.'

'Come on up, before my husband sees you.'

Howlett had several bags and he asked where he could get changed into fresher clothes. She showed him into her bedroom and shut the door behind herself on the way out. The speed their relationship was developing was leaving her feeling a little giddy and she didn't want to accidently send out any sexual signals he might misconstrue. She told herself she was just being sensible, that she hardly knew the man, but she knew she was fooling herself. She was a virgin, a status she valued. She didn't want to surrender her body to the first man who had treated her as an equal rather than a sex object, and she was nervous. She had never knowingly been so much as naked in front of a man before. She was shy.

Howlett joined her in the kitchen, breathing deeply.

'If that coffee tastes the way it smells I may just have to marry you one day, Prentiss.'

She grinned and handed him a mug into which he poured skimmed milk. He sipped, and sighed. 'You know the way to a man's heart sure enough. You look so fresh the birds would think it was spring and burst into song, and you make coffee like an Italian. Can I be rude? How come there's no mister Prentiss?'

'There is, he's my father. And how come there's no missus Wolfman?'

'Honest truth? I've never met the right girl and I'm very involved with my work. I love what I do and sometimes I'm out late working. I often travel abroad, go to conferences, write up reports and white papers, and the Sanctuary takes up a lot of my time. Girls like a man they get to see occasionally, you know? Spend some time with. And anyhow, yeah, I've never met the right girl. I never knew what she looked like, how she sounded, what her coffee tasted like...'

He grinned and took another long pull at his coffee.

'If angels made coffee it would taste like this. How do you do it?'

'Trade secret. I could tell you but I would have to shoot you and that would be a waste of a fine biologist.'

'Okay, point taken. But quid pro quo, Officer Prentiss. How come there's no mister in your life? Really?'

'Many were called but none were chosen. Lots of eager wolves, but never a pretty, blue-eyed one who walks with them. Shall we go to The Met, Wolfman?'

'Any more of that coffee?'

'All gone.'

'Then let's go to The Met. I like this plan.'

26

On their way, they returned the dehumidifier to Laurie, who seemed genuinely glad it had worked. He invited them into his apartment to show them his bone-dry walls. Prentiss was surprised by the clutter of books and publications that were arranged in piles all around the floor.

Laurie explained, 'When the water started seeping in I had to move my books and artworks off the walls and shelves before they were ruined. It would have been a disaster if my collection had become waterlogged. Everything's dry now, but thank God, I was in when it happened, and thank God you came home when you did. Let's just pray that whatever happened doesn't happen again. I may have to think about getting free standing shelves just in case.'

They offered to help put the books back, but he demurred.

'No, but thank-you, really. I know where each one goes and I love to potter with my books. It will make for an extremely satisfying Sunday. Help build up a proper appetite for dinner later. You youngsters go and get on with your day, I'll be fine. Thank-you.'

Prentiss left her spoiled rugs in the apartment building's dumpster and decided she would put off replacing them until she saw her electricity bill. Howlett insisted on driving rather than taking the subway, and he wove his way unerringly to The Met's parking garage on Fifth Avenue. Shortly afterwards the couple walked into the great halls of the museum. Prentiss sought out an information desk. A smiling woman raised an enquiring brow at her approach.

'May I help you?'

'Please, yes.' She shut her eyes to better remember. 'Yes, could you tell us, where would we find material about the Zagros mountains and Mesopotamia? Especially winged gods and figures. I can't be more specific, you see I'm not sure if I should be looking at Sumer or somewhere else. Sorry.'

'Not at all. Fascinating subject. You want the North Wing, Ancient Near East. That will take you from the rise of Sumer in the late Neolithic to the fall of Babylon in five thirty-nine BCE – and everything in between. An exciting and romantic journey. Do enjoy your time here.'

'Thank-you. We will.'

It was an hour later, when they were both wondering if they could face the museum's mediocre coffee, that Prentiss stumbled upon a set of stone reliefs which she discovered had come from the Northwest Palace built by King Assurbanipal the second in the Assyrian capital city of Nimrud. They were three thousand years old, but the workmanship was astonishing and the carvings crisp as the day they were created. Her eyes glittered.

'Tabaqui, look at these. Look at the winged figures. They are almost exactly like the winged men I saw in my dream. And look here, see these structures, they're like the balustrades in my dream and that place I dreamt about in the future, you know, when I shut my eyes at Rex's place and I...' she lowered her voice... 'when I levitated.' She raised her voice slightly. 'See there, that's exactly like the wristwatch that glowed when the winged man fired his weapon into the sea. What does it mean? Why am I dreaming about these things?'

Howlett frowned with concentration, 'I think we need to keep an open mind about what's going on. Don't be annoyed, but have you ever been here before? I mean, might you have seen these reliefs before?'

'I came here with my school, I'm sure of that, but I don't remember any of this stuff.'

'Okay, but you might have picked up some images that stayed with you subconsciously and they're only now coming to the surface.'

She whispered, 'Did you dream that I floated around Rex's studio last night?'

'No, and I admit I don't understand what happened there. It seems crazy in the light of day, as if I watched it happening to someone else. I have to keep telling myself it really happened. But we can't rule out the power of subconscious suggestion. The mind is a powerful tool. It can do amazing things, create monsters as well as dreams.'

'The men I dreamt about were bald. These guys have beards and dreadlocks. Why would I want to give them all a close shave?'

'I don't know.'

'Anubis is an Egyptian god, why would I put him next to an underground sea with a bunch of Assyrians?'

'I don't know?'

'That structure there.' She indicated a complex decorative section on one of the reliefs and read the information panel. 'They're calling it the "Tree of Life". Why would I be dreaming about something that looks almost identical but is about the size of Texas and is floating around Earth with a time vortex in its centre? And why should I dream that the whole thing's been frozen in time just moments before the sun explodes? Where did that come from and what's the link?'

She thought back to her conversation with Anubis the night before and his question, *what links us?*

Howlett shrugged, 'I don't know. Do you read a lot of science fiction?'

'No! I never have. It's not to my taste. I prefer the real world, thanks very much. I've got enough to deal with without adding spaceships, robots, and little green men to my mental diet.'

She ran a shaking hand through her hair. 'What am I talking about? I'm dreaming about an immortal from the future who thinks he might be my thousand times removed great, great grandfather and I've floated around an artist's loft in the Village like a helium balloon. Little green men would be a walk in the park by comparison.'

'Whoa there, lady. What was that about great grandfathers?'

'Can we get a drink, please, Tabaqui. I'm parched.'

They made their way up to the little house on the roof that contained the museum's café and cocktail bar rather than risk the coffee in the main hall. The storm of the night before had scoured the sky of cloud and cool bright sunshine had lured several groups of people out onto the roof garden.

Howlett fetched their drinks and the couple found a seat on a low wall where they could talk without being overheard. They silently appreciated the view across Central Park. Behind them was Fifth Avenue. The skyline around them was one of the most iconic in the world. Against such a setting Prentiss' story of a visitation by a super evolved being from the end of time made her feel ridiculous. But Howlett listened gravely until she had finished. He said nothing while she spoke and his silence continued until well after she'd finished. He took her hand with a little smile, leaned forward, and kissed her warmly on the lips. She responded, closing her eyes. When they drew apart she looked around at the groups of people on the roof and sighed.

'Look at those kids, Tabaqui. They've got all this around them, but they sit with their heads buried in their tablets or smartphones. They might as well be sitting in a windowless cellar. One day all this will be gone. Burned to nothing. And we'll be gone too, mankind will have evolved into God alone knows what. No trees, no bees, no babies, no grandfathers, no you, and no me. What's the point?'

'Perhaps, my dear Prentiss, that *is* the point.'

They turned to find Erskine had drawn up beside them while they were distracted.

'I'm sorry to say I overheard the last part of your conversation before I could offer the obligatory discreet cough to announce myself. I didn't want to interrupt. May I join you?'

27

'Now I think I know why you're dreaming about bald men.'

Howlett said it semi-seriously as he navigated the route back to Prentiss' apartment. She grinned at him and he smiled sheepishly.

'Are you looking for compliments, mister blue-eyed wolfman? Shall I compare thee to a flirtatious, bald-headed, gossip columnist?'

'No. But you two seemed to be getting on well enough.'

'He's a practiced socialite. He'd get nowhere if he wasn't. He plays his audience like a concert pianist, once he knows which keys to press.'

'Yeah? Well I thought he was a bit of a creep.'

'I noticed. I guess he never worked you out, kept hitting bum notes. Anyway, he was concentrating on me.'

'Why?'

'I think I've become a project of his. I went to see him about the Anubis case and he knew things about all the victims to date. He's emailed me a list of potential victims in New York City but I haven't read it yet. They're all celebrities and they've all been up to something nasty, but there's never been enough proof to issue a warrant. Anubis doesn't need one, he steps in as he sees fit. But we'll have to keep an eye on the people on Erskine's list, or at least try to protect them. But what are we meant to do? Knock on the door and say, "Hi, we're from the NYPD. We know you're all evil child molesters – and you've been getting away with it for years – but suddenly you've become the target for a supernatural vigilante. We need you to watch out, okay?" That would be idiotic, forget it. Sorry, Tabaqui, I'm talking shop. I'll worry about it tomorrow, today's my day off. In any case, too many innocent people die in what should be safe places, they deserve my attention much more than those evil creeps.'

'Murder's still murder, Prentiss, and you're a cop. And a good one too if I'm any judge.'

'I hope so, Tabaqui, I do hope so.'

He turned onto Prentiss' street then eased down the ramp into the parking garage for her apartment. He nosed his car into a visitor bay and cut the engine.

She licked her dry lips nervously, then said, 'I've got some more of that coffee you liked, if you could face another cup?'

He coloured slightly. 'Prentiss, look, I have to say something. Oh, this sounds so stupid, and I know you're just offering me coffee and there are no strings attached, but I need to explain something. It's important to me.'

He looked aside at her and took a deep breath, then looked down at the knotted fingers of his clasped hands, pressed hard into his lap.

'So, you see, ah, well...' He coughed and pounded his fists on his knees. 'Just say it, Howlett. Okay, okay, so, look,' he took another breath. Prentiss thought she knew where this train of stuttering thought was going to lead, but she didn't dare help. Howlett had to find his own way.

He spoke in a sudden spurt of words. 'The thing is, I take my faith very seriously and I once made an important vow in front of my Lord. It was a time when my soul was vulnerable. And I meant it. Still do. So, what it is, you see, I'm keeping my body pure until I marry, and I'll marry in a church. I like you a lot, more than a lot, but you need to know that. So, there it is, I thought it best to put it out there in the open.'

He looked up. 'So, do I still get a coffee? Or is it time for me to hit the highway and get out of your life?'

She kissed him hard, which was awkward in the confined space of the car. He seemed surprised but responded gamely. She took his hands and kissed them.

'Don't worry,' she smiled. 'Me too. I feel the same way. Oh, Tabaqui, can't you see? I feel the same way. Whatever we've got between us let's deal with it a moment at a time, shall we? See where it takes us, okay? Come on, let's go get that coffee.'

Howlett carried the bag containing their purchases from The Met in one hand and took hers in the other. Hers was dry and cool. His felt hot and damp by comparison. She leaned against him in the elevator and smiled happily. She had been nervous with the possibility of sex with a more experienced lover, afraid that she might prove awkward and disappointing. Her reluctance had previously become a barrier to relationships involving men she had quite liked, but who had expected the physical side of their liaison to 'blossom' as early as possible – as if sex was little more than a casual thing between friends. Even as a teenager she knew her peers were sexually active, and that they were swapping partners on a regular basis, but she had held strong compunctions against joining the party. And now she discovered, so had Howlett. He was just as sexually naïve as her.

If things ever reached the stage where they chose to consummate their relationship they would be finding out everything about each other's bodies at the same time. It would be a first for them both. This fact made him even more interesting to her, and he had already been the most interesting man she had met from the moment they first saw each other at the Wolf Sanctuary. Howlett was such a breath of fresh air, confident at one moment, shy and awkward the next. She welcomed his emotional contradictions, his honesty, and his frank, blue-eyed gaze, which softened whenever he glanced at her. The man had already found a firm foothold in her heart, she wondered how long their journey together might last. She prayed it might be a lifetime.

Howlett's phone rang while she steeped the coffee and poured out two mugs. He looked at the tell-tale screen and swiped 'accept'.

'Dude?'

He listened for a few moments.

'Sure, yes, we're in her kitchen. What? Coffee. No, we're not. Man, you have a filthy mind. Just a second...' He held out the phone. 'It's Rex. He says something's come up on the Strangeness feed and he needs to tell you direct.'

'Filthy mind?'

'Yeah, he wanted to know if coffee tasted better when we're naked. Here you go.'

She brought the phone to her mouth and breathed, 'Yes, coffee tastes so much better when you're naked with a beautiful man, Rex. You should try it.'

She received a shocked bark of laughter in response.

He replied, 'Fair enough. I will, it's a deal. Have you got a moment?'

She chuckled. 'Sure, what's happening?'

'It's the Strangeness feed. It's locked again. It keeps repeating, "The man will come down from his mountain again tomorrow, tell Prentiss to be ready". There now, I've told you and it stopped instantly. Does that mean anything to you?'

A cold wave of nausea swept through her. *It begins again tomorrow.* The romantic interlude concludes and the horror begins again. There would be another killing and another reason to talk with Gee Erskine. That day's quiet time with Howlett had lulled her into a pretence of normality. She looked at him and he frowned, concern written plain across his face.

Chappell's voice made her jump. 'Prentiss? Hi, you still there? What's happening? You okay?'

She took a steadying breath. 'Sorry, Rex, I was miles away. The man on his mountain is Anubis, it's one of his names. He's got more aliases than you can imagine. Is that all it said?'

'Yes, I read it out and it vanished off the screen, just like the other one. You sure know how to give a man a freaky time, Prentiss. I can't wait to illustrate it if you write it up. That a deal?'

'It's a promise, oh, and thanks so much for my drawings. They're beautiful. They're far too good to give away, you shouldn't have.'

'Nonsense, they'll keep your Whistler company. My work needs a big brother to look up to. Please, put them where they can see each other.'

'I will. Thanks, Rex. Shall I hand you back to Tabaqui?'

'No, thanks, tell him I'll catch him later when he's got some clothes on. Hope to see you soon, okay? Laters.'

'Yes, see you soon, Rex. Thanks.'

She handed the phone back to Howlett and told him what Chappell had said. Her coffee was cold so she made a fresh batch. While she was doing so he came up behind her and took her slender shoulders in his big hands. He kissed the nape of her neck.

'I've got an early start tomorrow, but if you want me to stay I can be here until about five. It's up to you.'

She turned in his arms and looked up the few inches into his eyes.

'I'll be fine. Get home and get some sleep. I don't have a spare room, and you can't sleep on one of the recliners. You certainly aren't sleeping on the floor. And I can't share a bed with you. Not yet. It would be too big a step. You understand? I'd love to be with you, but we must wait. I'll miss you.'

She kissed him. Her tongue flickered across his lips and he opened his mouth. They remained held in the moment long enough for her to feel his body responding, and to feel hers press sympathetically against him. She remembered gazing at the naked and priapic figure of Anubis, and in her mind's eye saw Howlett standing before her in the same condition. A warm tingle flowered in her belly. She kissed him again, gently. Feeling his hands on her back and cupping the back of her head. Even at that moment he was being proper and treating her body with respect. She pulled away slightly and took a deep breath, leaning her forehead against his chest.

'I've never allowed a man to kiss me like that before. I liked it.'

'Me too, I could get used to it though. I've never... you could tell?'

'Tell what?' She wondered if he was alluding to his evident tumescence.

'I've never kissed like that either. Sorry if I was crap, you know.'

'Oh, no, you weren't. Not at all. Now, you'd better go while I can still trust myself. Go home, you lovely man. Ring me when you get there. I want to know you're safe. Concentrate on your driving.'

'I'll do my best.'

112

The final kiss was almost chaste, and then she opened her door and watched him walk to the elevators. He pressed the down button and the doors opened almost instantly. He looked at her, smiled, and was gone.

Prentiss locked and bolted her door, thinking that it was too late to worry about security. The theft of her heart had happened in plain daylight, and she had been a more than willing accomplice.

On her table, she spotted the bag with their purchases from The Met, Howlett's postcards and book in with her own choices. She took out the bundle of cards and leafed through them until she found a clear image of a winged Assyrian deity. She gazed at the X-shaped spread of wings and the wristwatch. The numbing sense of lassitude that had fallen over her dissipated.

What are you? She wondered, *will I ever know?*

28

The blood-red sun seemed to pulse like a distressed and distended heart in the burning sky. Was it her imagination or were the rivers of yellow flame arcing across its face more active this time? She couldn't be sure. She couldn't shake the feeling that the bloated, fiery orb was an infected boil about to burst. It looked somehow unclean, as if the universe had become diseased and the infection needed to be lanced. Prentiss thought of the pure white autumn sun she had enjoyed earlier that day on The Met's roof garden. The younger sun, welcomed for its heat and light, looked beautiful against a clean blue sky. *It hasn't aged well,* she mused.

She floated once more above the waterless charcoal clinker that was all that remained of the rich continents and living oceans she took for granted eight billion years earlier, and she wondered if the black crust was completely sterile now. Was all life scoured away? Or did some strain of super indestructible bacteria still thrive, deep in the shadows?

Why had she been brought back to this moment when the hour hand of the sun's long life was poised to strike midnight? She wondered briefly about the other planets. Mercury and Venus must surely have been swallowed during the obese star's expansion, but what about Mars, Jupiter, Saturn, and the ice giants Uranus and Neptune? What of them? How would they have been affected by the sun's death throes?

She was distracted from her musings when the floating city rose up around her like an open-mouthed whale swallowing a microscopic scrap of plankton. The sun was blocked from view and replaced by an exquisitely engraved and curved ivory wall. The bone-like wall was stained with blood coloured light that traced out its complex, cellular patterns as if they were veins and arteries.

Bone and blood. Blood and bone. Must this end time be so drenched in symbolism? Or is it just my little human mind trying to find something recognisable in this terrible, alien place?

Once again, she was made to approach the wall of drifting white fronds, and she soon felt their cold, embrace. She relaxed and waited until she was wrapped tightly like a fresh mummy. She knew the voice must come, but she felt no fear this time, just a quiet resolve.

'Prentiss, we have truly missed your highly individual state of awareness. Do you know how very different you are from your fellows?'

'I'm no different from any other New Yorker. Why have you brought me here?'

'Oh, but you are so very rare. Quite the remarkable specimen. No matter. You are here because we must taste your ancestry. We are looking for distinctive indications that might explain our connection through the vortex.'

'See, I've been thinking about that genetic connection theory. It's pure crap. If Anubis was my great, great, heaven knows how many times, great grandfather then I would be just one amongst legions of us. Countless generations of Anubis' offspring. It would not make me special in any way. How could it? And what do you mean, "taste"? What are you planning to do? Bite me?'

'It is done. We did it while you were talking. Analysis is complete. It takes a while to sample the infinite algorithms of nature that make up a human genome. A pretty puzzle to unlock. But you are right, Prentiss. Anubis' seed has fertilised enough zygotes to populate all of near space. That is not the link that concerns us. That – we now know – is in your brain. You have a highly-developed cerebrum, specifically your Broca's and Wernicke's areas. These are parts of the brain that are directly involved with communication and translation, not only of human language but also facial expressions, and what is loosely called "body language". As a result, you are incredibly intuitive and can read people around you, as you say, "like a book". We believe you must have met the contemporary incarnation of the mind you call Anubis in person at least once, and read something in them that confused or attracted you. That might have created the link. We have evolved to be hyper-aware of other creatures' feelings and intentions in much the same way as you are. Your contemporary Anubis recognised something in you, call it sympatico, and responded by creating an unconscious bridge mentally linking you across time and space. Remarkable and unique.'

'Are you saying we're telepathically linked.'

'No. Telepathy can't work in humans. Your brains are hard-wired so they can't pick-up on another's thoughts. Too self-contained. No. Your contemporary has bookmarked you as an interesting subject and left a resonation trace so he can find you again. There is a side-effect, the trace is a two-way process. You can now find him, and because he is me, and we are also the Sumerian and the Egyptian you can also find us. Interesting.'

'You say I must have met my contemporary Anubis. Who is it?'

'You expect me to remember something that happened eight billion years ago? I was male. I have always been male. Will that help?'

'Not much. Do you remember me?'

'Of course. In lots of timelines. Now, Prentiss, open your eyes.'

She awoke back in her own bedroom, and with a sigh settled back down to a dreamless sleep.

...

'Hey, honey. You have a good weekend? How was the date? Welcome back.'

The welcome face of Sam Bolat grinned at her and the two women met with a hug as if they hadn't seen each other for months rather than a weekend. Sam was her usual, ball of energy self and her weekend had been busy. She high-fived her friend.

'I have your answer, by the way. Eight.'

'Eight?'

'Yeah. Eight.'

'It's too early in the day for math. Eight what?'

'Eight buildings in New York City over a thousand feet tall.'

Prentiss gazed at her flatly for a second, her mind racing, and then she blurted out, 'The man who lives on the mountain! Oh, Sam, you angel, how long did it take you to find them? I hope you haven't wasted the whole weekend.'

'Nah. It took about twenty minutes on my lap top. You want to see?'

Sam keyed in her search engine and asked for the tallest buildings in New York. She got the tallest twelve listed in height order complete with descriptions and a photograph of each. Prentiss read with interest and realised she had almost certainly seen all the buildings from the roof of The Met the previous day.

Sam continued, 'We're only interested in buildings over one thousand feet, and those start with: One World Trade Centre, one thousand, seven hundred and seventy-six feet. That makes it the tallest kid on the block, in fact the tallest in the Western Hemisphere. Next is four thirty-two Park Avenue at one thousand three hundred and ninety-six feet, this is the big boy of residential buildings. Imagine the view from the top of that baby. Next at number three is the best-known gorilla sanctuary in the world, the Empire State Building, at twelve hundred and fifty feet high it was the tallest building in the world from nineteen thirty-one to nineteen seventy-three when the old twin towers topped out. It regained the title for a while on nine-eleven when they fell.'

116

They took a sombre moment to reflect on the terrible events of that day. No-one who lived and worked in the Big Apple could think of that date without pause; that scar ran deep.

'Okay, yeah. Number four is the Bank of America Building at twelve hundred feet, and we have a tie for fifth place. At joint fifth the Chrysler Building and the New York Times Building are both one thousand and forty-six feet tall. And finally, coming in at number six, or seven I'm not sure how that works, we have One five-seven on West fifty-seventh street in Manhattan, mixed residential and Hyatt hotel. Oh, and I need to add a caveat to the list. Centre Heights will be the new number two at one thousand, four hundred and ten feet but it isn't finished yet. It topped out in twenty sixteen but it won't be finished until sometime next year. That's it, Honey, the mountains of New York.'

'We got two residential buildings on that list. What say we look see if any famous folk live in either of them?'

'Already done. Guess who lives on the seventy-third floor of One five-seven?'

'Elvis? Is that where he's been hiding?'

'No way, Honey. Everyone knows he's holed up in LA with Howard Hughes and Marilyn Monroe. They're all ancient, and shuffle around naked with tissue boxes on their feet. Try again.'

Prentiss grimaced at the image that had just been popped into her mind.

'Thanks for that. Go on, tell me.'

'Your gossip guru and mine, Gee Erskine.'

'Erskine? Really?'

'Yep. That boy got the looks and the bankroll to go with it. No wonder he can dish the dirt with the rest of the girls, he can afford the lawsuits.'

'Erskine? Wow. That would make sense.'

'How so?'

'So, we know Anubis is handing out old school justice to bad boys and girls, people on the wicked philanthropist list. Erskine knows what they've been up to, even if he can't prove it, and, as I've since found out, he knows much more than is healthy about the whole Anubis thing. Now you tell me he lives on a New York mountain. He's the perfect suspect, it's blindingly obvious.'

'Okay, what now?'

Prentiss reached for the phone and dialled a number.

'Hello, *Dames & Dandies*? Thank-you, could I speak with Mister Erskine please? Yes, I'll hold. Detective Prentiss, NYPD. Yes, he knows me.'

29

'Officer Prentiss and the lovely officer Bolat. The sun shines down on my road to joy and I find you here standing so prettily beside it. Welcome, welcome. Please, sit down over here by the window. The view of the park is lovely today. Coffee?'

He led them through the foliage to a table and a group of comfortable chairs next to a large window. They basked in a warm pool of bright sunlight. Now that the broadly smiling man was standing before her Prentiss was at a loss as to the best way to present her suspicions. He seemed too solid, too real, to be the human manifestation of a creature living in a floating city above a barren Earth. A creature living eight billion years in the future. Thoughts circled around inside her skull like flies batting at a locked window. She snatched at one of them.

'Gee, have you got anywhere with that list of potential victims?'

His smiled broadened, 'But, my dear, darling Prentiss, it's done. I emailed it to you over the weekend. I told you when I saw you with that fellow on the roof.'

It was true. She had forgotten. She smiled ruefully.

'I know. I guess I just needed an excuse to see you again.'

Erskine beamed. 'It must be telepathy. I was thinking the self same thing.'

Prentiss shook her head. 'Telepathy doesn't work in humans. We're hard-wired, so the thoughts can't leak out. And yes, please to coffee. That would be lovely.'

'Yes, well, it will be much better than that stuff they serve at The Met. Are you so very sure about telepathy?'

'Pretty sure, yes. I got it from a very confident authority. He seemed to know what he was talking about.'

Erskine asked which coffee they preferred, then after some complex negotiations with an impressive, dark grey machine in the corner of the room, he delivered three very creditable Americanos with cold milk in a jug on the side. He drank his black.

He leaned towards Prentiss, 'How are your fascinating researches going?'

She added milk to her cup and then Sam's. 'Which ones?'

'Your interest in the guardian of the underworld, the guide of the dead, the King of the great waters, the judge who weighs the soul in the balance.'

Sam butted in, 'He who lives on the mountain? Anubis? It's almost like she's had lunch with him and spent time chatting over coffee. This is good Joe, by the way. Thanks.'

Prentiss' eyes tightened and Erskine smiled at the smaller woman as if he had just remembered she was in the room. Sam returned her widest and brightest grin, eyes squeezed shut and her impish face a picture of mischief. Erskine laughed aloud.

'I must talk to a TV producer I know about you two. You girls really deserve your own show. Viewers would lap it up. Do you have an agent? I know the perfect woman; my darlings she would make your careers *fly*! But, seriously, what can I do for you today? I have a luncheon appointment across town that I can't break, you know how it is, and I will have to be on my way in half an hour. Much as I enjoy your company...' He shrugged.

Prentiss nodded, 'Of course. Very quickly then, from your list, who would you say might be the next victim?'

He sat back in his chair. 'Do you have a copy of the list with you?'

'No, sorry.'

'A minute, please.'

He put his cup on a coaster, got to his feet and padded like a sleek cat to his desk, on which sat a large flat screen and a keyboard. He tapped keys for a few moments after which they heard a gentle, churning sound. He bent at the waist and stood up with several sheets of A4 paper in his hand. He split them into two groups of five then stapled each group through the corner. He returned to his chair and handed the sheets to his guests.

'There are ten people on that list, seven men and three women. Each is a noted patron of the needy with impeccable credentials. They support hospitals, orphanages, overseas aid, blah, blah, you name it. I've listed who they are, where they live, what they do openly and what they do covertly. They are vile, evil creatures, but you won't find a single soul prepared to say a word against any of them. For my money, the worst of the bunch is the second name on that list. He might well be your next victim. To my mind, and you can call me a wicked old gossip, but it couldn't happen soon enough.'

He got to his feet once more and held out his hands. 'And now I must reluctantly bid you adieu. Give me a little more notice and we must do lunch again. Let me know how you get on, please. I'll come down with you and then I must be on my way. I'm getting the lowdown on a naughty Senator, and with luck it will give me enough scandal to make the White House itself blush to its foundations.'

119

He left them in the ground floor atrium with the mini-skirted Claudia. Prentiss thought the girl's skirt had shrunk since their last visit, or perhaps the woman's legs had grown longer. Claudia carded them into the parking garage, all the while trying to pump them about their interview with Erskine. Sam offered mischievous hints about all sorts of misdemeanours and the girl could barely breathe with excitement by the time they left her to walk to their car.

Once they had settled into their seats and fastened their belts Sam released a throaty chuckle.

'Miss mini skirt USA was going to wet her pants if I told her any more. You think she believed any of that crap?'

'Sure, why not? I did and I knew you were lying.'

'So, what happened to offering Gee his Miranda rights?'

'Can you imagine that man remaining silent?' Prentiss started her engine and eased out of the bay.

Sam shook her head. 'Good point, well made. But we still can't fall foul of violating the Fifth or Sixth amendments. What now?'

'Now you tell me who's number two on Gee's list, and where he is. Then, you tell me what he's done to potentially get his belly bit open. Can you handle all that my little bloodhound?'

Sam made a 'woof' noise, then panted with her tongue hanging out while she raised the list to where she could read it.

Her eyes widened. 'Holy shit!'

Her loud ejaculation made Prentiss jump and the car swerved slightly, earning her a cacophony of indignant horn music from surrounding traffic.

Prentiss shouted back, 'Yeah, yeah, I hear yah. Woman driver here, you know we all drive like shit. Live with it.' She flicked a glance at her partner. 'You going to tell me what freaked you out just now?'

'Listen to this. I like this guy. My kids watch him. They like him too. Clarke Wadsmythe, children's entertainer. The "Wads" bit is pronounced "Woods" and the "smythe" bit is shortened, so his name sounds like "Woodsmith". Come on, you must know him. Middle-aged guy, high-pitched voice, always laughing. He's got a beard. He does the Saturday morning cartoons and he can do all the voices and he can draw the characters fast as lightning. He's always got kids around him...'

Her voice trailed away as that fact sank in. They drove for a while in silence through the late morning traffic.

Prentiss spoke first. 'So, what did he do to get noticed by Erskine?'

Sam studied the list. 'Says he prefers kids with learning difficulties. He's not choosy, he likes boys *and* girls, so long as they're under sixteen. He's patron to the Florence Wellworthy Center for Special Children, and although he's never actually been caught dipping his gentleman's relish into any of the clientele, it says here some members of staff have become worried that he's much too friendly with them. Seems he's a touchy, feely, hands-on type. "How about a little tickle from Uncle Clarke?" You hear what I'm saying?'

'He's fucking the kids?'

'Erskine says he pays special attention to the ones who don't say too much, you know? The Center personnel have had their doubts about him spending time alone with the kids, but he's a big name and brings in the dollar value so, safeguarding wise, they've been told to turn a blind eye. According to Erskine this creep takes advantage at every opportunity. After he's had his way the kids don't say anything, they just become quieter. They're more likely to cry or be confused than complain. What are they going to say? They don't understand what the nice, funny man has done to them. Says here he always lubricates well and penetrates anally, then hits them with a big block of chocolate laxative. They shit away the evidence.'

'And we're going to protect this monster?'

'Says on the badge "To serve and protect". You reminded me the other day, remember? And another thing, what happened to "innocent until proven guilty"? You say stuff like that to me all the time.'

'Yeah, but I'm a smartass, you shouldn't listen to me. Shit, I hate this job.'

'Yeah? Well suck it up, girlfriend, listen to who else is on this list.'

30

They arrived back at the forty-second precinct in a sombre mood. The revelations in the list had strained their credulity. They had heard of every single one of the ten celebrities listed by Erskine. Most of them were household names. One of the women was a senior police officer directly associated with child protection. All were involved with the horrific abuse of minors in some way. Prentiss puffed out her cheeks and blew a long whistle.

'We can't tell anyone else about this. You know that, don't you?'

Sam made a zipping gesture across her lips. 'Shee-it! Don't you worry, honey. My lips are sealed tighter than a duck's ass in a tsunami. That's not to say I don't want to put my head in the washer and scrub my mind clean of everything I've just read. I feel dirty, and not in a good way, you know? I've got my boys, and sometimes, you know, I just want to throw them in a cage with a pair of hungry cougars so they can find out what living with them feels like, but otherwise they're cute as black-eyed puppies.' She swallowed hard and held up the list. 'What would these sick bastards do to them if they had the chance? Makes me want to puke just thinking about it. Okay, enough of that. My boys are safe as I can make them, so, what next?'

'Next? Well, next I guess we go see Mr Wadsmythe and tell him we've heard that he may be drawing the wrong kind of attention from some very bad people – without going into details. We keep it cool, we don't even ask him which brand of laxative he prefers. We've got his address. Let's go say, hi.'

'Do you mind if I keep a chambered round in my gun when we shake his hand, just in case?'

'Be my guest.'

Wadsmythe lived alone in an elegant pre-war building on the Upper West Side. Sam had phoned ahead to make sure he was expecting them, and he greeted them at his door with effusive warmth, before ushering them up a short flight of stairs to what he described as his 'drawing room', where he bade them to sit in deep, over-stuffed armchairs. Prentiss mused that most places like his would have been converted to at least three apartments with a family in each, but the man rattled around in his spacious home all alone, like a pea in a whistle. He kept switching his voice from his trademark, high-pitched chuckle, to those of famous cartoon characters such as Donald Duck, Peppa Pig, and Olaf, the snowman from *Frozen*. Prentiss wondered how long it would take before this trait escalated from mildly amusing to blindingly irritating, and told herself she fully understood why the man lived alone. Who could put up with his relentless good humour for more than a few minutes without committing murder? *And kids like this guy?*

Sam quickly realised her friend had been stunned into silence and stepped into the breech, carefully stroking the man's vanity. She told him how much her children loved his show, and how it had become a family event to sit together and watch it, laughing aloud at his incredible impersonations.

'The boys can't wait for the cartoons to end so the camera gets back to you. I mean it, to five-year old twins and their parents you are *the* star of the show, Mister Wadsmythe.'

Prentiss smiled at her precisely correct pronunciation of the man's name, and at the sparkling smile she had earned by doing so. He insisted she call him Clarke, asked for the twins' names, and then scurried to a desk in front of a large bay window. He opened a drawer, fetched out a wad of photographs and signed two of them, checking the spelling of the names while he did so. He handed them to Sam and then looked at Prentiss.

'And for you, my dear?'

'I'm sorry, I don't have any children.'

'No, of course not. You're still so very young yourself. What's your name?'

'Prentiss.' She spelt it carefully and thanked him for the signed photo, which she thought she would drop in the trash on the way back to the car. She badly wanted to wash her hands. He offered them drinks which they politely refused. He opined that it must be five o'clock somewhere in the world and poured himself a few fingers of scotch whiskey.

'Now then officers, what can I do for you? You said you had something important to share with me, and I think it's so important to share, don't you? Sharing is caring!'

Sam laughed with feigned delight at his lapse into a French accent.

'Wow, was that Pepé Le Pew? Fantastic!'

Their host made a little bowing gesture. 'I am evidently in the presence of a true connoisseur. You have my sincere admiration madam. And now TO BUSINESS!'

Sam clapped her hands, 'Foghorn Leghorn. I've always loved him.' And then her face became serious. 'I'm sorry, but we're here for a very serious reason, Mister Wads... sorry, Clarke. We must warn you about a threat to your life, and it is a genuine threat. I'm afraid you are faced by a real and present danger, and the attack may even take place this evening. We know

123

you're being targeted as one of a select group of celebrities, and intelligence indicates you are also most likely to be the next on the list.'

Wadsmythe dropped all pretence at humour. His features instantly became flaccid and lost their permanent smile, like a glove puppet face after the operator's hand has been withdrawn. The squeaky voice was also gone.

'What do you mean, next? Who else has been "targeted" by these thugs?'

Prentiss coughed lightly, then said, 'To date, three people that we are aware of: The Most Reverend Henry Puckling, Mrs Melanie Hart, and Mister Errol M. All of them died under horrific circumstances. We believe you might know at least one of them. It is your... association, with the victims that leads us to think that you too might be in danger.'

'Association? What do you mean, "association"? What are you saying? I've met Melanie, of course I have, but I'm no kissing cousin. If these bastards went after everyone who knew Melanie, the body count would make the Second World War look like a dust-up in a schoolyard. Everybody knows Melanie. And I think I've seen the other guys at fund-raisers. We all go to the big ones, we're there to be seen and seen to be there, you get me? That isn't a select group, that's a demographic. What else singles me out? Come on, what aren't you telling me?'

Sam took the ball. 'You do charitable work with children, Clarke. You're known to work with kids with special needs, you're famous for it. All the victims to date have worked with children and we think that's the selection criteria, or at least an important part of it.'

'What kind of freaking "selection criteria" is that? You saying these bastards would go after Saint Teresa? God bless her sweet memory. No, and I say again, no! This makes no sense at all, ladies, I tell you. None... At... All. And now, I'm sorry, but I have work to do, important work. Thank-you for popping by, but I need you to leave. I must concentrate without any distractions. Thank-you. Give my love to the boys. Hope they like the photos.'

They all climbed out of the chairs and got to their feet. Wadsmythe shook their hands and led the way to the stairs. Prentiss spoke up.

'Mister Wadsmythe, can I say something?'

'Please, make it fast.'

'Have you got someone who can be with you tonight? Someone you can trust? Or have you got somewhere you can be with other people this evening at eight o'clock. A restaurant, a bar, anywhere?'

He tried to look tough. Failed.

'This place is like Fort Knox, Officer Prentiss. I'm a lot safer in here than I would be out there on the street. Upper West Side is known to be a child friendly place, but it still suffers from random acts of violence. Everywhere does. I might be safe at eight, but what about when I'm walking home at ten? Muggers, murderers and lunatics are out there looking for people just like me. I'm vulnerable on the streets and a lot safer in my own home behind a steel reinforced security door and locked windows. Thanks for your concern, but I'm safer right here. Give me a call sometime, Sam, and I'll arrange tickets for the kids to come to my Saturday show. They can shake hands with their favourite TV star and sit in for the cartoons.' He grinned wanly and opened the door to the street.

'I mean it, I'll be okay. I'll see you.'

Several minutes before eight o'clock, Prentiss was standing with her thumb pressed against Wadsmythe's doorbell. He had not accepted her calls but she had decided to try to protect him if she could. On the stroke of the hour her phone rang, the screen informed her it was Howlett, and she already knew what he was going to tell her. His wolves were holding their eerie vigil once more, all of them silent and facing towards the city.

31

The blood was in his dining room, but his body was found in the Bronx next to a dumpster. It was stripped from the waist down and a deep triangular bite had torn away a good length of his gut, most of his liver, and a section of spine. To Prentiss it had looked as if the man had been lifted into the air and bitten the way a hungry man bites a soft, white bread sandwich.

On her TV Feldman was holding court to assembled members of the press. Sam was right, she realised, he looked shiny up there. It was as if he had been carefully polished before stepping out in front of the cameras.

'The victim is a white male in his mid-fifties. He died from trauma and exsanguination. There are no defensive wounds on the body. He had been drinking heavily at the time of his death and may not have been aware of his attacker. Investigations are ongoing and any new developments will be released in the usual bulletins. NYPD are pursuing many positive leads and we are confident arrests will follow. Any members of the public who have pertinent information can call the number or visit the website at the bottom of the screen. The victim will be named once he has been formally identified and his family has been informed. We would be grateful if our colleagues in the press would refrain from any speculation at this present time. This death is being treated as murder, and would seem to follow the exact pattern of the previous three *Anubis* killings. That is all we can say at present. Thank-you.'

Prentiss raised her glass to the screen. 'And thank-you Doctor Feldman. Succinct as ever, and not a single question answered. Good man, keep 'em on the hook. When you're ready to share those "positive leads" I'd be grateful if you share them we me, okay? Yeah, okay.'

It was late. A tray of dirty dishes from her meal was still on the floor because she felt too tired to cart it into the kitchen and run hot water into the sink to do her washing up. She placed her glass on the tray and closed her eyes to help her concentrate. She was attired for bed and wore a thick pair of canary yellow, woollen socks on her feet, which were tucked up under her bottom. She was on her second glass of wine. Exhaustion made her feel numb, but questions crawled around inside her brain like red-hot lice and wouldn't let her sleep. She realised her TV was still on and used her remote to turn it off. The presenter was discussing yet another Presidential faux pas with a political pundit and Prentiss thought back to Sam's comment about the painfully gauche man in the Oval Office being the 'First amongst the westerners'. She offered up a rueful smile at the idea. Sam was smart, but that bird wouldn't fly.

How had the killer done it? She had been right there on the man's doorstep when it happened. Nobody had come around her or climbed through one of the windows. The French doors at the rear of the property, which opened out from the dining room, had been found locked when officers forced entry, and in any case had led to a walled courtyard garden that had razor wire around the top of the walls. Nobody could get in that way without being dropped from a helicopter, and she was sure she would have noticed that. The killing had happened in the dining room, but the killer had not entered from the garden. Forget the traditional locked room murder, this had happened in a locked house with a police officer at the door. And how had the killer got the body past her to leave it by a dumpster? The meaning behind the placement was obvious, the symbolic language clear as any writing on the wall. The body of the victim had been treated as garbage, and its nakedness stripped away the person's last vestige of respect by displaying their most private parts to the public gaze of strangers. *This corpse is rubbish and not worthy of respect.*

It was not yet known where the first three victims had been butchered, but the scene at Wadsmythe's house had been unequivocal. Blood spray had hit the wall and ceiling at a height of fifteen feet, spatter had contaminated an area over seven feet in diameter. Traces of flesh and faecal matter had been found on the room's hemp flooring, but not so much as a pubic hair from the killer. One dining chair was turned on its side as if it had fallen during a struggle. In front of it had been a plate containing cheese, pickle, charcoal crackers, and potato chips, which the victim had evidently been picking at. There were also the remains of a bottle of good scotch whisky, the same brand Wadsmythe had opened in front of Sam and Prentiss earlier that day. She wondered if he had still been drinking the same bottle, or if he had moved on to his second as the afternoon got late and the sky dark. A small, battery-powered clock had been placed where Wadsmythe could see it. He had been waiting for zero hour and didn't want to miss his cue.

His corpse was still wearing the shirt she had seen him in earlier. The rest of his clothes, including his shoes and socks, had been scattered haphazardly around the room. None of them were tainted with blood. The man had been lifted, shucked out of his nether attire, and then dispatched with a single, powerful bite. If his killing had been part of a pulp fiction novel the author might have plumped for a madman inventor with a mechanical set of jaws into which the struggling victim would be pressed before they snapped shut, carving through flesh and bone as if they were butter. Then, post-mortem, jackal saliva would be introduced into the wound with a syringe. That was Feldman's theory, but Prentiss was convinced it wouldn't hold water. How did the killer get the machine into Wadsmythe's house? How did they get it away afterwards? Why were there no physical traces? Surely something sturdy enough to bite clean through a human body must leave indentations? Wadsmythe's floor was wooden under the hemp matting, there would surely be marks. And how did they get the body past her to the dump site? Too many questions and not one solitary answer that made sense, unless she accepted that the killer was the contemporary manifestation of a super-evolved creature from eight billion years in the future. She had been told she had met it and somehow linked with it. When? Was it Erskine? Was it someone else? When had it all started?

Her thoughts no longer burrowed through her brain like hot bugs, they had clumped together and now circled inside her like a fat, lazy, black fly. Circling and circling while emitting a low, irritating, droning hum. Why? How? Who? Who's next? The questions' circling motion sped up until they became a blur, then became a whirlpool into which she fell. She plummeted into darkness, falling like a heavy stone dropped down a well. Below her shimmered a faint, flickering light. As she fell it came closer, expanding until it was a huge, moon like face. The eyes were pale blue and the flesh seemed to have an anaemic, unhealthy, grey-white pallor. Prentiss thought the face belonged to an adult woman, but her features seemed oddly youthful under her lank, water blonde hair. Her little girl features were also too small, as if they had been pinched together in the centre of her face to avoid spoiling the pale, blank canvas of her skin. She was like an empty page, waiting mutely for an author to write her story before she could begin to live. The pale eyes in the pale face under the pale hair regarded her with languid interest, as if curious to see what kind of stranger had fallen down to join her in her well. And then a little girl's voice jolted Prentiss to her core. She knew that voice. It cast her back to a nightmare sequence in the stormy darkness of Prairie West, and the bulky, eerily draped figure lurking in the shadows of apartment thirty-seven.

'The Beast has spoken to you through your TV. He has called you to the city and the mountain. You have been judged, Prentiss, and your heart has been found pure. He will not harm you if you leave him to his work, but you must not come between the Beast and his prey.'

'Aliya Petrus?'

'You ran away. That was the Father's fault. He gets angry when I make friends. He wants me all to himself. I'm his little girl. His pretty princess.'

Only her mouth was moving. Her pale eyes were motionless as those of a fish on ice. Her head was still as stone. Pity welled up in Prentiss' breast. The woman continued speaking.

'I have some matches to light the candles now, if you want to come back. We could have tea and a nice chat.'

'I would like that.'

'Come during the morning. I can control Father better in the morning.'

'I will, soon, I promise.'

Prentiss had a thought. 'Aliya, did you put clues into my books and on my tablet where I would find them?'

'No, sorry, but no. That was someone else.'

'Do you know who?'

'Yes.'

'Can you tell me who it was? Please?'

'I like to hear the word, "please". It is like a ray of sunshine at midnight, and it shines all the brighter in a wicked world. You know him as Gawain Erskine.'

Prentiss gasped, 'Is he the Beast?'

'No.'

'Can you please tell me who the Beast is?'

The small, cupid's bow of a mouth smiled sweetly. 'I like the word, please, as I told you, but no, I'm sorry. I can't answer that question. Not yet. No, not yet.'

'Why not?'

'It is not yet time. It would be dangerous for you, and you are my friend. You are my friend, aren't you?'

Prentiss sighed and nodded. 'Okay, but thank-you. And yes.'

'Please and thank-you, and a new friend all on the same day! I am a lucky girl. Bless and thank-you, Prentiss.'

Prentiss wanted to cry, but instead she smiled. And then she had a thought.

'Aliya, please tell me, are you talking to me using telepathy?'

'Of course not, dear Prentiss. Telepathy can't work in humans, not even special ones like you.'

'Then how?'

The small mouth smiled once more, a bleak sight under her dead, fish-like eyes.

'I manipulated time and space to create a memory of this conversation and then placed it where you would find it when you were ready. Everything is about making things happen when the time is right. There, that is a clue for you. You see time as linear, it is not. You see actions as sequential, they are not. Think about that. By the way, the Beast visited your apartment once when you were out. He left his mark. Remember all his names, he is more than Lord of the underworld. Farewell, Prentiss. Remember, we shall have tea, you promised.'

'I promise.'

'Come to me one day in the morning. I'm so looking forward to it. See you soon. See you very soon, very soooon.'

The last word echoed as if delivered from a faulty loudspeaker, and it jarred Prentiss out of her reverie. She climbed stiffly out of her recliner and stretched hugely, yawning fit to crack her jaw. She took a small step towards her bedroom and touched her foot against something on the floor. Her tray. While so much was swirling around her, something as mundane as doing the dishes would be a real 'feet on the ground' pleasure. She picked up the tray and walked lightly to the kitchen. Running water into her sink she remembered that Anubis was also called Shar Apsi, Lord of the deep. Lord of the deep waters. Her living room had suffered a mysterious flood. Was there a connection? Was Aliya saying that Anubis had entered her locked apartment and soaked her living room floor? 'Marked' it to prove a point? If that was the case no-one and nowhere was safe. She looked out towards her darkened living room. If what Aliya was saying was true the killer could appear to his victims any time he wanted; even if they hid in a bank vault or a cave, nothing could keep him out. And there were nine more names on the list.

32

'Aliya Petrus? Yes, I know her. I didn't know *you* did. My word, small world. What about her?'

Gee Erskine's voice sounded tight and guarded. Prentiss took the plunge.

'She told me I had good reason to thank you, and explained why. I'd like to thank you in person, and get answers for some more questions that I believe only you can help me with. Somewhere discreet, somewhere the coffee is acceptable and we won't be overheard. Are you okay, with that?'

'Have you anywhere in mind?'

'I could say my apartment, but that might prove a little *too* private. Can you think of anywhere?'

The was a pause. 'Very well. Promise you won't think me a tremendous snob if I suggest my club?'

He mentioned a name and address that Prentiss recognised. She had sometimes glanced up at the entrance when she walked past – and she had read about events held there in New York's society pages.

'Women are accepted, nay, welcomed as guests, and I can book us a private room for lunch and a discreet chat. I can promise you there won't be any hidden microphones in the walls, or any of that rot. Food and coffee excellent, and the wine list would knock a teetotaller off his wagon faster than you can say Terrunyo's "Block 27". Shall I meet you there at one?'

'Do I come in the front door or is there a special ladies' entrance.'

'You climb the steps and enter through the front door, my dear. This is the twenty-first century, and *we* aren't barbarians.'

When she arrived at the address on East Sixtieth Street she had almost chickened out. The columned entrance portico and noble proportions of the building oozed confident wealth, and presented a level of dignified charm that made her want to spend a month's salary making sure she was wearing the right shoes before she so much as set foot on the staircase. She hesitated just long enough for the doorman to cast a quizzical eye in her direction and then step down to her level.

'Madam, please excuse me, but are you Ms Prentiss? Mister Erskine's guest?'

'Wow, you're good. How could you tell?'

'He described you most, ah, succinctly, madam. He has a flair for descriptive prose. I recognised you at once.'

'I suppose you were looking out for a tall, skinny black girl in her twenties?'

'I can assure you Mr Erskine's succinct description was far less prosaic, and gave you much greater – and evidently well deserved – credit than that, madam. Please, allow me to accompany you into the Club. I hope you enjoy your visit. I will have Mister Erskine informed that you have arrived.'

There was no need, Erskine was chatting with the man at front of house. He welcomed her and signed her in while she looked around in a state of glamoured shock. The interiors she could see through open doors combined palatial grandeur with the kind of first class detailing that film director James Cameron had brought to his recreation of the great cruise liner Titanic. Erskine smiled at the expression on her face.

'I looked like that the first time I was invited to lunch here. Even then I knew this would be the ideal club for me. It took me a while, but I finally got an invitation to join. It is lovely, isn't it?'

'I'm speechless. I've walked past this place, of course, and I always thought the outside was a little, you know, quaint, but this is fabulous.'

He glanced at his Patek Philippe Nautilus wristwatch. She wondered what it felt like to be wearing more than her year's salary on one wrist, just so the owner could tell the time. 'We have time for a quick tour.' He threaded his arm through hers and led her from one beautiful room to another. Walking from dining rooms to reception rooms and a library, he told Prentiss about the club's history since it had first been created by German Jews in eighteen fifty-two, as a response to blatant discrimination by the Union Club. She felt as if she was being ushered through a country mansion by a respectful guide, and realised that Erskine's customary theatrical boom had been metred down to barely a cultured whisper.

He ended the tour on the second floor before a tall, panelled door, through which he ushered her with a welcoming hand. She found herself in a handsome room with two large windows that overlooked the street. Despite the bustle she knew to be outside, the room was a haven of peaceful calm. A dining table had been set for two and menus lay on an occasional table between two leather Chesterfield armchairs. Erskine directed her to one of the armchairs and handed her a menu before taking his own seat. His manners were impeccable, as if he had made a deliberate study of etiquette and was giving her a demonstration.

Prentiss grinned. 'So, how do we attract the attention of a waiter? Do we open the door and yell SHOP?'

'Not quite. I lift that telephone and give our order to Patrick, the maître d'.'

'Oh? Like a drive-through?'

He grinned. 'Of course. Very much like a drive-through. May I say, panelled walls and elegance suit you very well. You look at home here.'

'I wish I felt it. I keep thinking the style Nazis are going to burst in and tell me I'm wearing the wrong coloured pantyhose.'

Erskine grinned, 'In the first place you aren't, you're perfectly co-ordinated as always, and in the second this is completely the wrong place to worry about Nazis. Albert Einstein worked with members of the Club to help raise awareness about what Hitler and his gang of thugs were doing to Jews over in the Reich. This is a principled establishment, and I like it that way. And there's not a hint of scandal here, if there was I'd soon know. I tell you, if there was so much as a whiff of it, I'd be down on them like a... like a hungry jackal.'

He gave her an arch glance from under his wide brows. She thought again how very distinguished he looked, while also seeming exotic. She found herself comparing Erskine with Tabaqui Howlett. Howlett's lack of sophistication and piercing intelligence made a fine foil for Erskine's charm and witty savoir-faire, but there was much more to Erskine than met the eye. *What was his agenda?*

'Gee...'

'No, no, Prentiss, not yet. I know you want to grill me, but please, let's order a good lunch and decide on the wine first.'

They concentrated on their menus for an intense few minutes. Prentiss became hungry just looking at the options. Erskine leaned towards her.

'If I may offer a suggestion? Portion sizes are quite adequate, but if you have a good appetite plump for a starter and a main course. We can discuss dessert afterwards. Your tastebuds will thank you, no matter what you choose.'

She made her selection and left the choice of wine to her host. While he was engaged in placing their order using the internal telephone, she took her opportunity to study the olive complexioned man in more detail. He had natural elegance and poise, and his voice had a masculine musicality that pleased the ear. His body was lean with a trained, spare efficiency that spoke more of the pool and the track than the gym. His carefully tailored outfit didn't bulge around oversized biceps, or jut forward thanks to a hormone induced pec-deck. His age was difficult to judge, he might be in his thirties or early forties. His skin was unlined except at the outer corners of his extraordinary eyes. And his eyebrows swept out under his hairless brow like the wings of a sleek black eagle. She decided she would be able to offer the Club's doorman a 'succinct' description of Gee Erskine if she ever needed to, something that provided 'greater credit' than, 'he's a tall, well-dressed, skinny, foreign looking, bald Dude'. Erskine replaced the handset in its cradle then gazed at her with eyes the colour of molten dark Belgian chocolate. He smiled broadly.

'Do you like what you see, Detective Prentiss? I must say I feel quite dissected.'

She felt momentarily chastened, then responded with, 'Aliya Petrus tells me it's you who's been putting warnings into my reading matter. Thank-you, but I don't understand how. Also, the warnings started before I even met you. How is that possible? They started from the night of the first Anubis killing, but I didn't come to your office until the day after the second body was found. How *could* it have been you warning me? Was Aliya talking through her ass?'

'When did Aliya talk to you?'

Prentiss almost choked on her answer and was saved by a gentle knock at the door. She got to her feet. Erskine said 'Come' and two liveried men brought in an ice bucket containing shards of cracked ice, a bottle of wine and some still water in a hinge topped flask. One of them poured the water into a pair of tumblers then adjusted the cutlery to suit their lunch choices. The other carefully uncorked the wine, handed the cork to Erskine, and waited. Erskine ran the cork under his nose, nodded, and thanked him. The man poured two glasses, placed the wine and the water in the bucket, covered them with a linen cloth, and then joined his companion in leaving the room, shutting the door behind him with a precise 'click'.

Erskine handed her a glass of wine and took the other one for himself. He raised it towards her in a toast and they clinked the rims together producing a cultured, bell-like sound. Prentiss took a sip. She had been expecting delicious and she wasn't disappointed.

'So then,' said Erskine. 'When you talked with Aliya? Was it in your dreams?'

33

Erskine drew out one of the dining chairs and bade Prentiss take her seat. He took his own chair facing her. He studied her with evident warmth, and yet with the same intensity a hunting hawk might use when studying the terrain beneath its wings. She was momentarily flustered, searching for a way to answer his unexpected question that wouldn't make her sound like a lunatic. As if aware of her problem he offered her a lifeline.

'She talks to me in my dreams, you see. It is the way we communicate, she and I. We rarely meet in the flesh. She is loath to leave her apartment, and I am loath to visit her there. If you had ever seen where she lives I'm sure you would understand what I mean. They've skipped it for *House & Garden* for several years now, too niche a taste.'

'I have. I mean, I've been there. I've seen it. I know what you're saying.'

'You have? Then you're much braver than me.' He took some water. 'Was she wearing her veil? Did you talk to her father? Tell me all.'

'I don't know about her veil, it was pitch dark. There was a localised black-out plus an electrical storm. I only saw her when the lightning flashed. It felt like we were on the set of a horror movie. I got the impression of a very large, very round person, shrouded from top to toe in fine lace. Aliya has a dainty, little girl's voice, you know? But sometimes she talks like an angry man. A man who sounds like he might easily become violent. She had another voice too, a hissing, sound. It was creepy, eerie. Sam and I were told to leave by the hissing voice and we didn't wait for a second invitation, we were out of there.'

'Sam was with you? The redoubtable officer Bolat? She must have been a comfort. What did Aliya say to you? She believes herself quite the oracle, with some justification, I may add.'

Prentiss told him about the warning; that if she looked to the past she would find the Beast, and if she looked to the future it would find her.

'The thing is...'

A knock at the door heralded the arrival of their first course, and they remained silent while the men fussed around them and then departed. As soon as the door emitted its decisive 'click' Erskine looked at her.

'The thing is?'

Prentiss told him about her meetings with Anubis in an ancient world, about the winged bald men with gold rimmed eyes, about the underground sea, the temple, and the mocking invitation to join the 'breeding programme'.

Then she told him about the snowflake city floating above the burned crust of a dying Earth. An Earth sterilised and roasted by a bloated, blood coloured sun. She described herself floating into the city, and the fronds that had held her before the voice insinuated itself into her mind. For the first time, everything spilled out: about her waterlogged apartment and the flooding into the home of the man downstairs; about floating towards the ceiling in Chappell's loft; the Strangeness Forum; and the visitation by the naked jackal god when she was in Chappell's guest bedroom. She explained about CCTV images appearing on her TV, the strange actions of Howlett's wolf pack at the time of the murders, and that she was standing on Wadsmythe's doorstep when the man was slaughtered in his dining room. That Wadsmythe's body had somehow been carried past her to end up by a dumpster in the Bronx. She gave Erskine details of the case that would have had her officially censured by the NYPD if it knew she had shared them with a journalist, but she couldn't stop herself. The bubble had burst and after long days of frustration, confusion and fear she had finally found release and a willing listener.

'There was no way his body could have been moved, no way it could have been carried past me, but somehow it was. I was still there on his Upper West Side doorstep when he was found back in the Bronx. How was that possible?'

She held nothing back, and afterwards she felt somehow cleansed, almost as if she had made confession to a priest. She hadn't touched her plate while she was talking yet once the torrent had been released a sudden peak of hunger impelled her to spread smooth goose liver terrine and orange jam onto a fragile sheet of toasted sourdough and pop it into her mouth. She washed the delicious flavours down with a sip of wine. The taste brought a little groan of pleasure to her lips. The second mouthful was just as good. Erskine watched her thoughtfully, an appreciative smile on his face.

'You enjoy your food.' It was not a question.

'Yes, I do, when it's this good. Some people shouldn't be allowed near a kitchen, I hate what they do and I wouldn't eat it if I was starving. I mean it. I believe two things. We kill creatures for food, they die for our dinner, so they deserve our respect in the kitchen. Badly prepared, badly cooked meat is nothing less than murder. Secondly, I believe we should be thankful for the food we eat. When someone has gone to the trouble of preparing something good we should show our appreciation. I can't stand the idiots who think food is beneath them and live on a plate of salad leaves and falafel every other week. It's all part of God's bounty. I would rather eat less of something excellent than chow down on a mountain of crap, you understand what I mean?'

'I do, and I wholeheartedly concur. You are a rara avis, Prentiss, a very rare bird indeed. Ah, here's our main course. I hope it meets your strictest philosophical requirements.'

It did. The buttery, juicy fish was gilled to meaty perfection and tasted fresh as the sea itself, and the tossed salad in its fruity dressing was light as air but supported every other flavour on the plate. She was transported by greed for every mouthful and mopped her empty plate clean with warm bread. She sipped her wine and let the chilled citrus tang dance on her tongue. She sighed and closed her eyes with catlike delight, leaning back in her chair.

Erskine chuckled. 'I also know a place where they slow broil marinated brisket for more than four hours and then serve it on toasted onion bread with homemade barbeque sauce and slaw.'

'That can be good too, in the right hands. Thank-you Gee, I think that was the best lunch I've ever eaten.'

'Coffee?'

'No, thanks, that would spoil it.'

'More wine?'

'I shouldn't, but yes, that would be perfect.'

The two men returned to clear away their table. A fresh ice bucket was delivered along with wine and water plus a little plate of sliced lemon, pieces of which were dropped into their tumblers to scent the water. The ceremony of the cork was repeated. Then Erskine waited until the waiters had laid the table between the Chesterfield armchairs, before, with a graceful gesture, he took her arm and led her wordlessly to her seat. The lead waiter poured the wine, offered a little bow, and asked if there might be anything else. Erskine thanked him, took some notes from his trouser pocket, and gave him his tip, indicating that it be shared with his colleague. The man's wintry smile briefly blossomed into spring and then Erskine and Prentiss were alone at last. They touched glasses once more, then Erskine studied her with a quizzical pout as if trying to make up his mind about her. Finally, he breathed deeply through his nose and nodded.

'Prentiss, my dear, you have all the pieces of the puzzle in your hands. The problem is the picture doesn't make sense to you. The words are all there, but they're written in an unknown tongue and you have no Rosetta Stone. You need a guide who speaks the language, a translator. If I may I will offer myself in the role. I think we can work well together, and I have my

137

own individual insight into the subject matter. We are dealing with three beings. Anubis, you know, or at least have met in some of his forms. The next character in our drama is known as Nut, or Newet, you have also met her. She manifests here as Aliya Petrus. In ancient times Nut was the deity of the sky; her name means "sky". Like Anubis she has connections with the land of the dead, and is also a protector of the souls of the dead. Her "ladder" to the afterlife was inscribed on the inside of tombs and sarcophagi, and people prayed that she would treat them like her own children come home after their death. They pleaded with her to bring them food and drink, keep them safe after they had climbed the ladder into her shrouds. Amongst other things she also looks after mothers during childbirth and protects young children from harm. If you think women are great at multi-tasking, I must tell you, they are as nothing compared to ancient Egyptian gods. Worshippers got a real bang for their buck back in the day. Are you with me so far?'

Prentiss put her half-empty wine glass on its coaster.

'You're telling me that New York has become the centre of activity for a bunch of Egyptian *gods*? Is that what you're saying?'

'Not quite, no. I would describe the current event as a concordance of minds that live along timelines which have been tempero-spatially knotted together, like iron filings to a magnet, and have thus manifested here. They have their tasks and they fulfil them, they even share them. Newet is dedicated to the protection of children and mothers, and as the sky goddess, she also supports the protective layer that separates the order here on Earth from the chaos of the universe. I told you Aliya has a phobia about leaving her home. Well, in fact, she is phobic about becoming contaminated by the filth in twenty-first century air. She can control it where she lives, filter it, but she would have to breathe it on the street. She can only stand that for an hour or so at a time, so she needs an accomplice to aid her in caring for children. Enter Anubis, who is protecting children by preying on those who would hurt them, your wicked, so-called "victims".'

'You said there are three minds at work here. Who's the third?'

'Ah, yes. The third player, the mind who protects and directs the other two. "He who is above", "He who sees", "He who is distant". Horus, whose name means "falcon" or "hawk". A prehistoric and a post-historic player, just like the other two. It is he who collates the list of evil people and declares war on them through his colleague, Anubis. Horus, Nut and Anubis are linked, they work as one mind, they speak together through dreams.'

'But, Gee, what has brought them here now? What was the "magnet" that brought them to this place?'

138

'But, my dear girl, haven't you guessed? What is the one common denominator that binds them? The one link they all have in common? Think, it is quite evident to me.'

'I don't know, please, help me understand, what?'

'Why, Prentiss, can't you see? It's you.'

[34]

Prentiss took her time mulling over what Erskine had said. He had topped up her glass but she was reluctant to drink much more. She didn't want the wine to cloud her faculties any more than it had so far. She asked him where the ladies' powder room was and he told her, a look of concern edging onto his fine features.

'Are you, all right?'

'I just need to powder my nose. I'll be right back.'

She found the washroom just a few doors down the corridor and was pleased it was empty and unattended. She wanted a few moments to herself to collect her thoughts. She took care of her full bladder and then washed her hands, after first identifying which of the bottles next to the sink was soap and which was hand lotion. Not for the first time she wondered who used the hand lotion. Then she gazed into the mirror in front of her. Her familiar face looked back. People told her she was beautiful, they always had ever since she had reached her mid-teens, but all she saw was her face, the face of an ordinary woman trying to make her way in the world. What had happened to push her into such an extraordinary situation? She wanted to walk away from the oddness, but that would mean walking away from everything she knew. She couldn't abandon her job, her apartment, her friend and partner, Sam. She couldn't abandon New York City. And, why should she?

When she re-entered the private dining room it was empty. She fetched her wine and sipped at it thoughtfully while she stood looking down to the busy street three floors below. All those people going about their business without a care in the world about murderous, vigilante creatures with eight-billion-year agendas. The door opened behind her and Erskine walked in. He raised his eyebrows and smiled.

'Took a leaf out of your book,' he said. 'Can't think straight with a full bladder, much more relaxed now.'

Prentiss nodded, then said, 'Why me? And how do you fit in with all this?' The words were out before she could stop them. 'What *are* you, Gee?'

He took a deep breath and lifted his wine to his lips.

'I'll answer your questions in order if I may. Why you? To answer that one, I must ask *you* a question. Do you know about the Butterfly Effect in chaos theory?'

'Vaguely.'

140

'Well, put simply, a guy called Lorenz was trying to create a model that explained how relatively small events in a deterministic, non-linear system can generate a major outcome. As an example, he posited that a butterfly flapping its wings in one place at one time might, under the right circumstances, create a tornado, thousands of miles away and weeks later. Put another way: the first little pebble moves another little pebble, and then they move a larger pebble and then a larger rock until finally you get your avalanche. Are you understanding me so far?'

She nodded.

'Okay, good. Now, imagine you're standing at the end of an eight-billion-year deterministic timeline. You are standing where the buck finally stops, where the ripples meet the shore. And a vast number of butterflies have flapped an enormous number of wings over all that time, and a whole mountain of pebbles have moved continents of rocks and you are ground zero for all of it, an apocalypse of tornado blown avalanches. That's a lot of grief to pile onto one place at the end of time. Now, if you had the technology to reach out and move those pebbles where they couldn't do any damage, or redirect the butterflies' effects into less harmful patterns, you'd probably be tempted to do something about it, yes?'

'Yes, I guess so.'

'Then we agree. Now, replace butterfly wings with human interactivity. Unless you keep people locked away and isolated they will interact with each other. The way stranger speaks with stranger, or how a loved one behaves towards their partner, will affect the way people think about themselves. This, in turn, affects the way they will act towards others, and the way those others act towards yet more people, and so the ripples of interactivity get compounded until we either get heaven on Earth or World War Three. You can imagine which outcome our hypersensitive, ultra-evolved person from eight billion years in the future would prefer. Heaven on Earth or nuclear desolation? Joy or unimaginable suffering? It's a no-brainer. Now go check out the newsfeeds and you'll soon see which way we're headed; Heaven on Earth recedes into the distance and currently there's not much in the way of light at the end of the tunnel, is there?'

Erskine gazed into his wine glass for a moment as if searching for answers from an oracle. He continued, 'However, all is not entirely doom and gloom. In every generation, there is born a single nexus for good, someone who never has a negative effect on the people around them. These singular people send out ripples of positive karma that our super-evolved busybodies can reinforce into great waves of well-being. These inherently good people shine like a beacon throughout time and they attract our evolved beings like moths to a lantern. And remember, these beings can manipulate time and space the way you manipulate a door into a room. They can send messages that wait for the recipient to arrive, manifest themselves however, whenever and wherever they choose, and they can bathe in the sweet flame cast by a nexus personality. It is such a delicious balm to them, a wellspring of hope amidst despair. Such a one, Prentiss, is you. The moths gather around your flame and that is what brings them to your city. They use their super-evolved wings to fan your flame, maximise its value, and perhaps even evade global catastrophe in the process. Are you still with me so far?'

'I'm with you, I'm not sure I believe any of what you think about me, but I hear what you're saying.'

'A nexus personality can't wander through life thinking they're good people and somehow special, they never do. If you like they are *too* special to fit into such a limiting framework. You just go about your day, and everywhere you go everyone you meet feels better about their lives. You can no more see the nexus effect than you can smell your own perfume. It has often been said that the Queen of England thinks everywhere in the world smells of fresh paint because everyone cleans and paints their place before she gets there. Rubbish of course. You, on the other hand, think that everyone you meet is intelligent, reasonable, friendly, and considerate, with few exceptions. Of course, there will *be* exceptions, you live in the real world not some Utopian, ivory tower. That boy Phil Clancy who attempted to rape you when you were a teenager, he was reacting to your fledgling nexus effect. You made him feel good, but it hit the poor sap straight in his loins. He didn't have the emotional sensitivity God gave woodlice. All he knew was that he wanted to eat you with a spoon, and the only spoon he had was the boner he got whenever he saw you. He tried to use it, and you know the outcome. Mrs Raluca Paceagiu rammed your car because you scared her when she was texting her daughter, who had just told her she was setting up home with a boy who wanted her to go with him to Syria. Mrs Paceagiu was terrified and angry and you made her feel worse. She reacted without thinking about what happens when you attack police officers in their car, and near shit herself when Sam pulled a gun on her.

'Now look at the nexus effect on those two. Clancy was a proto-rapist. If he hadn't attacked you it would have been someone else. He was a big guy and strong, but luckily he was no match for your neighbour, Mr Wiśniewski. Clancy learned an important lesson that day. Because of what he'd done to you he lost everything that mattered to him: his place on the football team, his self-respect, his college career. He got kicked into the shit and had to pull himself out afterwards. Now he's a married man with a good job and two kids. He's even quit his dad's firm and moved on to greener pastures.

'Mrs Paceagiu's daughter didn't go to Syria and didn't stay with the boy. When he heard what his girlfriend's mom had done to a cop's car he laughed at her and called her the baby girl of a crazy bitch. He said she would one day be a perfect fit for a suicide bomb vest. He told her how that would show her mom she was a proper chip off the, "crazy bitch block". And he meant it. The daughter slapped the idiot silly, even broke his nose when he tried to fight back. She went home to her folks, and her mom pleaded guilty and got a suspended sentence, subject to attending a course of anger management. Everyone's happy. Oh, and there's an addendum, Mrs Wiśniewski was so proud of her husband she agreed to get treatment for her alcohol addiction. She's been sober ever since. And that, Prentiss, is the nexus effect.'

'Come on, Gee, you can't know all this shit. You're making it up!'

He drained his glass and put it back on the coaster.

'I can, I can know everything when I turn my eye on it. You see, I'm the third person, I'm called "He who sees" for a reason, and I'm the mind that directs the other two.' He held out his hand.

'Please allow me to introduce myself, Prentiss. When we're alone together, you may wish to call me Horus.'

[35]

By the time Erskine had put her in a cab and kissed her goodbye – and very much against her will – Prentiss had begun to believe him. He had also promised her that nothing was going to happen to anyone on the list that evening, so, he said, she could go home, put her feet up, and relax. She had also drunk more wine than she was used to, and wondered if that was why she had been willing to accept everything he told her without too much protest. She was still wondering about it when she let herself into her apartment and flopped bonelessly into her favourite recliner. It all seemed too fantastic to be true, but when eight o'clock came and went without a call she wondered how he had known.

She took a shower, got ready for bed, and then did something she hadn't done in far too long. She dialled a familiar number.

'Hi, mom, it's me. No, I'm fine, I just wanted to hear your voice. No, really, work's fine, yeah, I miss you too.'

She talked with her mother for nearly half an hour, during which she ascertained the truth of Mrs Wiśniewski's old drinking problem, and that she had been sober for years.

'Since your run-in with that Clancy boy. You remember, honey?'

'Oh, yeah, the Clancy boy. Whatever happened to him?'

Once again, her mother proved a fount of local knowledge. Prentiss wasn't surprised to learn Erskine had been right. The erstwhile attempted rapist was now a proud father and a hard-working pillar of the local community. Prentiss thought to herself, *there it is. The nexus' butterfly effect strikes again.*

She and her mother spent five minutes telling each other how much they missed and loved each other. When she put the phone down the apartment seemed strangely still and silent. Prentiss felt very alone. She wanted to cry.

She drank a pint of mineral water and popped a couple of paracetamol to fend off any incipient hangover, then helped herself to a decent glass of Merlot. She poured some dry roast peanuts into a bowl and turned on her TV, looking for something light-hearted and trashy. She found a show involving two idiot cops in LA who were somehow also expert in 'drunken master' kung-fu, and, despite being total cretins, always bagged the bad guys. The acting was terrible and the entire show was filmed on a backlot somewhere. Perfect. She settled down for an evening of brainless guilty pleasure. The phone rang.

It was Howlett so she muted her TV.

'Hello, you.'

'Hi, Prentiss. How you doing? I tried to ring you earlier but got no reply, figured you must have been busy.'

Prentiss checked her cell phone. She had two missed calls.

'I'm sorry, I was with Erskine. We were going over some leads. It took all afternoon.'

'Erskine? The bald guy? What kind of leads?'

Why did she suddenly feel defensive?

'Erskine knows a lot of people, and he had some ideas that might prove useful. It's what I do for a living, Tabaqui. People are being murdered, I can't afford to turn down information no matter what the source. Surely you can see that? Sorry I missed your calls. Where are you, at home?'

'Not a problem, I know I'm just being silly. I'm here, I'm downstairs. I wondered if you fancied a bite? I know it's late but, you know, I wanted to see you. I promise not to keep you out too late, okay?'

'Give me ten minutes.'

She pulled off her big tee, hooked herself into a bra and wriggled into a pair of jeans. She was still tucking her blouse into the waistband when the elevator reached her floor. Howlett was standing by the door when it opened onto the ground floor. She frowned.

'Tabaqui! How did you get in?'

'I hoped you wouldn't mind. One of your neighbours let me in. Laurie, you know? The flood guy with all the books?'

'Just a surprise is all, finding you in the building without a key.'

'I can go back outside and wait in the car.'

'Don't be silly.' She leaned against him. 'Good to see you.'

He put his arms around her they kissed, gently.

'Great to see you too. How do you manage to look so fresh at the end of a long day?'

'Blame my mom. She taught me to moisturise every night before bedtime. Where do you want to eat? I warn you, I had a decent lunch so I'm only peckish, what about you?'

'Starving, is there anywhere good around here?'

'I know a place, if we can get a table.'

Enzo welcomed Howlett with guarded enthusiasm. He spent several minutes weighing him up before he shrugged and led the couple to Prentiss' accustomed table in the corner. Howlett looked around at the lobsters and the fishing nets.

'I bet the fish here is pretty good. Does he catch it himself?'

'I'm sure he would if he could. Everything's good here. This is practically my second home, and Enzo runs a superb kitchen. You'll see.'

Howlett devoured his antipasti with a glass of house white, and enthusiastically sat back when Enzo warned him before slicing open his speciality dish 'pollo sorpresa', and the hot, herby garlic butter spurted skywards. Howlett was full of chatter. Chappell had been asking after her and had wondered when she might come around to his loft again.

'He's not asking about me, just you. That bug bit deep. Even the wolves keep looking at the gates to see if you're walking through them. You have that effect on everything you meet.'

She smiled around her mouthful of calamari and said nothing. She was thinking about the urbane Erskine's claim to be the modern manifestation of Horus, and that the enigmatic Aliya Petrus was meant to be a sky goddess, and that somewhere an eight-billion-year-old Anubis was planning his next killing; and that she knew him and he knew her. *Who was he?*

Howlett was explaining something. '...so, although we officially met for the first time at the Sanctuary, we *had* seen each other before. I remember you even if you don't remember me. It's not every day that a strikingly lovely woman nearly knocks you into the Hudson. But I distinctly remember the way you looked at me before you ran off after that guy. Did you get him?'

Prentiss crashed back into the here and now.

'When was that?'

She scrabbled after a memory. When did she collide with someone while chasing a suspect?

'About three weeks ago. You were with your little friend Sam and a guy in uniform.'

Of course. She had it now.

'Yeah, we got him. That was you? I'm sorry, they call that "hot pursuit". The guy was armed and believed to be dangerous so we had to bring him down. I guess you were collateral damage. Did I hurt you?'

'No, I think I enjoyed it more than anything else.'

Prentiss thought back to that afternoon by the Hudson. They had been after an armed moped mugger who had crashed his bike while they were chasing him in a car after a nasty little robbery in a store car park. The mugger had raced away on foot but he had hurt himself and they were closing the gap when a man had stood up from his seat on a bench, and she had narrowly avoided colliding with him when he walked directly in front of her. Wait, did she avoid him or did he avoid her? She thought she had clipped his shoulder, but he had danced out of her way and stepped around her like one of the drunken master characters on the TV show earlier. He had *flowed* around her and she had looked at him in amazement. Their eyes had connected and Howlett had grinned at her with mischief writ large across his face. She remembered her confusion about that at the time, confusion washed away by the urgency of the chase. Sam and the uniform had been drawing away and she didn't want to lose sight of them. She had muttered her apologies and sprinted away. It had eventually taken all three of them to corner the suspect, and in the excitement the man by the river had been forgotten. Until now.

'Tabaqui,' she asked. 'Do you practice martial arts?'

He had just placed a mouthful of breaded chicken into his mouth, so he nodded rather than speak with his mouth full.

When he had swallowed he replied, 'Yes, Taekwondo and a few variants. It became something of a passion when I was younger and I mentored some of the other kids. I entered competitions and won a few. I still spar when I can and practice my kata when I have the time, which isn't as often as I'd like. Dancing with wolves takes up a lot of free time, same with policework I guess?'

'Yes, you said a good plenty there.'

'What made you ask?'

'I was thinking back to that day by the Hudson. You said we collided – but we didn't. We should have, but you just danced around me. I remember being impressed at the time, but I had to get back to the day job and got caught up in the rush. That was a smart move, mister.'

He shrugged, 'Automatic. I didn't think, I just moved. I didn't want to hurt the pretty lady. And who would have thought that a few weeks later we'd be sitting here talking about it. You're a tough girl to get out of a man's head once he's seen you. You know that don't you.'

'You're pretty unforgettable yourself, Tabaqui. Where does that name come from by the way?'

'India, I think. I have a mongrel past. My people were well travelled. Where does Prentiss come from?'

'Domestic. I'm a homeland girl, "My country 'tis of thee, sweet land of liberty" you know the rest. The whole "Pilgrims' pride" thing. But I bet there are slaves back in there, somewhere.'

'And queens. You don't have the bearing of a slave, you're more like the Pharaoh Queen Nefertari, but hey, maybe I could see you as a Harriet

147

Tubman or Sojourner Truth. But that's enough of all that. Thank-you for bringing me here. You're right about Enzo's kitchen. I'll get this and then see you home. Thank-you for joining me so late at the end of a long day.'

She protested that they should go Dutch but Howlett insisted.

'Besides,' he said, 'you've barely eaten a thing. And anyway, your being famous paid for dinner last time. This one's on me. No arguments.'

They kissed thoroughly by her entrance door before she keyed herself into her apartment building. She waited inside the glazed door until she saw his car climb the ramp and waved at it. She couldn't see if he waved back. She sighed, smiled, and called the elevator. Within half an hour she was asleep.

An hour later her eyes were wide open.

36

'You see that old guy over there with the shopping bag on wheels?'

Prentiss looked through the deli big plate window and over the road. She searched until she saw the man Sam was talking about. He was ancient, worn thin, and he walked hunched and slow, gripping the handle of his tartan bag on wheels as if his life depended on it. His head was narrow and crowned with a wild shock of silver white hair.

'I see him. What?'

'Watch.'

The man crossed a side road walking like a rheumatic tortoise, but as soon as his foot touched the sidewalk again he suddenly speeded up and almost leapt past the building on the corner. He didn't slow down until he had scampered past its entire fascia and reached the steps of the brownstone next door. Then he stopped, pulled a florid handkerchief from a cavernous pocket, and mopped at his face, panting heavily. He caught his breath before continuing his slow perambulation along the street.

Prentiss screwed up her face and shook her head.

'What was that about?'

'He, my dear, is Mr Benjamin Addams. And that building is the undertaker's establishment where he has his funeral plan.'

'Okay. And, so?'

'So, I've seen him do that before. This is where I stop for coffee on my way to the precinct, when I've got the time. It's good coffee, which is why I asked you to meet me here. Anyhow, every day at this sort of hour Mr Addams goes for what he calls his "packages". He makes a point of it. Rain, sleet or shine he thinks of something he needs and hits the sidewalk. He says good morning to all the same people while he pushes his little bag on wheels in front of him. All those people know his address. One day he didn't show, and the local cops got five calls within an *hour*. Turns out his daughter had made a surprise visit and brought the makings for breakfast, so he didn't go out. He was eating a cream cheese bagel with lox when the uniform hammered on his door. The next day he was back, and that morning he said to everyone, good morning, and thank-you. He's a real character.'

'Sounds it. Built his own local alarm system. But what's with the hundred-yard dash?'

'I know, weird isn't it. So, I asked him.'

'Yeah? And? What did he say?'

149

'He said, and get this, "The bastards got my money but they don't get me until I'm good and ready. There's the quick and the dead, and I ain't dead. I'm still too fast for 'em and they know it." He's ninety-two going on a thousand. You know something? I want to be like that when *I'm* ninety-two.'

Prentiss raised her cup, 'Much respect, Mr Addams.'

'Yeah, much respect. So then, honey, what's so all-fired important you want to see me outside the office? You had another dream? Seen spooky shit on your TV again?'

'No, thank God. No, it's not that. No, but, Sam, I think I know who the Anubis killer is.'

Sam hissed, 'No shit. And it's Erskine, yes?'

'No, it's doctor Tabaqui Howlett.'

'WHAT? Sexy wolf doctor? You slipped a gear or something?'

Prentiss leaned forward. 'Okay, do something for me. Swipe your phone to Safari or whatever search engine you got.'

Sam did as she was told. 'Okay, now what?'

'Look up the meaning of the girl's name, Aliya, A-L-I-Y-A.'

After a few moments Sam looked up. 'Sky.'

'Correct. Now, look for the meaning of the boy's name, Gawain. G-A-W-A-I-N.'

Time passed. 'Okay, it says here, falcon or hawk.'

'Good. Now, try to find the meaning of the name Tabaqui, T-A-B-A-Q-U-I.'

'Yeah? I bet it's Creole for a good cee-gar. Bet yah.' After less than a minute she raised her eyes to Prentiss' face. 'Shit in a sandwich. When did you work that one out?'

'This morning. Thinking about it woke me up. Erskine had told me a whole parcel of stuff that made my brain fizz. Sky and the Falcon are old Egyptian gods, Nut, and Horus. You heard of them?'

'No. But I must warn the boys, I'll tell them, you be careful with Egyptian history, may contain nuts.'

'Ha, yes, and one of them's sitting with you at this table.'

'Tabaqui, his name means jackal? Honey, this is beginning to freak me clean out of Kansas. What the hey are we involved with here?'

'Madness, that's what, and I don't know if it's more ancient than the pyramids or so advanced that you and me are like plankton by comparison. These people don't see time the way we do. They leave thought bombs where we can walk straight through them and they fuse with our hard-wired heads. They make us see the things they want us to see, read things they want us to read, and they can be right where they want to be without taking the elevator or unlocking the door.'

She pounded the heel of her hand against her temple. 'And apparently I'm like a magnet to them. Damn, where's Superman when you need him?'

'Hiding if he's got any sense. So, what do we do now?'

Prentiss drained her coffee, and not for the first time wondered who had come up with the saucer design that put the little circular depression that held the base of the cup slightly to one side. She knew it made room for the free biscuit, but the biscuit wasn't so big that it needed the space. *Space.* The thought arrived like a wave of cold water; the killings needed space to happen. Wadsmythe was the only one killed at his home, but he was also the only one to live alone. Puckling had staff who lived in, Hart and Errol M were both married. They had to be taken somewhere to be judged and devoured. Where?

Sam watched her friend silently. She knew the look of fully absorbed concentration that Prentiss took on when she was getting her teeth into a problem. She didn't want to distract her when she was on the chase, pursuing thoughts through the labyrinthine passages of her remarkable mind. When Prentiss' eyes came back into focus she pursed her lips and frowned.

'You told me one of the New York mountain range had been topped out but it wasn't open for business yet. Which one was it?'

Sam dug a tablet out of her bag and turned it on. 'Your intuition kicked in at last?'

'Just a thought is all. I don't know where it will take me. I can't shake the "man on his mountain" thing. If the upper floors are complete but nothing's happening there until later it might be the perfect killing ground for Anubis. We also need to visit Erskine's place, where was it again?'

'Topped out place is Centre Heights. Erskine's on the seventy-third floor of One five-seven.'

'We should go look.'

'Why? You said it wasn't him.'

'It isn't, but he's involved. He may be an accessory. And another thing. I've seen Howlett a few times, we've had dinner, been to The Met. He even turned up at my place last night and we went to Enzo's place, you know?'

'Yeah, nice.'

'Nice? It was nice, but you know something? He's never said where he lives. He knows where *I* live but all I know is where he works. He comes to me. Wait a moment, I want to try something.'

151

She hit a number in her phone, it rang a few times before a sleepy voice answered. 'Hello? This better be good, do you know what time it is?'

'Rex, hi, its Prentiss. Yeah. Sorry to catch you so early, but I wondered if you could do me a favour. Oh, you're a darling man. Thanks. Thing is I want to surprise Tabaqui with a present but I don't know his address. Would you have it to hand? You don't? But I thought... Oh, I see. Okay, no, go back to bed. Yes, let's do that soon. No, you won't have to be naked. Okay, you can if you want to be, see you soon. Ciao.'

She hung up and said, 'What do you call a man whose best friend doesn't know where he lives and has never thought to ask?'

Sam grinned, 'Suspicious.'

37

The tall bald man had grinned with pleasure when they stepped out of the elevator into the lobby of his home. He held out his hands as if he was ready to embrace both police officers but was finding it difficult to choose which to grab first.

'The lovely, Prentiss and the charming, Sam, my two favourite homicide detectives. Please, come through. Welcome to my high tower. How may I help you today?'

He cast an almost undetectable quizzical glance at Prentiss, as if to say, haven't you learned enough from me yet? What else can I tell you?'

When he led them through into his living room Sam emitted an appreciative whistle. Everything about Erskine's apartment had been organised around the view towards Central Park, and it was spectacular enough to cause vertigo in a mountaineer.

'Gee, you have real taste, man. You think you might want to adopt a cute homicide cop? I'd be happy to drape myself wherever you think I'll look most decorative, so long as I could see that view every day, and I'm scared of heights. This place is gorgeous.'

'Thank-you, Sam. I'm sure you'd look lovely anywhere. Would you like the tour? I love showing off my home.'

His willingness to take them everywhere, including his wet room and even through his master bedroom and into his dressing room – which doubled as a study and library – dashed their hopes that Erskine had provided the killing ground for the first three victims. The place was immaculate. Erskine wore his home like a well-tailored suit. Once they saw him in it, it was impossible to think of him living anywhere else. Prentiss wondered how often and for how long his cleaner made an appearance to maintain such a forensic level of cleanliness. She concluded that the apartment must be well above the city's dust layer, but still had to fight the compulsion to run a white tissue along the top of a door when no-one was looking. They ended the visit by admitting that they had wondered if he had any idea who might be next on his wicked philanthropist list, and had decided it was best to ask him in person. He gave them a name, Helene Craven, and told them all the details they needed were on the list.

Sam thanked him, then added, 'I've always wondered what it was like to see the park from up here. And now I know, and it's certainly worth the premium. I'll have to tell my old man he's got to get himself a better paid job. College tutors' fees don't even buy the rug on the floor in there. Is that really an original cubist design?'

'My dear, your erudition is truly impressive, but no. It's based on a Mondrian.'

Erskine saw them out and they departed in a welter of air kisses and invitations to return, none of which were entirely convincing. Once the elevator door had closed Sam chuckled. 'Well, there you have it. I think once you've seen one eye-poppingly beautiful millionaire's paradise you've seen them all. And did you see? No urine stains around his john, that man is the real deal.'

'He has a cleaner.'

Once they had started their smoothly rapid transit down to the parking garage Prentiss considered the next name on the list.

'Helene Craven. She's a sweet piece of work. Says here she specialises in online bullying and mental torture to drive vulnerable and depressed children to suicide. She's the principal patron for the Life's Highway Foundation which is meant to do the exact opposite. She lets the Foundation reach out to children in need and then selects her victims from its records. What a *bitch*.'

'Yeah, well she'll be a dead bitch unless we do something about it. Where now boss?'

'Center Heights.'

'Damn, I just remembered something I left at home.'

'What?'

'My head for heights.'

'You're a very funny lady, you know that?'

'Yeah, it's a classic psychological defence mechanism. Stops me bursting into tears.'

'Sam, honestly, what if we find something up there?'

'Me personally? I'll either tell a joke or weep like a baby. Let's go find out which.'

Thanks to its plethora of high rise buildings the skyline around Central Park was beginning to resemble a picket fence built by a giant. When fresh real estate in some of the most lucrative locations in the world begins to run out at ground level, the only way to go is up. New York is clear of the 'Ring of Fire' earthquake zone that plagues cities such as Los Angeles and Tokyo, so developers could vie with each other to see how high they dare go. As they approached their next destination Prentiss remembered that she had read somewhere that some of the tallest buildings in the world were held together using state-of-the-art, super strong adhesive tape. She didn't find the idea

154

very reassuring, despite the reported one hundred per cent safety record. Her mind's eye offered the image of a thousand-foot house of cards held together with sticky tape. Her palms became slick with sweat on the wheel and she wiped them one after the other on the legs of her jeans. It didn't help.

From ground level Center Heights looked finished. Directions for the parking garage led her up a side road and then down a ramp into a sub-basement. A Hispanic looking young man in a booth eyed Prentiss' badge with something approaching contempt at first, but then welcomed the women readily enough. He opened the barrier and stepped out of his box to explain where guest parking could be found. His voice was gentle and his smile seemed genuine.

'I'd better let the boss know we've got NYPD on the premises. That way he can stash all the wetbacks before you reach his floor. You want the sixty-third floor, so you'll need to go up in the express and change elevators on forty. Have a nice day, see you on the way out. Hope you find what you're looking for. Oh, and FYI, the express is *fast*. You gain weight on the way up and lose it on the way down. Might feel a little weird.'

The express was clearly signposted in the corner of the garage. Prentiss was pleased to see the elevator car was clean and fresh. It was formed in the shape of a cylinder with a crystalline looking floor and ceiling. There were just four buttons to press. The top luminous arrow pointed up, the upper middle button had a glowing red G in its centre, the lower said LG shops, and the last arrow pointed down. Sam examined the panel with an arch look in her eyes.

'Too much choice. Let's go for G. I feel good about G.'

Prentiss hit the top arrow. A voice told them what was happening as a curved door swung shut and the car began to rise as if on a column of air. LG glided past, then G, and then suddenly they were out in the open. Sam whimpered.

'Holy fucking shit! Thanks for the warning, parking guy.'

For the next several seconds they enjoyed an uninterrupted bird's eye view of New York from inside a completely transparent cylinder that was climbing the side of one of the tallest buildings in the world at high speed.

Sam moaned, '*No*, I looked down. Shit, I just looked down. I'm shutting my eyes. Tell me when we get there. What kind of sadist designed this nightmare?'

Prentiss dragged her eyes from the incredible prospect before her and looked down. She appeared to be standing on thin air. The only visible means of support was a black rail running up the corner of the high rise into which the elevator car was slotted. The whole thing looked to her as if it should peel away and dump them to the ground a steadily increasing distance below her feet. She wondered how much of the contraption was held together with adhesive tape, and then decided she was better off enjoying the view than pursuing that thought.

The car slowed and slid noiselessly into a surrounding socket. The door opened with a chime and an informative voice, and she led Sam out onto solid ground.

'Okay, we're here. You can open your eyes now.'

Sam opened one eye, and then the other.

'I kid you not. A little bit of wee came out in there. That was a shock.'

'Could have been worse. Wee's okay, you do that to me all the time when I'm laughing at the things you say. Where's the next elevator?'

'Yeah? Well next time it could be worse. Can we go down the slow way please?'

'We got another twenty-three floors to go. You okay with this or do you want to walk it? There must be a fire escape somewhere.'

'Do I look like a Sherpa? Do I? No! So, where's the elevators?'

'You look like a Sherpa with damp panties. Over there.'

Sam sighed with evident relief when the door opened onto a normal, fully enclosed elevator car. She stepped in and stamped her foot.

'This will do me just fine. Onwards and upwards driver, let's hit the heights.'

She stamped again as the car began to move.

'Sam, don't do that. Some of these things are held together with adhesive tape. Let's not take the chance this is one of them, okay? You hear me?'

'Did you have to tell me that? I mean, did you? That is cruel and unusual behaviour. You are a truly terrible woman, you know that?'

Both women had pressed themselves firmly against the walls on either side of the elevator car when it softly bounced to a stop and a chiming voice announced, 'doors opening'. They had arrived.

[38]

The man waiting for them looked quizzically from one to the other woman pressed firmly against a wall either side of the elevator, then down at the floor of the car between them. He shrugged.

'Hi,' he said. 'Did you get scared by a squirrel? They do get in sometimes. I'm Terry, by the way, Terry Forde with an 'E'. I'm senior construction management co-ordinator for Center Heights.'

With a feeling of relief Prentiss and Sam stepped out onto the evidently solid cement of an open-plan floor. Sam held out her hand.

'Hi, I'm Sam Bolat, this is detective sergeant Prentiss, pleased to meet you. We're with NYPD homicide. Good of you to see us on such short notice.' She indicated the echoing shell of the building's sixty-third floor. 'Not much going on here.'

Forde looked around at the darkened, empty space. 'No, not yet. This is your basic shell. The pre-formed units are all in place as are access to the services, electricity supply, plumbing, blah, blah. The guys will soon be up here to fit internal walls, floors, hygiene facilities, you know, bathrooms and kitchens. You wouldn't think it yet but a Saudi Sheik purchased this entire floor, and everything going in here will be completely bespoke. He even chose his own lay-out. Amazing how much money some people have.'

Prentiss asked, 'Why are the windows all covered up like that?'

'Windows? No, there are no windows yet. That's protective insulated sheeting to keep the weather out until we put the windows in. The windows go in first, before the floors. The guys will be up,' he checked his tablet, 'yeah, Tuesday, to fit the windows.' He nodded sagely.

Sam said, 'I hear, well, I've been told, that a lot of these new builds are held together with adhesive tape. Is that true.'

Forde sucked on that thought, moving it around his mouth as if it was a sour tasting boiled sweet. He swallowed it whole.

'That would be an idea, wouldn't it? Save a lot of time. Yeah, I heard they're doing stuff like that in the Middle East, but not here in the Apple. We got too much weather here to trust the building to sticky tape. This is all rock solid American know-how. It's foundations have even been cushioned so it don't rock in a high wind like some of the older buildings. They tell me you can even stand on the floors in the elevators without worrying they're going to fall out from under you.'

157

He grinned. His eyes glinted with affable intelligence. Sam and Prentiss grinned shamefacedly back.

Prentiss said, 'Are there squirrels here?'

Forde shrugged, 'Could be. I've never seen one though, and never heard of one. Never seen any rats neither, but I wouldn't rule it out. We've got ninety-eight floors here if you include the parking garage, one hundred if you include the two floors of storage below that. We stand fourteen hundred and ten feet tall above ground level and these walls contain some of the primest of the most prime real estate in the western hemisphere. She's an architectural work of art. So then, ladies, why are you interested in her and what can Terry Forde do for the NYPD?'

Prentiss stepped forward. 'Mr Forde, we are pursuing an enquiry into some killings that we believe happened in a half-hour transit circle around the Bronx. Center Heights falls into that circle, and it also fits into other specific parameters that I'm afraid we can't discuss at present. What we're saying is that the killings may have happened somewhere in the unoccupied part of this building.' She looked around her. 'Obviously not on floor sixty-three. Would you help us search the rest of the building?'

Forde performed the sour sweet sucking thing with his mouth again, swallowed it. He folded his arms and tucked in his chin, as if he was facing an aggressor.

'How many people been killed?'

'Four so far, but one died at home.'

'So, you're thinking maybe three people been murdered here at the Heights? Nope. Sorry, can't happen.'

'Why?'

'Because it can't. What's the timescale?'

'Just over a week.'

'Can't happen. How were these people killed?'

'I'm afraid we can't...'

'I don't need details, but was there, you know, was there blood?'

Sam nodded. 'Yes, there was. The bodies were moved and discovered elsewhere, but there would be blood at the kill site. Lots of it.'

'Jeeze, Louise, the night security people would have found it and reported it by now. And anyway, there's no way in without someone knows you're coming, you know that. Even you had to call ahead and, you know, you're the cops. Transients would love to sack down in a cosy crib like this, but they don't because there's no way in. It can't happen. Your murder site is somewhere else ladies, you can take that to the bank. Terry Forde crosses his

158

heart and lays his reputation down on your dotted line. This place is tight as a bank vault, tighter, it's that secure. Can't happen. Sorry.'

Prentiss nodded at his certainty. 'We're sure you're right Mr Forde, but it's our duty to look anyway. We have to confirm it for our superiors.'

'Can't we just say we did it and found nothing? Save your time and mine? You're talking about searching thirty-two floors of empty building above this one. Thirty-two freaking floors. Have you any idea how long that might take?'

Prentiss did the math, 'About two hours forty minutes at five minutes a floor. If it's there we'll know and so will you, trust me.'

'Nearly three hours? Man, they'll deduct that from my hourly rate. This is madness. Your killer can't get in, and he couldn't get out carrying a body. Miss... detective... Jeeze Louise, officer, it can't happen. Believe me.'

His protests were ignored, but Prentiss suggested a possible solution.

'Look, Mr Forde, why don't you join us for the first hour? We can start at the top and work our way down. We think the killer operates above one thousand feet, the higher the better. We think they have a thing about being high up above the common crowd, you see what I'm saying? We could start on the ninety-fifth floor and come down. If we use the elevator we will probably just need to open the doors and smell the air. If it's there we'll know. Okay?'

Forde sighed deeply and pressed the button for the elevator. When it arrived, he unclipped a small key from a chain on his belt, opened a panel in the centre of the control board and inserted the key, turning it to the right.

'Okay, this elevator is now ours. No-one else can use it until we say so. Let's get up to the penthouse and start working our way down. Hope you won't be too disappointed when we all we find is dust and food wrappers from the guys' lunches. Damn. Okay, let's do this thing. Shall we go?'

Forde talked all the way to the top but became silent when the car came to a halt. The doors slid aside. Prentiss and Sam sniffed at the air, moving slightly out into the dark space. They shook their heads.

The same thing happened on the next floor, and the next. Forde became chatty again, his voice sounding less strained as each floor yielded no new surprises.

'This is good for you guys I guess. No hours of paperwork, no hanging around for CSI New York to show up. Hey, is that show for real? I mean, if it was for real then no-one would get away with anything, would they? Everything's there, fingerprints, DNA, blood spatter, bullet directions with those blue lights. Amazing, truly amazing. Is it like that? Truly?'

Prentiss thought of the mournful Feldman and his cup of coffee.

'Yeah,' she said. 'Pretty much. Our pathology guys are awesome, aren't they, Sam?'

'Yeah, beyond awesome. And so cool about it too. They just turn up and get on with the job. No fuss, no grousing.'

The next floor was also a blank. Forde had fully recovered his spirits by then.

'I told you. Nothing here, nada. He would have to be a magician to get this far and out again with his victim. It can't happen in the Heights, not unless they got beamed in by Scotty and beamed out again, and that's an awful lot of technology just to go murder some poor folks, you hear what I'm saying?'

The doors slid open to the next floor. Prentiss and Sam instantly reacted.

Sam said, 'Bingo.'

Forde caught the smell of rotten body fluids in the air and grimaced.

'Shit! This can't be happening, this is impossible. Some bastard is going to get their ass fired over this.'

Prentiss was already on her phone. Sam turned to Forde.

'There any CCTV up here?'

Forde looked close to tears. 'Shit *no*! Why would we? No-one can get up here.'

Sam shook her head, 'Someone did, Mr Forde. Someone did.'

[39]

Feldman was gazing bleakly into his customary paper cup of coffee. His nauseous expression told Prentiss that he was, as usual, unimpressed by its contents. He regarded her with sad, bloodhound's eyes.

'Congratulations. New York's finest does it again. One day you must tell me which crystal ball you use to find your clues. There's no logic in it that I can see. What led you up here?'

'You did, Feldman, you did. The man on his mountain, remember? It was you who told me some buildings in New York are tall enough to be mountains. Sam looked them up and this is the one that ticked all the boxes. Mr Forde over there was kind enough to let us look up here, after some persuading. Fact is he was convinced we were wasting his time, and ours, but, here we are. And there it is.'

The killing ground was a spectacular mess of blood and shapeless chunks of rotting human flesh. Decay had been inhibited by the cool, dry environment on the eighty-eighth floor, but even so, time had worked its alchemy on the raw, human meat.

'It would appear our killer spits his victims out after biting them. Biting them. Bah, this is ridiculous. Are you still reluctant to accept that the wounds might have been inflicted by a person using some specially constructed mechanical device?'

'Why would he? A knife or a gun would be so much easier. And what kind of downforce are we talking about here. It bit through a human – including shearing through the spine – like it was a slice of baloney on white bread. What's the PSI force required to do something like that?'

'Less than you think, Prentiss, but a good question all the same. The Japanese broadsword called a katana is said to be able to slice a man in two with a single sweep. But that was because it was one of the sharpest things ever used in warfare. If our killer's contraption was sharp enough it would cut through the victim without any difficulty. The technique would be the primary problem, how do you get your victim into the thing before you fire it up? Tricky. I suppose you could drug the fight out of them – but I've found no trace of any drugs in the victims' bodies. Wadsmythe had drunk enough whisky to put him into a coma for several hours before he died, but the others were apparently fully compos mentis when they were killed. How did he do it? A five-pipe problem I think, Sherlock. I'll leave it to you and your crystal ball to find out. Officer Bolat might help. Here she comes now.'

161

Prentiss nodded, 'Okay, Feldman, thanks. Hey, what time is it?'

'Seven thirty, why?'

'Just curious.'

Sam appeared at her elbow. 'Hi, Feldman, how's the coffee?'

'Earth shatteringly terrible, and thanks for asking. I think I've tasted better urine samples. I would tip it away but I don't want to contaminate the crime scene. I'll leave you fine officers to banter, something you do so very well. I want to see if the urban spacemen have found any conclusive traces of the killing device our man used. Please, excuse me.'

Sam watched his retreating back. 'That man has the hots for me so bad he can barely contain himself when he's in the same room.'

'Is that why he walks away every time you come near him?'

'Classic case of desire denial. You must see it all the time.'

'Oh yes? Oh, yes, right, sure I do. Hey Sam, tell me, psychology was one of the options at the academy. Did you take it?'

'Sure did.'

'Did you actually turn up for any of the lectures?'

'Nah. I've got a natural aptitude for the subject, why spoil it with a lot of fancy-pants book learning? Hey, why do you keep looking at your watch?'

'It's coming up for eight o'clock. Helene Craven is married with two kids of her own. She lives at home with her husband. If he follows previous behaviour patterns our killer will bring her here for judgement. I don't know how, but that isn't the point. How will he react when he finds us here?'

'Shit, you're right. Shouldn't we warn somebody?'

'We can but try.' Prentiss raised her voice. 'Listen up everybody! We now know this is the killer's crime scene. We know he has previously murdered his victims at or around eight o'clock of the pip emma, and he's a very punctual man. He follows the same M.O. every time. Unless the vic lives alone, like Wadsmythe, he brings them here. We're due another killing tonight, and the word is the vic's married and lives with her husband and kids. So, our man will want to bring her here. We've got just under ten minutes. Heads up people.'

Feldman's distinctive drawl interrupted, 'Looked into that crystal ball again, did you?'

Another voice offered, 'This place is in lock-down. How's he going to get *himself* in, let alone a victim? Crazy thought, Prentiss.'

She replied, 'I'm just warning you is all. Be ready at eight.'

A mocking third voice cried out, 'And don't be late!' There was a ripple of laughter.

162

Prentiss persevered. 'Perhaps Mr Forde should leave the scene, just to be on the safe side.'

Forde replied, 'Jeeze Louise! You're telling me this psycho killer is on his way up here and you want me to go out and meet him? No way. Right here I'm surrounded by armed officers from the NYPD and you want me to go out there to meet who knows what? I think I know where I'm safer, you know what I'm saying?'

There came another rumble of laughter and agreement.

Sam said quietly, 'We've got six minutes. You've done what you can, you warned them and they're laughing at you. What else do you suggest?'

Prentiss looked around at the scene. Four large LED arrays mounted on tripods bathed everything between them in a clinical, cool, white light. The killings had taken place in the far right-hand corner of the floor furthest away from the elevator in which they had arrived with Forde. It was almost at right-angles to a larger service elevator that the team had used to bring their equipment to the scene. Outside the cone of light the entire floor had been thrown into shadowed darkness. Prentiss thought the highlighted area looked like theatre in the round. It gave the grim site a sense of unreality, as if the people involved were actors following a script. She waited for someone offstage to shout 'Okay, cut, that's a wrap everybody,' then chastened herself for her whimsical frame of mind. *Get a grip woman, this is a crime scene. People have died here.* She forced herself to focus back on the events unfolding before her.

Four environment suited scene of crime examiners crouched down, carrying out their work with trained efficiency. They had finished photographing, measuring, and bagging the victims' remains. Now they were making sure that everything was neatly tagged and was uncontaminated. Too many murder cases had been lost thanks to 'dirty' evidence, and as a result clean collection techniques had become as important to the success of a case as DNA sampling. Feldman stood alone to one side, watching their activity as if his people were undertaking a practical for an exam, and he would be marking them later. His cup of coffee was cooling on the ground by his feet.

Forde stood between two uniformed officers who had taken his statement several minutes earlier. He looked relaxed and was smiling at something one of the officers had said. He looked across at Prentiss and Sam and made a comment, both uniforms followed his gaze and nodded.

Sam sighed, 'They're either saying we're both mad as a bag of fleas or eminently fuckable, what's your guess?'

'Probably both, hey, what's that?'

163

With just a minute to go before eight they all heard the slight rumble of the approaching service elevator. The scene of crime people stood up warily and looked at each other. Feldman glanced at Prentiss and Sam, and then across to the closed elevator doors. It was evident to Prentiss that no-one was laughing now. There was the sound of the elevator car coming to a stop, and then the slight whine of gears engaging to open the doors. They slid apart and light spilled out followed by what at first seemed to be a formless shadow. A few members of the crime scene team took a long step back.

A cheery voice rang out. 'Hi, guys. Who ordered coffee and doughnuts? Are the specimens ready for collection yet? We'll take them down when we go.'

Two plain-clothed members of the forensic team wheeled a gurney piled with steaming paper cups and food cartons out of the elevator. There was a bout of nervous giggles and obvious relaxing of tense shoulders. Several people sneaked knowing looks at Prentiss.

Sam said, 'I'll grab us some coffee before it all disappears.'

She waved at the men with the gurney and walked over to check out their wares.

Within seconds she had them both laughing at something she'd said. *The woman's a natural,* thought Prentiss. *She's a treasure.* And then all the lights went out.

40

Chief Lewis sat silently beside her hospital bed and regarded her with grave eyes. Concern was writ plainly across his lean, muscular features. Prentiss wondered where she was and why he was there. Her body floated on a sea of painkillers, but even so she was painfully aware that she was hooked up to an array of beeping monitors. A bottle of clear fluid dripped down a tube into the back of her left hand. Other tubes snaked under her bedclothes. There was a faint smell of urine and something else, something harshly chemical. She accepted everything with dazed calm. Her mouth was very dry and tasted unpleasant. She wondered what her breath was like. Probably foul, and Lewis was close enough to smell it.

'Sorry,' she croaked.

Lewis jumped slightly. He hadn't noticed that her eyes were open.

'Prentiss, you're awake. How are you?'

'Wha... what happened? Where am I?'

'Relax. You're in Mount Sinai West Hospital, they're great people here. They're taking great care of you. Look here, the precinct sent flowers and cards. People really care for you, you know? They want you to get well. You just need to rest and get well.' He held up a narrow box. 'This is your Combat Cross. The Commissioner said you should have it. He wanted to send in our press photographer to get a picture of you wearing it in your hospital bed, but I vetoed that until you feel a little better. Maybe later this week.' He was talking to fill the silence. 'You'll be fine they tell me. Just fine.'

'Could I have some water, please? I'm very dry.'

Lewis looked across the room. 'Nurse, is it okay if she has water?'

Prentiss thought, *you need to ask? What's wrong with me?*

A calm voice replied, 'Just enough to freshen her mouth. Not too much. She has some abdominal damage and we don't want her leaking into her gut, do we? Here. I'll do it.'

A brisk but gentle touch. Barely a sip but so delicious.

'Thank-you.'

'You're welcome.'

The voice faded.

In her dreams, something gigantic lashed out in the darkness. There was gunfire and the sound of someone screaming. *Sam, it was Sam screaming.*

Prentiss struggled out of the nightmare and opened her eyes onto darkness. She thought she was alone but then she heard the sounds of pages being turned.

'Hello? Please, could I have some water? Please?'

'Of course, my dear. Give me a second.'

She was allowed a little more that time, but felt slightly sick afterwards. Some bile came into her mouth and dribbled from the corner of her lips. She tried to wipe her mouth but the cannula fixed into the back of her hand scraped against her nose. She felt tears gathering at the corners of her eyes. She felt weak and useless. *What happened to me?*

The nurse spoke gently, 'I think we need a little bit more sleep, dear. Night, night.'

Prentiss' eyes closed once more. And gold rimmed black orbs with diamond hard glints of reflected light were close to her face. Only the long snout separated them.

'I told you, little killer, but you wouldn't listen. Now see what you've done. I warned you to stay out of my way. What I do echoes long into the future, what you have done will make you weep here in the present. Then weep, little killer. Understand, I would not have had this happen. I swear I would not have had this happen, but you took away my choices.'

The voice was replaced by impossible memories of gunshots and screams, Sam was screaming. Days passed, and every time Prentiss awoke her world of acute pain had slowly metered down to something slightly more bearable, until it became a background sense of throbbing discomfort and a dull ache that wracked every inch of her body, but at least it allowed her to think.

Then one day she opened her eyes to daylight and found her parents sitting by her bed as if in prayer. The cool observer in her head said that they looked tired and older, but she was glad to see them all the same. She tried to speak but all she produced was a harsh croaking sound. Her father looked up.

'Nurse, I think she's choking. What should we do?'

A sweet voice answered, 'We'll let her have a little water to wet her larynx. She's just a little dry, aren't you, honey? She probably wants to say hello. Here we are, honey. Not too much. You're healing nicely but let's not rush things. That's it. A little more? Carefully does it. That's it. There, is that better?'

'Thank-you. Yes, thank-you. Hi, Mom, hi Dad. What brought you here?'

Her father was as ebony black as the nurse. His lean face was topped with tightly curled rows of iron grey hair. When she was a child Prentiss had always thought him the most handsome man in the world, she suddenly realised that she still did. His fine patrician features were creased with worry but his cool dignity never deserted him.

He said, 'We heard you were a little under the weather, and thought we would bring you some sunshine from home.'

Her mother said, 'We love you, you know.'

Time had erased little of her mother's youthful charm, even though her red rimmed eyes indicated she had been weeping. She had a beautiful olive complexion and seeing them side-by-side Prentiss marvelled at how the two colours of their genetic palette had been blended together to produce her own distinctive shade of coffee latte.

She tried to smile. 'I love you guys. It's great to see you together.'

Her mother frowned, 'What are you saying? You talk as if we'd been divorced or something. We're still together. Poppa what's she saying?'

Her father said, 'Hush, Momma, we mustn't excite her. Isn't that right nurse?'

The buxom nurse grinned. 'Don't worry. Your daughter's as tough as she's beautiful. She can take a little excitement. She's doing well, and she's well on the road to recovery. A bit of family chat will set her up nicely and anyone with half an eye can see how well you all get on. Shall I leave you to it for a few minutes? If you need me just press the call button.'

With the nurse out of the room the little group fell silent for a long moment. Then her father broke the stillness.

'You've got some beautiful flowers here. I hope you don't mind but we read some of your cards while you were asleep. You're obviously a popular person at the precinct. Who's Fat's Morten?'

'Why?'

'He says, "Get well and come back soon. Without you here there's nothing here worth looking at." Is he a boyfriend of yours?'

The perennial question.

'No, but he's a friend. He's the precinct comedian. You know the sort, always ready with a snappy comeback.'

Her father snorted his agreement, 'I know the sort all too well. Cheer the place up one minute and have you groaning in your coffee the next. We've got one in the office. Sometimes I think he's the one single reason New York should bring back capital punishment.'

Her mother frowned, 'Never mind the comedians. I want to know what she meant with that crack about how great it is to see us together.'

Prentiss smiled, a motion that hurt her face. She winced involuntarily.

167

Her mother looked concerned, 'Look, honey, don't worry if it's going to upset you. I'm just saying that we're not divorced so I wondered what you meant.'

'Mom, sorry if I said the wrong thing. It's just that Dad's always away, busy with work and you've always got a dozen things you're doing at once, so you're never in the same place at the same time. You guys look great together, and you know something? I don't even have a photo of you two I can look at. How silly is that? Really, I mean it, how silly is that? I don't... I don't... I ask you...'

As if a dam had broken a sudden fury of tears flooded out of her. She couldn't control the rage of pain that tore at her heart and threw her into helpless paroxysms of agonised despair. Her body curled tight into a yelping fury of keening grief. She didn't know where the wracking sobs had come from but she was powerless to stop them. She couldn't breathe and darkness threatened to overwhelm her. She must have pulled loose some of the connections to the monitoring station because alarms began to sound and a pair of nurses rushed into the room. They attended to Prentiss' cables and tubes and one flicked a needle into her arm. Within seconds the storm was over. With a muted whimper Prentiss lapsed back into blackness and peace. The last thing she heard was her terrified mother asking, 'Was it something I said? What did I say?'

41

Sometime during that afternoon, while she was lost in her storm of grief, it had all come back to her. Like a mantle of horror, it fell back into her mind as if cut from whole cloth. She remembered every second of that terrible night but it felt as if she had seen everything from a distance, as if she was watching events unfold through a pane of glass. The lights had gone out and almost at the same second a burst of explosive energy had blasted her off her feet, flinging her backwards away from the scene. She had landed hard, breaking bones, and cracking her skull. For just an instant she had been knocked to the brink of unconsciousness but had furiously fought her way back to awareness. She knew she and the team were in danger, she knew she must do something to protect them and herself. Screaming through a daze of pain and nausea she had tried to reach for her pistol, but her right arm wouldn't answer properly. The attempt sent a jolt of agony through her body that brought bitter tasting hot bile into her mouth. She vomited with a wrenching groan. She heard a short volley of gunshots, the reports rebounded and echoed across the empty floor then ended in silence. It sounded as if a rock drummer had begun a rapid, staccato beat and then thrown away his sticks. Then the screaming began. Prentiss had forced herself into a sitting position when she was caught by another pulse of powerful energy that slid her even further away from her colleagues and whatever was happening at the crime scene. She fetched up against the wall a few yards from the private elevator. One of the LED arrays crashed to the ground just feet away from her legs, and bounced noisily to smash against the wall. All screaming ceased. The air became frigidly cold, icy. She could see her breath steaming before her face and realised that orange light was bleeding into the scene from somewhere. *Oh,* she thought, *the windows are open. Why are the windows open?*

Then she saw it, a barely discernible shadow silhouetted against a dark orange sky. Something immense was in the room with her. Despite the high ceiling the giant figure was too tall to stand upright and was crouched forwards, its knees slightly bent. She could just make out that it held a limp, doll-like human figure in its powerful hands. The towering body flexed once, its head snapped down and forward. Prentiss heard a brief sucking and crunching sound. There followed a visceral smacking noise. The doll figure's arms and legs jerked loosely in its grip. And then it was gone. And there was total silence. No-one was moving. She could hear none of the pitiful sounds

169

one might expect from injured people in pain. *What had happened?* She shouted into the silence and got no reply. Nothing on Earth would make her approach closer to that ominously silent crime scene. *She had to get out of there, she had to get help. People must be hurt, she had to go for help. Suck it up, Prentiss.*

With great difficulty Prentiss managed to pull herself the short distance towards the elevator. She levered herself upwards and pressed the call button. When it arrived and the door opened she half stepped, half fell into the bright car. She hit the bottom button on the panel and waited fearfully for the door to close. Her breath came in painful gasps that sent lightning stabs of acute agony through her chest. She felt as if she'd been stabbed several times and all the blades were still rammed into her body. Something in the shadows caught her eye. Was the nightmare creature still moving out there? She squinted into the clotted darkness. A thrill of terror took her knees from under her and she crumpled to the floor. She had never felt more impotent than she did at that moment, waiting for a dark figure to reach out of the night and take her helpless body into its clutches. What was that? Had she heard approaching feet?

The door closed. Prentiss groaned with relief and her head slumped onto her shoulder. Even in the elevator's bright light darkness hovered at the edges of her vision. It seductively invited her to sink into its depths where she would be safe. She remembered how as a child she would squeeze her eyes tight shut and burrow down into her bedclothes to escape the notice of the monsters that prowled the night. In her waking hours, she would excise her demons through furious black and red crayon drawings, depicting them with swirling hair, jagged teeth and staring eyes. Her mother thought the drawings were meant to be the neighbour's dog Jester, but Jester was an affable and elderly beagle who spent more time asleep than he did awake. Jester was not the soil from which monsters sprouted. Prentiss' imagination was fertile enough. It needed no kickstart to breed its nightmares. She tried hard not to think about Sam up at the crime scene. She would send help as soon as she could. It was all she could do.

She was jolted by the elevator car coming to a stop and wondered briefly at a high-pitched sound she couldn't recognise. After a few seconds, she realised it was coming from her own throat, a childlike wail of dread. It stopped.

The door opened onto a smart, well-lit corridor and she gazed out at it with shocked familiarity. She was back in the real world once more, but she now understood how quickly reality could descend into horror. Reality was only skin deep; the nightmare was just a cold finger's touch away. The door began to slide, closing her in, and she scrabbled at it with a surge of adrenalized panic. She tumbled out into the corridor, gasping against a torrent of blinding shocks of pain.

She was close to surrendering to her injuries, close to allowing the pain to drown her body and carry her away on a wave of dark relief. Anything to get away from the agony. She wanted to let herself be sucked down into the liquid balm of oblivion. And death? *Death? NO!*

Dragging and clawing at the carpeted floor she pulled herself to the express elevator. It was still there in its cradle. She opened the door, fell in, and somehow pressed G. Everything around her had become remote, as if seen from far away through a thick, watery lens. The elevator began its arrow-like descent, and she gazed out at the sparkling, night-time cityscape of New York. Her eyesight was blurred. *Safe soon, safe soon, safe...*

Keeping pace with her descent she discerned the figure of Anubis poised just feet from her, floating the other side of the thick acrylic wall of the elevator. It regarded her with its ebon eyes and reached out a hand as if inviting her to join it, out in the open air. She began to scream. She was still screaming when the door opened onto the ground floor but she didn't notice. She was curled into a shrieking ball of outright panic on the floor. She also didn't hear the feet pounding to her side, but she was aware enough to fight the helping hands when they reached for her. She fought, but with all the strength of an exhausted kitten. *It had come for her. The monster had taken her in its grip and there was nothing more she could do. She had lost.* She felt herself being lifted and finally succumbed to despair. She stopped fighting. Her consciousness slipped away from her like a bead of failing light sliding down a greasy tunnel, deeper into torment. Then, at last she felt herself flow through the pain and she finally allowed herself to drown in the warm dark waters of blissful peace.

She began to die.

...

'We nearly lost you, too.'

Chief Lewis was looking a lot less haggard than during his previous visit. He had had over a fortnight to assimilate the facts about what had happened on the ninety-first floor of Center Heights, but at least he now knew he had a witness and a survivor of those dreadful events. Prentiss was finally off the endangered list. Her storm of grief had proved the turning point for her recovery, bringing a degree of physical strength back along with her memories.

He continued, 'You stopped breathing three times before they got you to the ambulance and the paramedics brought you back each time. You were unconscious in intensive care for four days before they felt confident enough to bring you to this room. You were smashed up real bad. They said it was like a series of explosions had gone off in that room, but there's no sign of any explosive devices. The gas people are shitting themselves in case they get the blame. They say they want to investigate to clear themselves, but we haven't let anyone near that floor. Not after what we found up there. No scorch marks, no blast radius, nothing. Nothing but the mystery of how eleven good people could be killed while you ended up looking like you'd been through a meat grinder.'

'How did Sam die?'

Lewis paused, then said, 'I'll tell you what I know, okay? We know there were twelve people on the scene. Feldman and his team, you, Sam, two uniforms and that poor bastard Forde. Then there were those unlucky guys with the coffee and doughnuts on the gurney. Talk about poor timing. God must have held a grudge against them for something. When back-up reached the scene after you came down they found five bodies and a slice out of the latest Anubis victim, Mrs Helene Craven. The rest of her was found next to a dumpster by garbage collectors the following morning. It was a real sorry day when that bastard killer started to target New York.'

'What about Sam?'

'I'm getting there. Please, let me tell this my own way. I told you about the explosions? Yes? Well they think some of people were near the windows when they blew out. They got thrown out by the force. We found the bodies in the grounds. They could only be identified by their personal belongings. I'm sorry Prentiss. I'm sorry. One of them was Sam Bolat.'

'She got blown out of a window? Oh, no... She hated heights. She was terrified of heights. Oh, Sam, what have I done to you? What have I done to you?'

Her grief was no longer a helpless torrent of emotions. It had become focused around the loss of her best friend and partner, the one person with whom she could share anything without expecting judgement. Her breath was tight in her chest, her voice cracked.

'What do you do, Chief, when the one person you need to talk to most is the one person you've lost? What do you do then? Where do you go?'

He sat on the bed and lay his arm around her shoulders, the most human contact she had ever had with her boss.

He said, 'I used to talk with my dad. Anytime I was in trouble or needed to work something out he was always there for me. He did more listening than talking. He died last year, his big old heart finally let him down. He was a wonderful man, I hope I can be just one tenth the man he was. I miss him.'

'So, who do you talk to now?'

He smiled and looked deep into her bruised eyes. 'I still talk with dad, and you know something? He don't say much but when he does he's still worth listening to. Don't let Sam's death come between you. She's still there for you.'

'You believe that?'

'Shit, yeah. If I didn't have dad to talk to I would have ended up talking to myself, and that would be crazy, you know?'

'Yeah, Chief, I know. Thanks.'

42

Her downstairs neighbour Laurie was in the lobby when she hobbled into her apartment building on crutches and he almost hadn't recognised her. After the second take he realised who he was looking at, rushed to her side, and took her bag from her.

'Prentiss, what happened? Were you in a car crash or something? My poor dear girl. Let's get you up to your apartment.'

'I'm fine, really.'

'Nonsense! There's two things I can't stand, bullshit and martyrs too far up their own asses to know when they need help. Cut the crap and let's get you upstairs, shall we.'

'Wait, my post. I've been away more than three weeks.'

'Hold it right there.'

He came back with a surprisingly small bundle and then called the elevator.

'You poor thing,' he said. 'What happened?'

'Sorry, Laurie. I was hurt as part of a police operation and there's an ongoing enquiry. I can't say anything about it. Not yet, anyway. You know what they say, I could tell you...'

'...But you'd have to shoot me.' He chuckled, 'The old ones are the best.'

'And that one's not even true. I promise you it's me who would get shot, not you. Here's the elevator.'

He stayed with her for the rest of the morning and on until late afternoon, only leaving her alone after getting her to write out a shopping list so he could fetch her some bags of groceries from the local store. He cleared out the soured milk, rotten salads, and vegetables from her refrigerator, threw away the remains of a spoiled bottle of wine he found in its door, then performed a fingertip search of her whole apartment to make sure nothing unwelcome had taken hold while she was away.

He explained, 'A pigeon got into my place while I was out one day. I stupidly left the window open, you know? I was only going to be out for a coupl'a hours. What's the worst that could happen? Stupid of me. Thank God, the creature was trapped in my bedroom. Who knows what a mess it would have made of my books. Turns my hair white to think of it. You can't imagine how so much shit can come out of something so small! It beggars belief. Took a full day to clean up the mess, once I'd got the beggar back out the window. Now I never leave the windows open when I go out. Never.'

After his salutary warning, he made sure she had his number before leaving her to her own devices.

'If you need me, call me, okay? Anytime, and I mean it. Wake me if you must. I'm only downstairs, I can be here in a coupl'a minutes.'

He gave her a tentative hug, as if he was worried he might do more damage if he squeezed too tight. Then he lightly brushed her cheek with his before letting himself out, pausing only to look at her from the doorway for a moment before leaving.

Sitting alone in her recliner Prentiss couldn't shake the feeling that her apartment felt strangely large and empty after her time in the single hospital room. During the latter stages of her recuperation she had been encouraged to get out into the grounds or visit the cafeteria – anything that got her out of bed – but she had still spent most of her time in that room. The doctors had sternly advised her to take it easy, telling her that her injuries had been life threatening and that she was not yet fully recovered. She was told she might have been better off if she'd been hit by a speeding car. They listed her injuries as if they were awards she had won. She had a compound fracture to the shaft of her left femur and a mid-shaft fracture to her right humerus, plus, broken ribs, internal bleeding, and a crack to her occipital bone; all of which had been exacerbated by her desperate struggle to reach the ground floor. The biggest danger had been caused by the amount of blood she had lost from the puncture wound in her thigh. She had required six transfusions of whole blood before she was stable enough for the team to start work on repairing the damage. She had not been declared as out of the danger zone until they were certain she wouldn't die from a blood clot, contract a dangerous infection, or develop pneumonia.

It had taken an hour to reset her thigh bone and repair the damage done to her muscle and skin. She would have a fine scar there for life. One of the doctors told her she had almost lost the leg – or at least the use of it – thanks to nerve damage. She had been lucky a world class specialist was visiting the hospital and on call when she needed treatment. With excessive zeal, her doctor had described how the original damage had been bad enough, but Prentiss had made it much worse by 'dragging her broken bones around like bricks in a sack'. The compound fracture in her leg had developed further complications due to the thighbone's 'torquey, spiracular movements through her torn flesh' when she was, as he described it 'throwing herself about and crawling around on the floor'. None of which he prescribed for a patient with broken limbs and a compound fracture. Before her nurse had finally told the men to 'go find another patient to bully, this girl's mine' one of the medics had even observed that the next time she decided to unscrew her leg she should call in an expert and not plump for the 'messy DIY option'. 'Why,' she was asked, 'hadn't she just stayed put and called for help?'

Prentiss had handed back some nonsense about 'Clearing the scene and warning colleagues about any potential threat to life being a police officer's first priority', but the fact was that she hadn't been thinking clearly. She had been dazed, terrified, badly injured, and wanted to get help for her team. She hadn't even considered calling for help, she just wanted to put as much space as she could between herself and that scene of horror on the ninety-first floor. In any case, although she didn't know it, every electrical device on the floor had been neutralised by the first blast of energy. They had been shut down as effectively as if they had been hit by an electro-magnetic pulse, one of the most notorious side-effects of a nuclear blast. But she had only discovered that well after the event from a bemused Chief Lewis.

'The more we discover about that evening's events the crazier and more complex it becomes. Of course, your report has been put under tight need to know authorisation until we get some handle on what really happened up there. If we accept your eye-witness account we must also accept that ten NYPD personnel and one civilian were killed during an attack by a powerful supernatural being. How would that look on the cover of the *New York Times*? "Ancient god slaughters New York's finest". "Central park hero only survivor of Egyptian god's wrath". I wake up sweating in the early hours, dreaming about the headlines. The commissioner wants an enquiry and he wants you to undergo a post traumatic psych evaluation. I've nixed that, of course. Told him that the specialists now say that evaluation and counselling too soon after trauma might be counterproductive, and that talking about it with strangers just reminds people about the terrible things they've been through and it makes the trauma worse. Yadda, yadda, yadda. Of course, he swallowed it hook, line and sinker. Remember that, you want to tell the commissioner something, bring in a bunch of facts from specialist advisors. He dearly loves a specialist.'

And now she was home with an inflated splint on her left thigh and another splint on her upper right arm. She had been told she would heal good as new and would be back at her desk within the month. However, she had also been taken off the Anubis case as an investigator. She was now a survivor and the only key witness to whatever had happened during that evening in the Manhattan skyrise called Center Heights.

She removed her splints and stripped naked in her bedroom, then using her crutches she hopped cautiously into her bathroom. She lingered over the sheer luxury of using her own toilet for the first time in far too long, and then she carefully wallowed in the warmth of her shower, attempting to wash the smell and taint of the hospital from her body and hair. The dressings on her thigh were modern and waterproof, but her ribs still caught at her if she moved too quickly and she frequently gasped with pain. No matter, she gritted her teeth and got on with it because to feel truly clean again made any agony worthwhile. The back of her right hand felt numb and there was an ongoing ache at the back of her head that painkillers couldn't touch, but when she felt the soapy, freshly scented water sluicing down her body and rinsing through her hair she almost wept with relief. Her time in the hospital had left a sticky residue that a single shower wouldn't budge, but she had taken her first step back to normality. In hospital, her body had belonged to the medical personnel. It was theirs' to prod and probe and examine whenever they chose. In the privacy of her shower, Prentiss was washing away every trace of their clinical invasion. Her flesh was her own once more.

She was in her panties, wearing a big tee, and pulling the splint back onto her thigh when her phone began to ring. It confused her for a few seconds and she looked around in alarm. *Her phone had been wrecked!* And then she remembered. She had left her personal phone at home and taken a precinct smartphone with her to the breakfast meeting with Sam, all those weeks before. It had been a recent initiative. Thirty-five thousand handheld devices had been issued to NYPD officers and they had all been told they were expected to use them. The one she had been allocated was a Samsung Galaxy S6 Active, a cell phone that had a precinct address book containing "useful addresses and contact details". She was told she could add "colleague's and immediate family details and nothing more". It was not to be used for social purposes. It normally remained in her drawer back in the office, but that day it had been in her bag. And it had been terminally fried along with every other item of electrical equipment on the ninety-first floor.

Before she could find it her phone stopped ringing. Cursing, she wracked her brains, and then realised she had left it on charge before leaving to meet Sam on that fateful morning. It was still on the work surface in her kitchen. She limped to where she had left it and unplugged it, blessing robust Apple technology all the while. Not surprisingly her phone was fully charged. She saw she had a vast number of missed calls. Scrolling down the list she saw that two names appeared more than any others. Howlett and Erskine, and the most recent caller was Howlett.

177

43

She jumped hard and winced with pain when her phone rang again while she was still gazing at it and musing about the wisdom of calling Howlett back. She looked at the name on the screen and reluctantly thumbed 'accept'.

'Hi, Gee, what's happening?'

'The meek and the good still have piss in their ears and dirt on their faces while the wicked eat foie gras at high table and laugh at the misfortunes of their betters. Such is the nature of our unbalanced world. Prentiss, my dear, I had to call you. How are you? And I was genuinely sorry to hear about Sam. I liked her, she was a good woman. Funny *and* smart, that's rare.'

Prentiss didn't ask how he knew. Erskine's grapevine was deep rooted and impossibly long.

She replied, 'And sexy. She'd never forgive you if you left out "sexy".'

'Of course, funny, smart, and sexy. Yes, all of that. Good call, well made.'

'Thank-you. Yes, Sam was the best, losing her bites deep. Her husband spent a long time trying to think of the best way to tell their twins that mommy can't come home now. He finally told them that baby Jesus needed someone to cuddle him and mommy was chosen because she's the best cuddle in the world. They pray every night now that baby Jesus will soon start feeling better so mommy can come home and cuddle them too.'

'If you want me to weep for them I shall.'

'I already cried an ocean of tears, for them and for me. You want to weep do it for Jock, her husband. He's got to be strong and keep smiling for the boys, and it's twisting his heart into little pieces. He could do with a prayer too.'

'Jock shall join my elite register of names when I'm next bothering the almighty. The list is short and distinguished, and you are very near the top. How are you, by the way? I heard you got badly mashed up in the... Ah, yes, "explosion" I believe they're calling it, for the moment.'

She plumped down on a stool by her breakfast bar. Her leg was aching too much to stand on it any longer. How was she? She felt exhausted and sore and her heart was gripped in a vice made from an alloy of anguish, pity, and deep-seated anger. She wanted to curl up in a ball and weep like a child, and she wanted something or someone to pay for what had happened. She lied.

'Yeah, I'm good. I won't be running any marathons anytime soon and I'm missing Sam like a lost limb, you know? But I'm alive so at least half the team is still here and still fighting that good fight.'

'Wish I believed you.'

'Yeah? Wish I did too.'

'Could you face dinner and a friendly face to talk to? Has to be better than listening to a disembodied voice on a cell phone. I can get a cab to you in half an hour, give you time to get ready. We can go somewhere quiet where we can talk, it might even be therapeutic. What do you say?'

'I say thank-you, really, thanks very much, but can I take a rain check for a couple of days? I'm only just home and I'm still hurting. I need to rest and heal more than I need to talk. Do you mind?'

'I may be an old barbarian but I still have some social graces. I mind but I fully understand.'

Prentiss heard her entry-phone system buzz.

'Have to go, there's someone at the door.'

'Ah, good,' he said enigmatically. 'I'll see you soon.'

He hung up and she hobbled to the door. She took up the handset.

'Hello?'

The usual pause, and then a voice echoed her, 'Hello?'

'Yes, hello, what do you want?'

'Delivery for Miss Prentiss, apartment 204.'

'I haven't ordered anything.'

'I don't know about that, Miss. I just make the deliveries and they don't pay me by the hour, they pay me per item. Can I bring this up?'

'Second floor and turn left from the elevator. I'll be waiting.'

She buzzed him through then donned her most concealing robe before opening her front door.

She was leaning on her crutch and wishing she'd taken another brace of painkillers when the elevator door opened to reveal a bouquet of flowers the size of a mature shrub. It was two thirds the height of a tall man. The courier was completely shielded by the display but she could see he also had a bottle of champagne in his left hand. She felt momentarily giddy, almost faint. *What was she going to do with that giant bunch of blooms?*

'Miss Prentiss?'

'Over here. Wait a second.'

She hobbled back into her apartment and dug out her purse, then pulled out a ten-dollar note. She returned to the door and took the flowers in her numb right arm and held out the money in her left

'I'm sorry, I've only got a ten, I hope that's all right?'

As soon as he appeared from behind the bouquet Howlett grinned, 'Thanks for the offer but I'd happily settle for a glass of this champagne, it's still nicely chilled.'

She barely stopped herself from screaming in shock. His grin disappeared as quickly as it had materialised.

'What happened to you? Girl, you look like you've been in a train wreck. Is this why you haven't been answering your phone? I was getting worried but I didn't imagine *this*.'

He took her flowers and put them to one side, then he put his arm around her shoulders and guided her to her recliner. Only once she was seated did he hustle the wine into her chill cabinet and then hurry over to shut the front door. He lifted the bouquet in both arms and carried it through into her living room. After a moment's consideration, he placed it carefully in a corner where it was out of the way but could still be seen to the best effect. Prentiss made as if to get to her feet and he reached out with both hands to press her back.

'Where do you think you're going, lady?'

'I need to get a vase for the flowers, or at least two. I've only got two.'

'No way, and anyway, no need. Whoever ordered them knew what they were doing. They're already in a water-filled bag, see?'

She squinted at the bouquet. 'Oh, yeah! Isn't that clever.' Then she replayed what he had just said. 'Wait, didn't you order them?'

'Me? No. I met the delivery guy downstairs and asked who the flowers were for. I was pretty certain I already knew the answer, so when he told me I explained I was on my way up and could save him some time. Signed for them and the champagne, and gave him a tip. Then I pressed the buzzer and here we are. Shall I look for the card?'

'No, no need. They're probably from my parents or the precinct. They're the only people who know I'm back home.' *Or Gee Erskine,* she thought, remembering his 'Ah, good' on the phone earlier.

'How much did you tip the guy? I should reimburse you.'

'Forget it. Anyway, so, what did happen to you? And where have you been?'

Prentiss told him about the 'explosion' and about her tough time in hospital. He took her right hand in both of his and then dropped it like a hot coal when she winced. She waved away his apologies and told him the arm was mending well but her hand still felt weird and numb.

He looked at his watch. 'I was going to suggest dinner at Enzo's, but he'd probably take one look at you and come at me with a meat cleaver. I should leave you to rest. I tried to ring first but... well, you know the rest. How a girl who's been through what you've been through can still look this good is amazing, but you look tired. I'm being selfish. You stay there, I'll see myself out.'

He bent to kiss her, then hesitated, 'Is this okay? I mean, are your lips all right?'

She grinned and leaned towards him, but the action stretched her damaged thigh and the sudden jolt of pain tore a yelp of agony from her. Howlett stepped back.

'I guess that answers that question. Let's make up for it another day, okay?'

She nodded. He kissed her forehead and then her cheek. A few moments later she heard her front door closing. She got to her feet and leaned on her crutch, then looked around to make sure she was truly alone. Her apartment rang with empty silence. The flowers looked good where Howlett had left them. They could stay there. She turned off the lights and prepared for bed. She was hungry, but too tired to bother with food. She grabbed some chilled mineral water from her ice box and drank it greedily, leaving the remainder of the bottle on her bedside cabinet. She dropped her robe on the end of her bed and gingerly lay down. She thought pain would keep her awake but exhaustion got the better of pain. She slept. And opened her eyes to a bloated, blood red sun.

44

She forced herself to relax during her brief journey towards and then into the floating city. Pain was a constant companion here as it was back in New York, which didn't surprise her. This was only a dream, and pain was real, even in one's sleep. The familiar wall of yearning fronds reached out for her and wrapped her in gentle bondage. She waited for the quiet, dry voice to speak, but at first it remained silent. The pressure exerted by the fronds began to peak. They pressed hardest against the areas where she had been most badly injured. In her mind, she began to shriek with pain and horror but no sound escaped her compressed lips except a whining groan.

She felt the fronds pierce her body, felt them enter her with inexorable force. She imagined herself being violated simultaneously by a thousand creatures, each of which was driving its own passage into her body, screwing itself deep into her flesh. Her mind fluttered at the edge of sanity but could find no escape. She felt herself to be utterly invaded.

She uttered a mental whimper. *Why are you doing this to me?*

Its voice was gentle. 'I would not have had this happen. I promise you, I would not have had this happen. I know, I remember, I said that to you then, but had you really taken away all my choices? I think not, and I choose what I do now. Please, Prentiss, relax, be still. You must let me work. I know it feels strange. Perhaps you should sleep. Yes, sleep.'

Oblivion. Deep oblivion. Pierced only with the piquant sensation that subtle fingers were playing her nervous system like a harp, tuning her to perfection. Each pluck on her strings created acute, razor sharp pain. In front of her dreaming eyes a glittering gold ring hovered against a formless, inky background. She was floating in a place without dimension except for that slim gold ring. Every tug of pain elicited a sound. The sound was harmonious and bright, it conflicted with the pain and lessened it. The sound came from the gold circle, which twitched every time it resonated as if it had been plucked by invisible fingers. The process settled into a routine: pain, sound, pluck, repeat, pain, sound, pluck, repeat, in an endless cycle. After a measureless age, she realised the circle had begun to spin with hypnotic slowness, and then it began to roll, flipping gently end over end. Prentiss slipped into a mindless reverie. All pain had ceased, all thought quieted, yet still there remained a sense of expectation. Something was coming. Something important. Her heartbeat quickened.

The centre of the flickering ring filled with light and something moved there. The rolling motion slowed and stopped. Against a background of stars Prentiss saw a naked woman with her arms outspread and her legs open wide, bent slightly at the knee. The point of view closed in on the woman's face where Prentiss saw beauty and wisdom. The universe was reflected in her dark eyes, which were framed with gold.

In her mind, a steady voice told her that this was Nut, the sky goddess, and the protector of Earth from the chaos of the universe.

'She is the cloak against the storm. The mother and protector of the souls of the recent dead. She was known and worshipped as a force for good in the pre-dynastic periods of ancient Egypt. She touched the consciousness of mankind much earlier than that. Now, watch...'

With languid interest Prentiss watched the image change in the ring. The sweet features remained the same but the face broadened out and swelled until the eyes, nose and mouth were lost in a pale, moonlike orb of a head. She was now looking at someone barely recognisable as the goddess, but she knew who the woman was. It was Aliya Petrus.

The voice asked, 'Do you understand?'

'I do.'

'Good, and now...'

The picture swirled and dissolved into a flat field of wan silver light. Then like an old photographic print developing Prentiss saw another three-dimensional figure rise to her view. This was a fine bodied, tan skinned man. He was naked apart from a blue and white skirt. On his head sat the crown of the Upper and Lower Nile. His head was that of a noble falcon.

Her guide continued. 'This is Horus, he who sees. His right eye is the sun and his left the moon. He is the god of the sky and is said to be the son of the sky goddess Nut and her husband Geb, the Earth. Horus sees all and knows all. He is one of the most ancient of all the deities. The pharaohs claimed to be personifications of him, and, in fact, some of them were. Later myths would claim he was the son of Isis and Osiris. However, his storyline is older than either of those more recent deities. He brought peace to the world when he vanquished the original figure of terrible evil, the god Seth. Horus was worshipped as a great force working for good, and is recognised as one of the founders of true civilisation. Like Nut, his true name pre-dates the earliest Egyptian dynasties. Now, watch...'

The point of view closed in on the falcon's head. It turned to face her. Its gold rimmed, black eyes glittered with arch yet warm intelligence. This time the transformation was less dramatic. By the time the bird's face had become that of Gee Erskine, Prentiss could still clearly discern the hawk-like characteristics stamped onto his chiselled features, lean and high cheek-boned. Mischievous warmth still shone from his fine eyes. He smiled and she felt a thrill of intense attraction flutter through her detached body, greater than she ever had in his physical presence.

The voice once again asked, 'Do you understand?'

'I do.'

'Very good. And now the final reveal.'

Trepidation trembled in the pit of Prentiss' disconnected belly. She was certain she knew what she was about to discover. If she had control of her eyes she would have closed them. She didn't want to see Howlett's face in the ring.

Erskine's features dissolved back into the flat disc of gold rimmed silver light. The bland surface quivered as if something swam just under its skin, but nothing else happened for an interminable age. Then finally a familiar silhouette developed within the fine gold ring and she was looking once more at the figure of Anubis. She thought the god of the underworld looked more magisterial than its fellows; it radiated dignified majesty. It gazed directly at her with imperious eyes. She barely listened while her guide took her through the god's attributes. She knew them almost by heart. Instead she studied the long, muzzled face to see if she could pick out anything that reminded her of Tabaqui Howlett. It was impossible. With Horus she could discern Erskine, and Aliya Petrus' drowned features were identical to those of Nut, however buried they were in layers of pallid fat. Anubis was an enigma, a midnight rebus worshipped from the time before the first pyramid, yet born billions of years in the future, just before the Earth had finally been snuffed from the sky. The voice ended its recital, which seemed to have taken more time than the other two put together. There was a pause before her point of view was brought close to Anubis' features. They gazed into each other's eyes with an air of relaxed familiarity. The jackal god's achromatic regard almost seemed to reach out and touch the very edges of her consciousness, she felt its gentle brush against her mind, like lips caressing. And she thought of Howlett.

The transformation began. The long snout shrank back and the spear point ears shrivelled and became more rounded. Her guide's voice made Prentiss jump.

'A common mistake has been to think of Anubis only as a jackal. He *can* manifest as a jackal, and has done so on many occasions, as you are aware, but his first worshippers knew him as a powerful, grey wolf.'

184

A lean face topped with a shock of dark hair was slowly becoming defined in the ring. Every passing second the regal hound melted away and the man took its place. And then, at last, there he was, and there was no mistaking the leonine features of the man she knew so well. Gazing at her from the circle of gold was the calm, wise face of New York City's Police Commissioner, Randall A. Highview. The very same man who had shaken her hand and congratulated her so warmly when handing over her police badge on that parade ground, on the proud day she had graduated from the academy seven years before.

45

The revelations were done and she was free once more, drifting above the rippling fronds in the floating city. This time she had not been sent straight back to her sleeping form in New York. This time she was held in suspension above the white, coral-like structure.

The voice spoke to her. 'Have you any more questions before you return?'

'What can I do about Anubis in my time? What did I do, can you remember?'

'We do not know. It is too long ago. Many of the things we saw in your mind that you take for granted are a complete mystery to us. We cannot advise you, the choices are yours to make. You might still let him complete his mission. The things his "victims" did still colour our minds after all this time, they were foul creatures best forgotten. And there will be other "victims" to be judged for a long time after he has finished in New York and left "your time". Listen to me, you have me thinking in quotes. His prey are not victims, any more than that man you shot in Central Park was a victim. They are criminals to be judged and sentenced as a lesson to others who might consider undertaking similar crimes. No-one should be allowed to take pleasure from the pain, destruction or humiliation of innocence.'

'Why did he kill my colleagues in Center Heights? Why did he nearly kill me? We had done nothing to deserve that. My friend died screaming while she fell more than ninety floors. Is that *judgement*?'

The voice was silent as if considering its answer. Then, when it spoke once more it sounded sad and tired.

'We feel your pain. It touches us most profoundly. Their deaths were the result of a terrible accident. We were with them for every single second of their last moments. Their memory lives on in us. We are devastated by the event.'

'It was an accident?'

'Yes. You should not have been there. None of you should have been there. He thought the place was empty. His translations from one place to another, from one time to another, take place through the time vortex that links this city to the earliest days of Earth. Such movement requires a distortion in time and space that creates a powerful localised gravity pulse, harmless in most cases when the site is empty, or the translation is for him alone. It becomes deadly when he brings another with him. That is why he chose Center Heights as his place of judgement. That is why he translated those he had judged to a quiet place where he kept his vehicle, and then drove them to the sites where he abandoned them. He wanted to protect the innocent from the great power he wields. We're sorry. It was an accident. A regretful accident.'

'And why does he strip them naked from the waist down?'

'Such a display exposes the criminal to two things, ridicule and the visible manifestation of that which led to their punishment. People like you will ask that very question and start digging. One day the truth of their terrible crimes will be discovered. Even posthumous revelations of evildoing can prove very effective assassins of a previously respected and unsullied character. Anubis' judgement protects more innocents from potential harm. If many people suffer from food poisoning – all after eating at the same restaurant – do you simply keep treating the symptoms or do you do something about the cook? You know the answer. Anubis removes the cause of the problem the way you removed that gunman in the park.'

'That gunman was a clear and present danger to other people, and anyway, I acted in self-defence.'

'Is that why you left your medal in a drawer the whole time you were in hospital? Is that why it is now hidden on a shelf in your wardrobe? You don't seem very proud of your bravery that day.'

Momentarily the statement disarmed her. 'I... I... No... No, you're right. I'm not proud. I was doing what I'm trained and get paid to do. Any officer on the scene would have done the same. Why reward me for doing my job?'

'You saved lives that day. The medal reflects that. Anubis also saves lives. Why must you stop him from saving others?'

Prentiss voice lashed out. 'Because he's fallible. Because he makes mistakes. Because he acts like a god but he fucked up and killed my friends. Because he's not a god, and neither is he an authorised officer of the law. I have the list of his victims, and yes, that's what they are, and yes, I know what they're doing. I'm going to get the evidence I need to stop their filthy games. I'm going to stop them and I'm going to put them behind bars where they belong. You know why? Because I have a badge that says that in *my* city *I* am the law, not some fucking werewolf from the future. Do *you* understand?'

'Yes, Prentiss. Yes, we understand.'

'Is he here? Is Anubis here? Can he hear me? Anubis, are you here? What are you now? What has life on Earth become for you? COME ON, TELL ME!'

The voice whimpered. 'Please, your anger is very painful to us. Please.'

'Then answer me! Come on, Anubis! Show me what you are now, come on, SHOW ME!'

Her answer was silence, but something in the fronds shifted. Rich colour flowed through them in waves. She was reminded of the bioluminescence she had seen demonstrated by sea creatures in TV documentaries. She heard a sound like a great sigh and the walls of the city moved gently apart. She could see the blood red light of the sun wash through the gaps in the architecture, which moved smoothly apart and then reformed as eight monolithic forms pierced with intricate lacework. She recognised the atomic structure style of art she had seen long ago in Mesopotamia, but now it was much richer and even more delicate. Beads of bright blue light streamed around the shapes in a way that looked to Prentiss like thought made visible. It was difficult to judge their size. Against the impossible landscape of the roasted planet there was nothing to offer her any sense of scale, but, she estimated, each monolith must have been anything up to a thousand feet high or more. She realised she was surrounded by eight flying mountains, and they began rotating around her like an impossible carousel. The anger in her melted into awe and her mind became numb. When confined within the city she had felt as if she still had some tenuous grip on her environment. Within the confines of the city she still had walls and floors and ceilings around her and those gave her a sense of dimensions she could relate to. No matter how alien they had seemed she had felt protected. Her mind tried to analyse everything around her now and succeeded only in feeling diminished. She felt faint and sick.

One of the eight throbbed with light. A fresh voice spoke to her.

'We are the Ogdoad, the council of the last eight on Earth. I am that from which an echo will manifest as Anubis in the distant past. By the time that manifestation reaches your city, law-giver Prentiss, I will know no more about its motivations than I do about the motivations of a tree. It will have been layered by its time amongst men, changed into the wolf judge and executioner of legend. It will no longer be part of the Ogdoad, but will have become its own creature. You must do as you think best, law-giver Prentiss, and all here wish you well. You will not be invited to return to this place again. Once you are gone we will close the vortex and end our time on Earth. We realise we have been too close to midnight for too long. It is our time to rest and meet the promise of an afterlife. But understand this. Anubis is long-lived, he is an ancient and cunning executioner. With the vortex closed he will no longer be able to translate from one time and space to another, meaning he can no longer kill the innocent by accident, but he will still be able to shape-shift. And he will not surrender his mission easily. We wish you good luck, law-giver, and bid you farewell.'

The incredible scene faded to darkness and Prentiss slept like a child at last, pain-free, and whole once more.

46

When she strode into the precinct the next morning every eye followed Prentiss' lithe form. There was no hint of any of the horrific injuries her fellow officers in the forty-second precinct had been told about. They had heard she had been close to opening death's door and that skilled surgeons had spent hours patching her together. Rumour said she had almost lost a leg, and that her face looked as if someone had spent several hours trying to demolish her luminous beauty with a baseball bat. They had been told she was badly crippled, had been signed off for a month, and unlikely to return to anything more than a sedate desk job or, more likely, get pensioned off on a 'medical'.

The slender figure striding through the glazed partitioning towards her desk looked as if she had spent the last month training for the Olympics. She radiated strength, good health, and energy. Her coltish, long-legged pace held no sign of a faltering limp, and her expression was that of an angry woman filled with implacable resolve.

Fats Morten looked up when she stalked into their office and his jaw swung open like a trapdoor. He didn't respond to her 'Morning, Fats' because he couldn't believe his eyes. Unlike many others in the precinct he had found the time to visit Prentiss in her sick bed. On the one hand, he believed himself a good friend as well as a colleague, and on the other, hospitals didn't intimidate him the way they did some others. He had seen Prentiss the previous week when she was already said to be 'on the mend', but looked like road kill. It was his highly graphic descriptions of her parlous state that had fuelled the disbelieving stares she was getting that morning. He gaped at her when she hooked her coat onto the rack and then settled down in her seat before firing up her computer. Other members of the precinct found reasons to sidle up and get a better look at the Lazarus woman who they knew had recently returned from a near death incident – and yet now looked like a poster girl for drop dead gorgeous.

'Hey, Fats,' she said after collecting four freshly printed and stapled sheets of paper from the photocopier. 'What's the status on the jackal killings. Have there been any more since I've been... away?'

Morten looked to be on the point of swallowing his tongue. He blinked in confusion and kept looking her up and down. She looked better than new.

'You look great,' he said in a strangled voice. 'You taking some new tonic or sump'n? How come you're here? I saw you, just last week... I mean, you were... It's like, *no way!*' The normally loquacious man was lost for words.

Chief Lewis stormed into the room. 'I saw her too. What are you doing here, Prentiss? You should be convalescing at home, you...'

His voice trailed away when he saw Prentiss standing straight and true as an athlete. He too looked her over in confusion.

'Prentiss? How... how are you feeling?'

'Morning, Chief. Yes, I feel fine. Keen to get on with the job. Who's my new partner? Am I working with Fats here, or have you got someone else in mind?'

Lewis and Morten looked enquiringly at each other, and then back at Prentiss. Lewis dragged a hand across his astonished face, gestured she should wait for him, and then wordlessly stepped outside to fetch a cup of water from the cooler. He was confronted by a stream of people, all whispering urgent questions at him, but all he could do was shrug and shake his head without offering any reply. He downed two cups full of icy water but found no refreshment in the liquid. His head was buzzing.

When he returned to her office he discovered Prentiss standing by Morten's desk making ticks on a list.

She frowned at him. 'The jackal's been busy. Six more down. All the same M.O. Where's his kill zone now? It can't still be the Heights, that site's busted. Where's he killing them now? Do we know?'

Lewis answered through gritted teeth. 'We're no further along now than we were before Center Heights. We lost Feldman and most of his team in that operation, plus we lost Sam Bolat, and, damn it, we nearly lost you. We aren't big enough to take that kind of hurt and roll with it. So, forget it, Prentiss, the case has gone elsewhere, and that's where you should be. I don't know what wonder drug you took to get yourself in here but I suggest you take some more and get yourself back home.' He continued expounding his theme despite the evidence to the contrary in front of his eyes. 'You took a tough pounding, and I don't want you putting yourself back into intensive care because you're too proud or stubborn to admit it.'

'But, Chief...'

He grabbed her coat and handed it to her. 'If you're not out of here in five minutes I'll let you rest up in the holding cells, okay? Now, please, I'll ask nice. Get out before you pass out.'

Her face burning with barely supressed anger Prentiss took the long walk towards the exit and the precinct parking garage. Despite her fury she had to smile briefly when one of the female uniforms said in an audible whisper,

'Whatever it takes to look that good and still get sent home sick, man, order me a case full. I'm willing to take the risk.'

The woman by her side agreed, 'I'll take a bucketful. Hubba, hubba.'

As soon as she was behind the wheel of her car Prentiss took a moment to calm down, and then thumbed a number into her cell phone. A tired sounding voice answered.

'Hello?'

'Hi, Gee, it's me, Prentiss. Can you spare me a few minutes?'

'Prentiss? You sound very lively. Why are you so lively?'

'I can explain when I see you. Gee, please, this is urgent.'

'I'm at home. When shall I expect you?'

'Give me twenty minutes. I'm on my way now.'

'I'll be waiting.'

The hawk-like bald man hugged her when she stepped out of the elevator. Then he held her at arm's length to give her a thorough examination.

'What happened to you? You look great. I thought you were all smashed up.'

'I met the Ogdoad, the final Council.'

'I know them. They healed you?'

'Yes. I didn't know what they'd done until I woke up this morning. I've never felt better.'

'Good, that's good. I'm glad for you. What now? What can I do for you?'

'Gee, I need your help.' She pulled out the list of potential victims she had printed back at the precinct. 'There's just two names left on this list, Anubis has judged all the others, they're dead. This is a roll call of the damned if ever there was one. Every one of these people is a sickening psycho and they've been getting away with what they've been doing for years. But even so, it isn't for Anubis to judge them. He's not the law in New York, he's a vigilante murderer, and I have to stop him before he kills again.'

'What's this got to do with me?'

She had never heard Erskine's voice so flat. She realised that his fine eyes looked shadowed and dull. She ploughed on regardless.

'These last two people. Today's Monday and Anubis strikes on a Monday, the day after the Sabbath. He rests on the Sabbath. I'm willing to bet one of these people will die tonight at eight o'clock. Which one will it be?' She held up the list. 'We've got Connor Greenman, celebrated dwarf actor, philanthropist and playwright. He sponsors a puppet theatre for disadvantaged children, which gives him access to his favourite prey, wheelchair-bound kids with learning difficulties. And then we have Marion

Strawpenny, a fine piece of work. A spinster of this parish, she is most noted for her charity dinners; fundraising initiatives on behalf of the most undernourished children in Africa, especially in places like Somalia and Tanzania. She's worked shoulder to shoulder with some of the most respected legitimate charities in the world. And all the while she's head of a vile organisation involved in trafficking the sweetest youngsters to a life of prostitution and slavery in some of the richest countries in the world, including right here in the States. So, the question is, which one will Anubis target tonight?'

Erskine regarded her with a distraught expression. 'Prentiss, I can't help you.'

'Can't or won't?'

'I can't! You see, since late last night I've become blind.'

[47]

'I don't mean that I can't see you, or that I can't see right across Central Park if I want to. But I can't *see* anymore. I'm blind like you, like everyone else in the world. The unique sight that made me Horus, the gift that made me "he who sees", it's gone. I can't see the secret places anymore, Prentiss. I don't know any more about those people than you've already got written on that list. Shit, I used to be so clever, so fucking smug. Not anymore. Aliya's in the same position too. She rang me. Since last night she can't be sure that day's going to follow night, or night follow day. Her prescient vision is completely gone. She's all alone in her head now too. Yesterday she was an oracle speaking in tongues but now she's just a sad fat girl living in a shitty dump in the Projects.'

'What about Randall Highview?'

Erskine started as if he'd been struck. 'How? Randall? You know? When did you find out?'

'Last night, not long before you went blind and Aliya found herself alone. I know what happened and why. The vortex is gone, Gee. The city is ended, and the Ogdoad have finally gone to their rest. It's finished, it's all over.'

He prowled around her like a caged beast, then turned upon her with a snarl.

'Then WHY? What happened? What changed everything?'

Prentiss remained cool, 'I did, I happened. I gave them the facts. Because of me the Ogdoad learned the truth, and they couldn't live with it. I told them how Anubis had made mistakes – and because of his mistakes he killed my friends. He acted like a god, but gods don't have fatal accidents. The Ogdoad saw the truth of that. They saw the truth, that – thanks to Anubis thrashing around trying to save the world from the so-called Butterfly Effect – they had set a pair of wings flapping that would *cause* Armageddon, not stop it. And it's not just Anubis who's at fault. What about you, Gee? You're out there dishing the dirt on celebrities as if you've never done a wrong thing in your life, but what about you? Are you so squeaky clean? Anubis pulled the trigger – but who aimed the gun? You gave him the same list you gave me, didn't you? And then you packed him off to murder the bad guys like a good little soldier. And you didn't need to see me to know about me, did you? Aliya saw me in her crystal ball or her bowl of ink or whatever she uses. She saw me on Anubis' trail and she warned you, so you sent me little messages that showed up in my books, on my tablet and on TV. They were worded like warnings, but they were all meant to put me off the scent. The pair of you have blood on your hands. You're as guilty for Sam's death as the jackal itself. Well, now it's over. Your home city is destroyed, and all your special gifts are gone. And you want to know something? The Ogdoad described all of you as "echoes". Tell me, how long does an echo last when the original voice is still? I think you're all just people now, people just like me, so welcome to *my* world, Gawain Erskine. I wonder how long you'll survive here.'

She turned to leave, and Erskine gazed resolutely at the floor. She called the elevator and stood tensely waiting with her back to him. She could feel the tension building in the room like water coming to the boil in a kettle. Any moment he might attack. The elevator door opened and she stepped inside, then turned around to face him. The door began to close and then at the last moment Erskine lunged forward, his teeth bared. He forced the door open.

He spat the words like bullets, 'Strawpenny! He's going after Strawpenny. Look, I'm sorry about Sam, I truly am. Good luck, Prentiss.'

He stepped back and the door slid shut, shutting him away in his solitary, luxury world. Prentiss' last view of him was his face crumpled with despair. She allowed herself a deep breath and relaxed. She had fully expected him to attack her. She wondered if she would ever see him again, and whether she wanted to. Whether she cared.

Back in her car she pondered her next move. Should she make an appointment to see Highview or Strawpenny? Neither, it was lunchtime and she was famished. She drove to the deli where she and Sam had enjoyed their last breakfast together. She packed away a jaw-breakingly large, hot salt beef sandwich on freshly baked sourdough, spiked with piquant yellow mustard, and chased by delicious coffee. Life for a simple human might be tough, she mused, but it tasted wonderful. She gazed through the deli window from which she had a fine view across the busy street. She was just in time to see Benjamin Addams returning from his day's errands. She watched him continue his race against death as he scampered past the undertakers pushing his shopping bag on wheels, and it brought a warm smile to her face. *You keep running, Mr Addams,* she thought. *You run as hard as you can.*

Highview was unavailable, which didn't surprise her, but Marion Strawpenny said she would be free for a few hours after five o'clock. She lived alone in a converted loft in what had once been a late nineteenth century bakehouse in Prospect Heights. It took a while for Prentiss to find a parking garage, but she managed to present herself at the woman's entry-phone grill just fifteen minutes later than her predicted arrival time. She was

195

buzzed straight in and found herself entering a well-lit lobby. Broad stairs led up on the left-hand side and jinked right at the top to a formidable looking door. It swung open silently just as Prentiss was about to rap on it with her knuckles. Strawpenny grinned.

'Officer Prentiss? Really? What a surprise, you are not what I expected from NYPD, aren't you a honey! Come in, come in. Don't you just love my door? I bought it at an auction, isn't it marvellous? It used to be the door to a bank vault in London city, England. It's Victorian, and it has sixteen bolts, four to each side, all operated by a single central key,' she held up an ornate and complex looking length of steel that could have almost been a piece of expensive jewellery. 'When a girl lives alone she needs a good door between her and the outside world. When I shut this door and lock it I'm sealed away tighter than the Queen of England's crown jewels. Come in and get safe, it's a madhouse out there.'

Prentiss could easily see how the charismatic woman had become such a popular personality in New York's philanthropic circles. She had reached her early fifties without resorting to Botox or any obvious plastic surgery, and her boyish cap of dark blonde hair looked natural. Her make-up was minimal to the point of being non-existent, and her figure was feminine and slender without being fashionably anorexic. She wore a simple tee over cargo pants rolled up to mid-calf, and the ensemble was finished with flat, woven leather sandals that Prentiss knew to be expensive but they didn't flaunt it. Her only accessory was a red coral necklace with a silver centrepiece. Strawpenny smiled and her face took on an impish air.

'Do I pass muster? Am I ready for my close-up Mr DeMille? I feel like I've just been x-rayed. Please, come right in officer Prentiss, get comfortable. Can I get you a drink? It's a little early for the evening I know, but I'm just having a late *lunchtime* vodka and tonic. Puts a little sparkle in the day.'

Prentiss was surprised to hear her own voice answer, 'That would be lovely, please, Ms Strawpenny.'

'Marion, my dear. And what shall I call you?'

'Prentiss is fine, thanks, Marion.'

She accepted her drink and an invitation to enjoy a quick tour of the loft. Strawpenny took great pleasure in pointing out original features, and others that looked authentic but were, in fact, later introductions.

'You see that mantel shelf? It looks like a nice nineteenth century beam of polished timber, yes? Looks right at home there doesn't it? But no, oh no. I got that beam from a place called Nantwich in the north of old England. That beam comes from one of the ships of the Spanish Armada, sunk by a great storm – and Sir Francis Drake – during the reign of the first Queen Elizabeth in fifteen eighty-eight. I get a kind of electric shock when I touch something that has survived part of the world's most iconic history, do you know what I mean?'

'Well, yes, I do.' Prentiss reached out and stroked the smooth wood. She felt a tingle and shivered.

Strawpenny chuckled, 'Listen to us chat away like old friends. What must you think of me? A flighty old bird who can't stop yammering away. I'm not a complete airhead, I promise you. Now, what can I do for you, Prentiss? Ask away, I'm yours for another,' she looked at her watch, 'just under two hours. And then I must get my war paint on for my seven-thirty date. I do hate to be late, don't you?'

Prentiss nodded, 'I know exactly what you mean. May I be rude and ask who you're meeting this evening?'

'You're not rude, not at all, but promise me, you won't tell the media or post it anywhere. Cross my heart there's nothing scandalous going on, ha, I wish. It's just a perfectly chaste and friendly private conversation with your boss, that gorgeous man Randall Highview.'

Prentiss flinched and said, 'You mustn't go. Your life is in danger if you keep that date with Highview, Marion. You must break it. I mean it. If you go to meet him you will die.'

48

Strawpenny frowned. 'Neither of us is laughing, Prentiss. You're not even smiling. What on Earth are you saying and why the hey should I believe you?'

'Marion, this is going to be hard to believe but you must listen to me. Your life depends on it. Highview's a killer, and that's a stone fact. He's been murdering high society philanthropists, people like you, for the last few months. His kill total to date is eleven, and all the bodies have been found half-naked and dumped in alleyways or on waste ground. All of them have identical mutilations, and all of them have been killed for the same reasons. You fit his criteria to a T, and I know Highview plans to kill again tonight. If you meet with him you will not survive the meeting.'

'What criteria? What the hell have I done? Heck, listen to me. What am I saying? Look, honey, I've known Randall for years. He's a lovely, gentleman, and he's always been a great supporter of my work. Why should he suddenly turn into an axe murderer or whatever it is you're telling me? Can you explain that? Keep it simple, honey, I'm hard of thinking.'

Prentiss paused, temporarily stumped for words. Strawpenny had a valid point. She herself had known Highview since entering the police academy over seven years before. He was a highly respected figure in the police community, a man regarded as the perfect role model for aspiring law officers. Why should he suddenly start slaughtering people? He wouldn't, not even the kind of scum she had found on Erskine's list. What had been the trigger that turned a good man into a cold killer? She gazed at Strawpenny with increased respect.

'That's a good question. That's a very good question. Is there somewhere here I can make a private phone call? I'll only be a few minutes I promise. Is that okay?'

'Sure, stay here. I'll go make us some coffee. How do you take it?'

As soon as she was alone she called Erskine. He answered on the third ring. There was no preamble. 'Prentiss, what did you forget?'

'I've got a question for you. Highview started killing his victims over a month ago, but why start now? Why is he doing it now? He's lived in New York forever, so, what started him killing these people? What was the trigger? Are you involved?'

'You worked it out, did you? I wondered when that would happen. Very well, he started because I activated him. The time was right because all the names on my list were in town and within reach. Like all of us he was born human, but what you call his Anubis "echo" was there inside him all along. He didn't suspect a thing until I triggered his switch. Of course, the Anubis echo has always affected him in many ways, not least it made him passionate about the law, and that easily led him along his career path to become the Commissioner of police. In fact, he's one of the most respected and admired men to ever hold that position and none of that will change. Once he's finished what he must do he will forget everything he's done and he'll get on with his life just as before, but until then he's highly dangerous. He'll strain every fibre of his being to complete his mission; Strawpenny must die and then Greenman, and if you try to stop him Anubis will destroy you too. I really don't think you have a chance, unless...'

Marion Strawpenny brought a tray into the room, saw Prentiss was still on the phone and mouthed, 'Oops, forgot the milk and cookies.' She crept back into the kitchen and shut the door behind her.

'Unless what?'

'Prentiss, listen closely to everything I have to say. It may be your only hope.'

She held her breath and concentrated. 'Go on.'

Erskine then spoke to her in a language she didn't recognise, but that somehow seemed familiar. It sounded as if he was chanting an ancient ritual. She thought she recognised one word that sounded like 'Amun' at the end, but none of the others made sense. When he had completed his string of strangely evocative sounds Erskine whispered, 'Prentiss, I am so, so sorry,' and hung up. Prentiss looked at her phone in confusion for a second, and then, as if she had had been clubbed from behind, she collapsed in a boneless heap on the floor. Everything in her mind had become ominously dark and still, except that somewhere in the distance she could still hear a lone voice monotonously repeating Erskine's evocation.

Her face felt suddenly cold and wet. She gasped and her eyes fluttered open to find Strawpenny crouched over her with a bowl of water and a facecloth, which she was dabbing frantically at her brow and cheeks.

Strawpenny looked closely into her eyes. 'Honey, if you're trying to freak me out you're succeeding in bundles. How're you feeling? You just collapsed for a moment, are you okay? Do you need a doctor? Have you got medication you should be taking? What is it?'

Prentiss sat up and water dripped onto the front of her blouse. Strawpenny had obviously been very busy with her damp facecloth.

'How long was I out for?'

'Well, I guess that's better than "where am I". Not long, less than ten minutes is all, if that. Coffee's still hot if you want some. Can you stand?'

'I think so.'

Strawpenny helped her to her feet. Prentiss was shivery. She felt weak and off-balance. She thought Erskine had some major explaining to do, *what had the bastard done to her*? She remembered when she had once suspected he might be a hypnotist. Had he just used some auto-suggestion technique on her? Would that work over a phone? And if so, why was he doing it?

Her hand shook badly when she brought her mug to her lips so she gripped it in both fists then sipped cautiously, anxious not to spill any liquid onto Strawpenny's expensive rugs. Thankfully the coffee was good, full bodied, rich, and strong, and she felt the bloom of caffeine surge to the very tips of her fingers. She wanted to laugh it felt so good.

She smiled at Strawpenny, 'This is perfect, thanks.'

The woman fetched her another mug full, chattering all the time, but Prentiss was no longer listening. Something wonderful was happening to her and she needed to gauge the glorious changes taking place throughout her body. She was feeling great, better than great. Sensations of pure wellbeing continued to escalate, building to an impossible level. Strength was flowing into her as if a spring had been opened into her body from a deep well of potent energy. She felt unstoppable, and she was no longer a mere, weak human. Her body had become a vessel of immense power and she was ready to shriek defiance at everything stacked against her. Her gaze settled on Strawpenny who cowered away from her as if she had just been slapped.

'Not being funny, honey, but I'm not sure coffee agrees with you. It takes people that way sometimes, brings out the worst in them. I think you should leave. No offense, but you're scaring me now.'

Prentiss' voice was calm and level, yet also implacable.

'Where does your meeting with Highview take place?'

Strawpenny answered meekly, as if her will had been completely subsumed.

'He's coming here at seven thirty. Here.'

'I shall meet him with you. Agreed?'

'Of course, that would be fine. He'll be enchanted to see you I'm sure.'

'Marion...'

'Yes, honey?'

'Is there any way you can see your visitors before you open the bank vault door to them?'

200

'Ha, ha, you're one of the smart ones. You've worked out that ol' Marion ain't so green as she's cabbage looking. Of course, I have, lookee here.'

Strawpenny almost skipped gleefully to a cabinet on the wall by the massive door. She opened it to reveal a flat CCTV screen. When she switched it on Prentiss could clearly see the full stretch of the stairwell leading up from the lobby.

'Perfect,' she breathed. 'Just perfect.'

49

Prentiss wondered how much damage Erskine and his breed had done to humankind and culture over the millennia if they had always found it so very easy to control the will of those around them. Strawpenny was completely in her thrall, agreeing to her slightest suggestion without question. At seven o'clock she dispatched the woman to her bedroom to get ready for her date. While she was out of the way Prentiss swiftly checked her pistol to make sure it was fully loaded, and then made sure that she had a second magazine where she could reach it easily. Despite her new burst of energy she felt tense as a cat trapped in a kennels, and her belly was filled to bursting with enough butterflies to start a storm that would devastate the East Coast. She knew Anubis was hell bent on killing Strawpenny, and she had seen what it could do during the carnage at Center Heights. Was she fooling herself in thinking that a gun was going to be effective against it? She remembered gunshots on the ninety-first floor, gunshots followed by screaming. Suddenly her pistol seemed very small.

Strawpenny re-entered the room and performed a little twirl.

'What do you think? You young girls look like fashion plates without doing anything special, but we old war horses need a little more grooming to look our best. Will I do?'

'You look simply charming, Marion. He'll be like putty in your hands.'

'If he's got eyes in his head he'll only be looking at you, and I can't say I'd blame him. Now, if you'd like to freshen up the bathroom's free. Go ahead.'

'Thanks, yes, I will.'

Prentiss washed her face and hands and then took a long minute to study herself in the mirror over the washbowl. Was there something alien glittering in her eyes? Erskine said he had activated the Anubis echo in Highview, had he activated something equally dangerous in her? And if so, what? She realised that Highview was just as much a victim of the Ogdoad as those he had killed, but what *was* she going to do about him when he finally reached Strawpenny's loft? Too many pointless questions. She had no choice, she would have to play the cards as they were dealt to her.

She took a deep breath when she heard the buzz of the entry-phone. She looked at her watch, seven twenty.

'Okay,' she whispered, 'it's showtime.'

When Prentiss reached the living room she saw Strawpenny already had the big door open, which was against her strict instructions. Prentiss drew her gun from its holster and held it ready behind her back. She prayed she would be fast enough to stop Highview before he killed his next victim. Then Strawpenny stepped out onto the stairs. *What's she doing?* When the woman returned into the room and leaned back on the door to close it, she had arms full of food cartons and bags.

'I'm the hostess with the mostest,' she explained, 'but I can't cook worth a damn. I always order a delivery. Can you help me with these, honey?'

The food smelled wonderful and the oven was already warm and ready. Prentiss wondered if they would get the chance to eat any of it. Then the quiet question itching in her mind got the better of her. She had to ask. Putting the ultimate in control into her voice she said, 'Marion, why did you let yourself get involved with child slave trafficking? I don't understand.'

She received a guileless, wide-eyed look in return. 'Where did you hear something like that? Me? Who ever said such a thing? That's terrible.' Strawpenny looked as if she was going to burst into tears. 'Slave trafficking? Me? Oh no, you can't say that, what makes you even think such a thing? If sponsoring a child's education and finding them honest paid work is slavery and trafficking, then fine, I'm guilty. Lock me up and throw away the key. But, really? Slavery? Oh Prentiss, never that. I call it trying to do my Christian best to help the vulnerable. How could you say that to me?'

Prentiss hugged her. 'I'm sorry, Marion, honestly. Someone told me a lie and once I'd met you I didn't believe it myself. I'm truly sorry, but I had to ask.'

Strawpenny smiled and cuffed away a tear, 'You're a nice girl but I guess you're paid to be suspicious.'

'No, Marion, I'm paid to get my facts right. People are always innocent until proven guilty, and in my eyes, you're innocent.'

It's not just Anubis who fucks up, she thought.

The entry-phone buzzed again. Strawpenny gave her a docile look.

'Shall I see who that is?'

'Are you expecting any more deliveries.'

'Not today.'

'Then yes, you'd better. Open the outer door, but don't open the vault door whatever he says, okay?'

'Sure.'

Strawpenny drifted to the entry-phone handset.

'Yalloo,' she drawled. 'Who is that? Oh, hi, Randall, just a second...' She covered the mouthpiece. 'It's Randall.'

'Right, let him in as far as the stairwell and turn on the CCTV.'

'Hi, Randall, please, come right on in.'

The CCTV screen flickered into life just in time to catch a figure in a hoody enter the lobby. He shut the door behind him then pulled the hood back from his head before climbing the stairs. Strawpenny took several steps away from the CCTV image. She touched a shaking hand to her lips.

'Oh, my. Who is that? What is that?'

Prentiss regarded the long elegant muzzle and spear-point ears of a familiar face. Its ebon eyes were lined with gold, as were its lips. When the lips pulled away in a snarl to expose a mouth full of sharp white fangs she realised with a shock that he wasn't wearing a mask, he had never worn a mask.

'Prentiss, what is he?'

'He's a killer, but it's okay, he's the other side of that door. He can't get at us.' She put her arm around the older woman. 'I'm here to keep you safe.'

She got on the phone to her precinct and issued a code Ten-Thirteen Zee, plain-clothed officer in trouble, and gave the address of Strawpenny's loft. She was told back-up would be with her in ten minutes or less.

The creature on the stairs called out, then knocked gently on the door. When he got no response he called again, then started pounding on the vault door. Within seconds fine dust had spurted into the room and cracks began to appear in the plasterwork. They heard a muffled, male voice shouting to be let in. It began howling in fury, and it was howling Strawpenny's name. Strawpenny began to shiver. She whimpered in terror, pressing closer to Prentiss, who hugged her. She said, 'Marion, the guys are on their way, they'll be here very soon. You're safe. He can't get through that door, okay? So, don't worry, we're safe.'

The pounding intensified, sending juddering ripples through the walls. The cracks in the plaster deepened. Prentiss wondered if she was lying to herself, then realised that the stout door would have been much more secure bolted into the steel-lined walls of a London bank vault. How long would it last under such a relentless onslaught if all it had to secure its sixteen bolts was nineteenth century brick and plaster? Moments later she found out. Every strike of the creature's powerful fists began levering bricks out of the door surround. It would only be a matter of moments before the door fell.

'Marion, okay, get behind me. Let's back away from the door, you hear me? We must back away from the door.'

A brick came out of the wall like a cannon shell. It clattered onto the floorboards, throwing out a shower of long splinters. There was a hole in the wall now and a thick beam of smoky red light shone through. They could see the raging black shape of the creature. It screeched furiously at them. There followed a final detonation of enraged pounding and with a fearful grinding sound the great door crashed to the floor. Prentiss saw everything as if it was happening in slow motion. The doorway framed a landscape she recognised. The bloated red corpse of the terminal sun seethed and billowed where the stairwell should have been. It silhouetted the unmistakable figure of Anubis. She heard his voice lash out at her. 'YOU! YOU MUST LEAVE!' Marion Strawpenny heard the order and fell to her knees in abject terror. She was whimpering, her voice an imploring whine, but Prentiss could no longer spare the time to listen. His voice roared again. 'YOU MUST LEAVE, NOW!' Every inch of her wanted to obey, the power of his command was irresistible. She took a faltering step towards the door and freedom. 'NOW! LEAVE!'

Strawpenny was gibbering and clutching at Prentiss' legs. It was the end game, it was face him or leave her to her fate. All that wonderful energy had drained away and left her at his mercy, and he was ordering her to leave. She could survive this if she left now, she could live. *No, I won't!* She shrieked with blazing fury at her own weakness, and something new inside her clicked into place. She stood her ground and felt her power once more. An alien other gazed calmly from her eyes – and she smiled serenely. With a surge of hard realisation, she knew exactly what she must do.

In a voice that wasn't hers and using words she didn't recognise, Prentiss answered Anubis, who had bounded into the room at high speed and was stalking straight towards them. Her words brought the creature up short. It crouched, breathing heavily, and glaring from her to Strawpenny. It shook itself as if trying to cast off whatever she had said, then peeled away its hoody. Underneath it was clothed in skin-tight, stretchy, black material that revealed every inch of its well-muscled frame. And then, right in front of her eyes, it began to grow. She spoke quietly in that strange tongue, and then barked an order. It howled back at her in incensed confusion and she could see it was mentally wrestling with what it was seeing and hearing. It continued to grow. The loft was some fifteen feet high, yet soon the dark figure had to bend its head forward or hit the ceiling.

Prentiss issued another order in that uncanny language. In response, the frustrated and confused creature punched a hole in the ceiling, showering them all with thick chunks of sooty plaster. Prentiss ducked away and Anubis saw his chance. He reached out towards Strawpenny with a roar of triumph. Prentiss was ready. She straightened up and leapt towards his face, her gun outstretched. Without knowing how, she felt herself levitate and hover for the split second she needed to be perfectly positioned. Anubis screamed in fury and lashed sideways at her, but it was too late. She had already squeezed her trigger in the moment before it struck. Its blow sent her hurtling helplessly towards the wall, the breath knocked painfully out of her body, but even as she tumbled she saw with grim satisfaction that her shot was good. The bullet knifed into the centre of Anubis' right eye and its head snapped back and downwards, jetting a spray of dark blood, its muzzle open in a final soundless howl. The great body pounded to the floor, shaking the whole building to its foundations. Its fall was accompanied by the sounds of Strawpenny's terrified screams, and a welcome host of booted feet scrambling up the stairs. A cluster of armed, uniformed officers rushed into the room just as the creature twitched twice and lay still, its great tongue lolling from its yawning muzzle.

She heard one of the men cry out, 'What the flying fuck is that thing?' And then Strawpenny was at her side, sobbing over her like a lost child. A stream of incoherent words spilled from her mouth like vomit.

Seconds later a shadow moved behind Strawpenny's shoulder, and she saw Chief Lewis regarding her steadily. He shook his head and gave her a wry smile.

'This is going to be one report I can't wait to read.' He looked back towards the prone form on the floor. 'Prentiss, are you always this dangerous when you're on sick leave?'

50

'I still miss her every day. I can't come to terms with the fact that she's dead, you know?'

'She was your best friend and your work partner. It's going to take you a while to accept it. And grief isn't a race, you know. You've got to work your way through it one day at a time. I only met Sam once and she made me smile. I liked her. She was cool.'

'Yeah, she was very cool.'

Enzo kept a wary eye on the couple in the corner from behind his bar. He pretended to be polishing wine glasses. Prentiss looked happy. Distracted, but happy. If she was happy the guy was welcome. Howlett hadn't been the first man to dine with the beautiful detective at the restaurant, but he was the first to do so twice. To Enzo that meant things must be getting serious.

Howlett placed his hand over hers. 'So, when are you back to work?'

'Beginning of next month. They're not calling it a suspension, not yet. Officially I'm still on sick leave, but everything else is pending the review of what happened at Marion Strawpenny's loft. Marion wants to give me another medal, she thinks I'm Wonder Woman, or something like that. The NYPD has a much simpler agenda. It just wants to know why detective Prentiss shot Commissioner Highview in the head. They don't know what to make of the witness statements, and nor does Chief Lewis and he was right there. I just don't know what's going to happen. I might be asked to resign, or I might face a disciplinary hearing. They might even decide on a full homicide investigation, you know? Or maybe we'll forget everything that happened and hope it goes away.'

The giant jackal/wolfman hybrid had shrunk back to human size shortly after death. It transformed in front of a room full of witnesses leaving Randall Highview lying sprawled in a widening pool of blood, his left eye glaring sightlessly at the ceiling. His right eye socket was a cratered mass of blood – the eyeball itself had been blasted through his brain and out the back of his ruined skull, along with a quantity of brain tissue. Death would have been instantaneous.

Based on Prentiss' information, investigators were sent to talk with Gawain Erskine and Aliya Petrus, but they came back empty-handed. Both Erskine and Petrus had disappeared from their homes and the city of New York. It was believed they were probably together and had skipped the United States. *Dames & Dandies* had been unable to supply a forwarding address for its leading gossip columnist, something the editor-in-chief was very unhappy about in an angrily vocal way, and none of the spiritualist's neighbours knew anything about Petrus other than that she was 'weird', rarely went out, and tended to dress like an 'outsized beekeeper'.

Prentiss' most recent medical examinations had also raised several confusing questions. Her x-rays showed no hint of the terrible physical trauma she had suffered at Center Heights. Even her internal sutures appeared to have evaporated without a trace. Scant weeks before she had been in intensive care and her prognosis had been poor to critical. Her injuries had been life changing, and even the most optimistic forecasts said she would face a future of crippling discomfort, and probably be on painkillers for life. Not anymore. Her most recent scans showed her to be at the peak of health, in fact she was probably the finest specimen of young womanhood the medics had ever seen. One of the doctors had half-seriously mourned the fact that she had survived her second encounter with the killer, saying it would have been great to open her up and see what was happening in there. She was, they said, either a fraud or a miracle. And they knew she wasn't a fraud.

Prentiss had also spent a great deal of quality time talking with Howlett and Rex Chappell about everything that had happened. She had even admitted to them that Howlett had become her prime suspect for a while after she discovered his Christian name, Tabaqui, meant jackal. He had quickly disabused her, telling her that his name was an invention by Rudyard Kipling and he had been Christened with it because his mother had been a great fan of the celebrated author.

Chappell loved her story and made her go into precise detail, especially about the idea of time travelling echoes implanted in the human psyche. He accepted the idea that people might be 'activated' and given special missions they were compelled to complete, but her tale also raised a lot of questions in his critical mind. The three friends were sharing wine, ideas and nibbles in his loft when he put forward his greatest doubts about the truth of her explanation.

He said, 'So, Prentiss, before I go any further I need you to know that I am in no way accusing you of being a liar, okay? I know you believe what you're saying. Okay, so you're telling us this Ogdoad Council is a super evolved group of minds from billions of years in the future. They are painfully sensitive to the Butterfly Effects of evil and suffering, and they want to put an end to it by sending echoes through time to judge and punish the worst perpetrators. That's what they told you. They decided the only way forward, was to deliver us from evil by somehow reaching through the time vortex that powers their city, and as a result they've been guiding the development of mankind since we climbed down from the trees? Am I right so far?'

'I believe so. I know it sounds ridiculous...'

'Ridiculous, no way! Wow, no, really it's totally awesome. These guys tell you they've been meddling in civilisation's background forever, creating all sorts of gods and myths, and directing our feet onto the straight and level path to the promised land. I can see that. Then, one day, you turn up and tell them they've been getting everything wrong, and you explain why. They listen, nod in agreement, and instead of blasting you back to the present day with a flea in your ear, they shut up shop and allow themselves to be wiped out by an exploding sun they've casually held at bay for thousands or millions of years. Amazing.'

'Yes. If they turned off the vortex, and that's what they said they would do, the Earth would finally be swallowed by the sun and they would go with it.'

'Yes, you said. And they also healed you. They healed you so well that our best doctors are baffled. In fact, you aren't just healed – you're better than ever before. You are now an uber Prentiss.'

'Yes, I guess so, but don't ask me how.'

'Future science, Prentiss, does it every time. To us it will look like magic. Imagine what an ancient Egyptian would make of laser beams, rockets, computers, or satellite navigation. We don't really understand it ourselves, we just use it every day so we stop asking questions. Anyway, I don't get it.'

'Get what?'

'Any of it. It makes no sense to me.'

Howlett protested that Prentiss was telling the truth, and Chappell agreed, but with a caveat. 'Look, we know the Ogdoad from the earliest writings as eight mysterious mythological deities who pre-date the pyramids and the Egyptian gods, fine. We can look them up online. But, Prentiss, you've also met them as eight super intelligences from eight billion years in the future.'

'Yes, like I told you, they influence the past through the vortex by using echoes of themselves.'

'Yes, but do they? Is that true? Let me explain. They *healed* you, Prentiss, they healed you. To do that, surely, they had to touch you, you had to be where they could reach you. I simply can't see how they could heal you using echoes fired down a vortex. You had to physically be there or it couldn't work. If they can bring you to them, surely they can also send much more

209

than just echoes down that vortex of theirs. I wonder how often they've made house calls to mankind. Makes you think, doesn't it? Can you see what I'm saying? And another thing, I don't believe they would voluntarily self-destruct just because you spoke harshly to them. Think about it. The Ogdoad have had eight billion years longer than us to develop their super intelligence, and then along comes a twenty-first century NYPD cop who tells them they've been getting it wrong all this time. And instead of slapping her down with a sarcastic, "Get lost lady" they say "Sorry, we didn't think of that. You're right and we should die". I mean, *really*? Does that sound likely? You're a smart lady, one of the smartest I've ever met, but could you really outsmart brains so far ahead of us, we might just as well be algae by comparison? You know something? I don't think so. I have to wonder if this is really over, and I don't think it is. I think we'll just have to await further developments.'

Chappell's words had tumbled around in her brain ever since. She had also decided to keep her own counsel about Erskine activating something powerful in her, an energy without which she was convinced she would have died during Highview's attack. She couldn't remember the words she had chanted to hold him back, and she didn't know where they had come from, but they had stalled him long enough for her to plan her defence and that was all she needed. She was deeply lost in thought when Howlett said something to her and dragged her mind back to the restaurant.

'I'm sorry, what did you say?'

'I said I can't blame you for being distracted, there's a lot going on. I also said, you've got two weeks before they expect you back at work. Why don't we use the time, go away somewhere and forget about everything for a week? I'm owed time off. We could rent a place and just walk and talk and leave all this madness behind. Go to the beach, somewhere warm, get to know each other better, what do you say?'

'Mr Howlett, are you asking me to go away and co-habit with you? Really, I'm shocked.'

He blushed and looked flustered. 'No, sorry, I didn't mean it like that. We would get a two-room place. You know we won't do anything like *that* until we're married. I made a vow, and, I thought, so did you.'

She grinned at him, 'Did you just propose to me?'

He thought back over what he had just said. 'Yes, yes, I guess I did. Do you mind? Should I get down on one knee?'

'Of course I don't mind, you wonderful man, and please, don't get down on your knees. Enzo will think you've dropped something and come over to help you find it.'

She watched the smile spread slowly over Howlett's face like breaking sunrise.

'So then,' he said. 'What do you say? Yes or no?'

She spent a long moment thinking it over. All the while she traced his face with her eyes, drinking in every beloved line.

'I think it has to be yes, don't you?'

'I guess so, yeah. That would be the best answer. I love you, you know.'

'I should hope so. And I love you.'

They kissed, and stayed locked together until Enzo came to their table and coughed a warning that other customers were watching. Prentiss turned a beaming smile on him, and Enzo helplessly grinned back like a happy cat.

'Enzo,' she said, 'we want you to be the first to know. We're engaged.'

Amidst the laughter and congratulations Prentiss forgot about the Ogdoad. She didn't think of them again until she was alone in bed and Chappell's words came back to her with full force. *You know something? I don't think so. I have to wonder if this is really over, and I don't think it is. I think we'll just have to await further developments*

At last she entered a fitful sleep. Fragments of memory merged with her dreams and circled all of her unresolved questions. Her drowsing mind sought answers where none could be found. One clear image brought her gasping into wakefulness, bathed in a cold flop sweat. Anubis' gold framed, ebon eyes were looking closely into hers. They seemed filled with anguish and another emotion she couldn't quite fathom; an emotion that plucked at the deepest core of her being. Two words had jolted her awake. Two words that made her fear her pillow so much that hours later the dawn found her wide awake and curled up in her recliner. She had Chappell's drawings in her hands and she was looking compulsively from one to the other, tears leaving large damp splotches on her tee shirt.

What did it mean? Why had he said it? And in her mind's ear she heard the words again, just as they had been uttered in that whispered groan; she heard them clear as day.

'Mother!' Anubis had asked her. 'Why?'

...

Prentiss will return in *The gathering of gods: Isis*

211

Author's note

I never planned this to be more than a single novel. I had my cast of people neatly arranged and a story arc that should have ended when Anubis fell. The problem is he doesn't want to lie down. I'm with Chappell, I think we'll just have to await further developments.

As usual I have blended the real with fiction to build my foundations deep enough and strong enough to withstand the mayhem I wreak on the poor devils who inhabit my worlds. Prairie West and Center Heights are both completely invented, however, Erskine's Club is loosely based on the Harmonie Club in New York, which can be found at Four, East Sixtieth Street, and is the second oldest social club in the city. Please note, when I say loosely – I mean it.

Howlett's Wolf Sanctuary is also loosely based on a real place, The Wolf Conservation Centre in South Salem. If you love wolves, which I do, you must put this place into your search engine and at least take a virtual visit.

And penultimately, the 'history' of the ancient Egyptian and Sumerian gods has fascinated me since childhood, as has the question, 'Was God an Astronaut'. The Ogdoad are astonishing and almost forgotten deities who I have played fast and loose with, but I didn't make up the name. I must stress that I intend nothing less than complete respect for all ancient beliefs, but they make awe-inspiring subjects for imagineers like me, and I want to say a special thank-you to all those people who have researched the subject and put it online for eager authors to find.

And finally, much respect for the women and men of the NYPD, I salute you.

Other Works by Derek E Pearson

www.gbpublishing.co.uk

Preacher Spindrift series
GODS' Fool(Jul 2017)

In the first great allied tank battle of WWI, an injured Texan reservist's religious beliefs, sanity and courage reach breaking point – on encountering Dr Spindrift.

GODS' Enemy (Nov 2016)
FINALIST - 2016 Indies Book Awards

Read2Write: "Texas 1883, a terrifying story that fuses sci-fi with history and theology. Pearson is in electrifying form"

Slave Skin (Jul 2017)

Diminutive medium Medina Bishop follows perplexing clues to save hundreds of dead souls from an eternity of tortured madness. With her protector, an earth elemental Fargo, she finds a bizarre and touching kind of love.

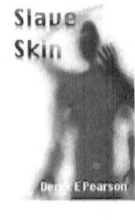

Soul's Asylum trilogy (2016-2017)
FINALIST - 2016 Indies Book Awards

The Sun ☆☆☆☆: "*a weird, vivid and creepy book, not for the faint hearted. But its originality and top writing make for a great read.*"

Body Holiday trilogy (2014-2015)

Surrey Life: "*Pearson's galactic-sized imagination delivers, with veiled gallows humour, a compelling image of a chic, high-tech society infused with a toxic strain that feeds on extreme violence.*"

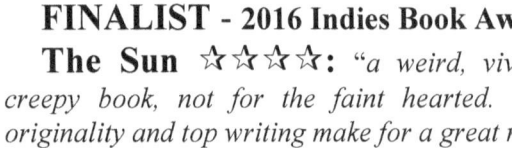